Blackwater Nights

By Donna R Brown

ISBN-10: 0692326200
ISBN-13: 9780692326206

Dedication

This book is dedicated to James Weldon Jones. In his lifetime he's been soldier, police sergeant, husband, father, grandfather and great-grandfather, as well as brother, uncle and friend. What his humility may never have allowed him to acknowledge is that as all of the above, he's been a hero. I love you, Dad.

Acknowledgements

To my parents, Weldon and Edie Jones, for always believing in me and to my Mom in particular for your endless hours of formatting, editing and revising. I could never have done it without you. To my daughter, Amanda Burlin and my dearest friends, Doug and Beth Banks, for the fruitful brainstorming sessions and your inspiring ideas.

My aunt, Shirley Gilbert, my brother, Sergeant Steve Jones, our friend, Lieutenant Roger Park, and our friend, Joyce Cloudt gave of their time to provide incredibly valuable proofreading skills and consultation. I'm thankful for their watchful eyes and attention to detail.

My love and gratitude for the people of Liberty, Texas, my inspiration for the town of Blackwater. And last but not least, to my husband, Tim, for being the love of my life, and for loving me in return. God has truly blessed me.

Chapter 1

Brynn Callaway surveyed the scene before her and hesitated briefly. As a nurse she prided herself on having a stomach of steel and nerves to match. As the mother of a twelve-year-old son, not so much. Blake, her son, was up to his knees in a giant aluminum tub, covered in suds. A heavy duty extension cord stretched across the back patio, through a puddle, and was flush against the tub where it dangled, a hair dryer loosely plugged into it. Sarge, Blake's giant German shepherd, was also covered in bubbles but wouldn't come anywhere near the tub.

"Blake!" she shouted. "Do not move!" Unplugging the extension cord from the outlet, she retrieved it and tossed it toward the door to the garage. "Why on earth did you have an electric cord out here with all this water?" She took a few deep, cleansing breaths while she waited for his answer.

"I have to dry his hair, Mom," Blake said, rolling his eyes. He stepped out of the tub and made a move toward Sarge, who was having none of it. With a good grip on his collar, the golden-haired gangly boy tugged and pulled to

1

bring him back to the tub. Brynn realized this was going to be a job for two, and pushed up her sleeves. Together they coerced him into the tub.

"You hold him and I'll scrub." Working her hands into Sarge's fur, she worked the shampoo into a rich lather. "See, there?" she sang out in a soothing voice. "This isn't so bad, right?" About that time, Sarge decided to shake as hard as he could. Water went flying, and Brynn turned her face to the side in a failed attempt to avoid being splashed in the face.

Before long, Brynn and her son had rinsed off the dog and lured him inside the house. He demonstrated his preference for air-drying over blow-drying and lunged from Blake's grasp, tearing down the hall.

"I've got 20 minutes to get showered and ready for work. Get your backpack and be ready. Your uncle will be here in a few minutes to get you."

"Cool!" he answered, grabbing his game system and shoving it into his backpack. Brynn smiled, glad her brother had such a wonderful relationship with her son. He'd grown up without a father, but had never lacked for a positive male role model. Ben doted on him. Brynn knew how blessed she was, especially with her life the way it was now.

She'd only been out of nursing school for a couple of years and had taken a night shift position. Hopefully it would only be a matter of time before there would be a day shift available. Being a single mom was tough under any circumstances, but on the night shift it was even harder. Having her brother and sister-in-law across the street, on the opposite corner, made it much easier for Blake to go back and forth with little if any disruption to his routine. He even had a room at Ben's house right across the hall from his little cousin, Annie.

Annie was a darling toddler, and was the apple of Blake's eye. She'd managed to work her charm on the entire family, and none of them were immune to her chubby little cheeks, blonde curls and cherubic smile.

Brynn heard the doorbell ring and then heard Blake's shoes squeaking across the hardwood floors while he raced down the hall to answer it.

"I got it!" he shouted. Brynn rounded the corner to see her brother just stepping in the front door with little Annie on his hip. He flicked a wave of golden hair out of his face. It was easy to see where Annie got her yellow curls.

"Hey, Sis. What's going on?"

"Just getting ready for work. Thanks for taking Blake," she said, leaning in to kiss Annie's delightfully chubby cheek.

"Hey, it's no problem. Ludie's home getting dinner ready, so we've got the evening free."

"Cool!" Blake said as he rounded the corner and came up behind his mother. "I can show you the level I reached on my game!" Blake's face was full of enthusiasm.

"Cool," echoed Brynn. "You can show him how you know all your vocabulary words!"

"Aw, man!" he said. "Maybe after?"

"Maybe after," Ben answered. "Come on. Are you hungry?" Blake was trailing him out the door, Sarge close behind.

Brynn couldn't help but smile as she watched them all head down the sidewalk: Ben in front with Annie on his hip, then Blake, with Sarge walking close enough for his haunches to brush against the boy's pants leg with each hurried step. Sarge loved his boy and, for that, Brynn was grateful. He had more than earned his treats and trips to the dog park, and then some.

Knowing her son would be with her brother was a great source of comfort to her. Her ex-husband, Mark Callaway, was never enthusiastic about becoming a father. They had gotten divorced when Blake was a baby. For a while Mark had made a few small efforts to be a part of his son's life, but they were few and far between.

By the time Blake was four years old, he had stopped watching out the window for his father. Even at that tender age, he'd finally figured out he wasn't going to come. Mark had never paid child support; Brynn had never asked. It still hurt to remember the sense of abandonment she and her son had both felt at the time.

A few minutes later, Brynn was showered and clad in light blue scrubs. She ran a brush through her auburn hair and pulled it into a neat pony tail. She preferred to think of herself as a redhead, but the truth of the matter was that her hair was more of a chestnut brown. Only when she was out in the sunlight did the auburn highlights start to show. Sometimes she wondered if her desire to be more of a redhead was because it usually came with such a bold personality, like the one of her friend, Roxy.

Altogether it wasn't so bad. Her complexion was nice, although she wasn't particularly pleased with the scattering of freckles across her nose and cheeks. Once she had applied a finishing touch of lipstick, pinned her hospital ID badge to her scrubs, and draped her stethoscope around her neck, she smiled with satisfaction. This, she reflected, was more than she could have dreamed of.

Graduating from nursing school and passing her board exams was the buttercream icing on the sweet vanilla cupcake that was her life. A growl from her stomach suddenly reminded her she'd forgotten to eat dinner. Sarge's bath had taken precedence, so she'd have to eat out of the hospital vending machine again. So, her life wasn't *all* cupcakes and sprinkles, but it was full and it was rich.

Her business, Blackwater Creek Candles, was thriving. Once she'd made the decision to follow her dream of nursing, her brother had stepped in at just the right moment, the critical moment, really. She'd been on the verge of selling the shop when he'd come forward. He and his wife, Ludie, had bought into the business and were managing it flawlessly, allowing Brynn to retain a smaller minority of shares while pursuing her career. It would make for a nice nest-egg for Blake one day if it continued on the same path.

Chapter 2

Blackwater Memorial wasn't a large hospital, but it managed to maintain a good reputation for quality care. Being a rural neighborhood hospital, it served several other small communities in the area. It was a small, university-connected teaching hospital and had provided Brynn with the perfect opportunity to learn and advance.

The medical and surgical unit, four west, kept a fairly large census and its patients presented with ailments that required a wide variety of treatments and procedures. Brynn loved the cohesiveness of her unit and had formed some great friendships. Facing life and death issues on a regular basis resulted in close bonds between staff members. They worked hard, but they played hard, too. Brynn didn't keep with the younger set, girls in their early twenties getting their first taste of life on their own in the real world. She had taken more of a maternal role with that age group.

She was of the belief that experienced nurses should take brand new nurses under their wings and nurture them. Even though she was a bit older, already in her early 30's, she still considered herself a fairly new nurse. Too many old school nurses had a reputation for eating their young, so to speak. They were often known to throw them to the wolves, which meant teaching them the basics and then tossing them out on the floor with a full patient load on their own. Brynn had been treated fairly and always tried to pay it forward. She had every intention of being fair once she'd become a more experienced nurse. When it came to socializing after hours, though, most of her closest friends at work were either also moms or were at least a little closer to her age range.

Lindsey Myers, her closest friend at the hospital, wasn't a mother yet, but she dreamed of it. She was very new to nursing, but was learning quickly. She was amazingly astute and had good instincts, two characteristics every nurse needed but couldn't be taught in the classroom. There was something about Lindsey, though, that Brynn had warmed up to. They shared the same warped sense of humor, which was a necessity when a job involved life and death as theirs did.

Tonight Brynn had six patients, so hopefully it would be an easy night. She immediately grabbed her report sheet and poured coffee into a Styrofoam cup. It was thick, and dark, and smelled of burnt coffee beans. There was no time to brew more so she took it and sat down across from the nurses' station. She began highlighting the names of her patients, circling their diagnoses with a red pen. Ernie, a tall, older nurse slid into the seat across from her, winded. That was never a good sign of an easy day.

"All righty," he said, breathlessly. "Are you ready for report? It's a busy group."

Brynn sighed, taking a long sip of coffee. Grimacing suddenly, she gulped, managing to swallow it down. "That's disgusting!" She pushed the cup away from her.

"They're not *bad* patients," he told her. "They'll just keep you busy."

"No, I meant the coffee. When did y'all make it? It's like thick, black sludge."

"There was no time for making fresh coffee before shift change, your highness," he laughed. "Didn't you hear I had a busy group? Room 421. Mr. Gonzalez, 59 year old male. He came in through ER, complaining of shortness of breath, chest pain." He began rifling through a stack of papers. "Here's the cardiac enzymes report. Apparently no MI, but keep an eye on him. He's had nitro sublingual twice, and he can have one more if he needs it."

Brynn scribbled furiously on her report sheet, careful to take down all the pertinent information. Each patient had very individual concerns and would need to be monitored accordingly. Out of the corner of her eye, she noticed Spencer Evans, a respiratory therapist who'd transferred in from another campus of the hospital. His well-muscled body moved with speed and easy grace. He kept his hair cut very short, nearly bald, which emphasized his strong, masculine features. He reminded Brynn of a cop. A cop or a soldier. He was definitely all man, virulent and masculine.

Ernie's voice broke in, bringing her back. "She's status post cholecystectomy, three small

8

sutured areas, no drainage." Brynn cleared her throat, pretending to focus on something he'd said on the previous patient. "Go back," she told him, "I was still thinking about 421's labs." She wasn't about to admit it was Spencer that had distracted her, so she blamed it on the labs.

As soon as he began, Spencer looked up from the desk and noticed Brynn and gave a quick nod, an irresistibly disarming smile, and bounced off to his next patient.

"I'm sorry, Ernie," Brynn stammered. "I'm just having a hard time focusing today."

"Yea, I can see that," Ernie remarked. "It's always the cops that get the women."

"Oh, Spencer's a cop?" She smiled, secretly pleased that she had nailed it.

"Yep. He was. He was with the police department in Houston for a while." He shrugged nonchalantly. "Something happened, and he ended up leaving. I guess all this glamour and glory we live every day in the hospital was enough to lure him in. He doesn't like to talk about his previous job much."

Brynn was curious, and found her thoughts returning to Spencer several times after she'd finished getting shift-change report and started her rounds. Ernie was right, this was going to be a busy group of patients. This was her "short shift," and by eleven pm, she was more than ready to clock out.

Life on a medical telemetry unit was stressful and the hangout around the corner from the hospital, the Star Bar had everything a mentally and physically exhausted hospital crew needed. Most everyone worked at least two 12 hour shifts per week, although many of them rotated an evening shift twice a week as well, working from 3:00 in the evening until 11:00 pm, which was about when things started settling down, in a manner of speaking. Twice a week, Brynn came in at 7:00 pm and stayed until 11:00 pm. Nights like this flew by, and the four hours were always up before she knew it. Every night, right before midnight, there was an army of scrubs-clad people scattered throughout the bar and grill. Some ordered dinner and relaxed with a drink or two. Others engaged in colorful competitions either shooting pool or throwing darts.

The Star Bar's evening patrons all knew the hospital staff would be filing in soon and that if someone had a queasy stomach it would be best not to sit next to their tables when eating. Nurses in particular weren't known for sparing details with one another when exchanging war stories from their shifts.

Brynn slid into a corner booth across from her friend Lindsey after a hectic night on the floor. Blake was spending the night with his Uncle Ben and Aunt Ludie so she was in no particular hurry to get home. Lindsey held her hand up with a peace sign, which was code for "Bring us two of our regulars." True to form, one of their regular waitresses showed up momentarily with two draught beers.

"Potato skins?" she asked, "or fried mushrooms this time?"

Brynn and Lindsey exchanged a glance and giggled. "Both!" they blurted at the same time.

"Must've been one of those nights, huh?"

10

She circled something on her order pad and disappeared to turn in their orders. Brynn took a long sip of her beer and set it down; Lindsey did the same.

"What did you think?" Brynn leaned back against the cool vinyl of the booth. "How did we handle it all?" she asked, her brows arched in question.

Lindsey, petite and perky, her sandy blonde hair pulled loosely into a bun, took a deep breath before answering.

"Incredible! That's how we handled it!" Her pretty pink lips turned up on the corners. "You're amazing! Once my preceptor, and now my hero! I absolutely *love* watching you in action." Lindsey had only been a nurse for six months and was still learning but showed incredible potential in Brynn's eyes.

"Oh, come on! I've only got a year on you, Hon. I was your preceptor by default. We're learning together," Brynn sang out. "And we got through this shift together!" She splayed her hands out in front of her, picturing the events.

"There you were, leaning over the desk, when telemetry calls a nine beat run of V-tach in 421." Brynn's auburn ponytail bounced as she continued, a few stray curls broken free, her voice animated. "You were fast, girlfriend! First one in the room! Only, you took one look at the patient, then at me, then hauled butt back *out* of the room!" They burst into a fresh bout of giggles. "What was that all about, anyway?"

"Hey, somebody had to get the crash cart!" Lindsey replied defensively, a smile playing at the corners of her mouth.

Lindsey raised a glass, and Brynn raised hers in response. "Cheers!" Their glasses clinked together in a toast.

"What are we celebrating?" said a very tall, very handsome man in navy blue scrubs who suddenly appeared at their table.

Brynn swallowed hard, embarrassed as she suddenly became aware of the noise she and her friend were making. Quickly gathering her composure, she dabbed at her mouth with the corner of a napkin.

"Oh, you can celebrate, too!" Brynn met his gaze, trying not to notice his dark eyes and how they seemed to focus so intently on her. His nearness was overwhelming, and she suppressed a shiver.

"Lindsey, scoot over," she gestured, "let's make room for Spencer. After all, he *is* the one who came to our rescue."

She felt her face flush with color when Spencer moved to sit down on her side of the booth, beer in hand. "It was no big deal, ladies," he said. "I was just doing my job."

Brynn was quick to inform him otherwise. "The guy with the ambu bag is *never* just 'no big deal'!"

Her pulse quickened the moment his arm brushed against hers. She tried, unsuccessfully, not to notice his masculine build, his strong features and kind mouth.

"You already had things under control when I got there," he was saying. It was just like him to deflect the glory off himself. It wasn't the first time she'd noticed his humility.

He gave her a smile that was nearly as intimate as a kiss. Perhaps it felt that way because he was sitting so close.

They spent a while laughing and talking and, when the waitress brought their appetizers, he dug in, not shy at all. They had their appetizers in baskets in the middle of the table and each ordered a second beer. By the time they'd emptied both baskets, Spencer moved to stand up. With one raised brow and a cocky smile, he challenged Brynn to a game of pool. A playful dimple on his cheek made him even more irresistible than before.

She took the challenge. The night flew by quickly and, when she crawled into bed a few hours later, Spencer invaded her thoughts repeatedly. She worried momentarily about being unable to sleep but, before she knew it, she'd drifted off into a sound, dreamless sleep.

Chapter 3

The next afternoon, her thoughts returned to the previous evening at Star Bar several times... to Spencer. She made a mental note to pick up Sarge from Ben and Ludie's before time to pick up Blake from school. Wherever Blake went, Sarge was usually nearby, with the exception of school. Sarge had been with them since Blake was in preschool. He'd begun training as a service dog, but had been disqualified from the program due to a slight hip deformity. *Dysplasia,* they'd called it, but as far as Brynn and Blake were concerned, he was absolutely flawless. His veterinarian kept him in good health, and his limp was infrequent, and even then only slightly noticeable

They'd only had Sarge for a few months when Brynn had noticed something miraculous. She was passing Blake's room when she saw Sarge tugging on his pajamas. She rushed in to investigate when Sarge responded by issuing a low, steady growl. It had struck her odd that Blake didn't awaken, until she noticed he was clammy. She'd immediately raced to retrieve his glucose meter and a cup of juice. As she rushed back into his room, she was stirring a thick clump of sugar into the juice to help quickly raise Blake's blood sugar.

Cradling the back of his neck and lifting him from the pillow, she spoke to him firmly and placed the cup to his lips, dribbling a small amount of the sticky juice into his mouth. It was only after he'd begun to regain consciousness that she dared take a moment to check his sugar. It was 41, still dangerously low for any diabetic.

The entire time she'd worked with him to return his levels to normal, Sarge had continued his growling, though he'd ceased to tug at his clothing once Brynn had taken over. Once the boy was able to talk to his mother and drink on his own, it took a while to coax Sarge away from the bed so Brynn could get him into the kitchen to eat breakfast. That morning was the first of many times Sarge had literally saved her son's life. Though he'd been unable to complete his training as a service dog, she knew he had been the cream of the crop all along.

Since that day, her affection for Sarge had grown exponentially, and she now found herself eager to retrieve him from her brother's house. Having him nearby gave her a sense of security. Grabbing her purse and keys, she got into her car and crossed the intersection to Ben and Ludie's.

Ludie answered the door after one knock. She'd been expecting her.

"How did it go last night? Did Blake give you any trouble about getting his homework done?" Brynn asked, following her inside where little Annie played on the floor. Sarge was lying quietly next to her, patiently tolerating her attempts to include him in her play.

15

"Great," Ludie answered, gesturing to a chair. "His homework was done by 8:00 and he and Ben played games till bedtime. Want some coffee?"

"No, thanks, and I don't even have time to sit. I've gotta just grab Sarge and go pick up Blake from school."

Glancing at the clock, Ludie said "Oh yeah, I didn't realize it was this late! Let me get the leash."

Brynn bent down and swept Annie up into her arms, planting a kiss on her chubby little cheek, dimpled from smiling. Brynn set her back down and watched while she began playing as though she'd never been interrupted.

"All right," Ludie answered, handing her the leash. "Y'all come back anytime." Brynn gave her a quick hug and thanked her for keeping Blake.

It was nearly 3 o'clock when she pulled up to the circle lot in front of Blake's school. He opened the door and threw his backpack onto the back seat before climbing into the front seat next to her. She smiled and asked "How was your day?" Before he could answer, he was reaching over the back seat to greet Sarge.

"It was all right," he answered. "I'm hungry." She wanted to hear more about his day, but he made it clear it was time to move on. Being twelve years old, he had a separate life of his own, his own friends, and his own social scene.

She longed for the time when she had known every single person he came into contact with, from play dates, preschool, church. His life and hers had once been so intertwined that it was hard for her to accept that he now had a whole world outside of hers.

A few minutes later they pulled into the driveway and Blake ran up the back steps, Sarge close behind. He threw his backpack on the bar and went straight for the refrigerator.

"What's to eat?" he asked, pulling out a string cheese and an apple. She was just about to answer him when the phone rang.

"Check your sugar," she said, pointing to his backpack, where he kept a glucose meter.

He was old enough now to check his own sugar levels. Once she finished with her phone call, she would manage his insulin. She leaned across the bar and snatched the phone.

"Hello?" she answered, pausing to listen.

"Aunt Sylvia!" she finally said, taken aback by the unexpected call. "How are you?" she asked. "Where have you been? And how is Piper?" All the questions seemed to rush out of her.

Leaning across the bar, she glanced at his blood sugar level. No insulin this time. Good. She gave him a thumbs up as she continued listening to Sylvia. She busied herself wiping down the countertops while listening, then paced back and forth, attentive to the conversation. Once they'd spoken for a good while, Brynn hung up the phone and stood staring out the back window.

Sylvia had been the dearest friend of Brynn's mother. The two had been inseparable, and had considered each other family. When Brynn was fifteen, Sylvia and her ten year old daughter, Piper, had moved away. They didn't go far; they were still somewhere in the Houston area, but their families had lost touch after a while. Brynn was never sure why, and her Mom never spoke about it much.

Brynn didn't remember much about that time, she only knew that Aunt Sylvia had taken a position with a school district near Houston. Brynn never knew Piper's father. As best she could remember being told, he'd been a long haul truck driver and had never stayed in Piper's life for any length of time. Brynn nor her mother had ever met him. Brynn smiled at the memory of her mother. Her sadness felt newer, fresher somehow, after talking to Sylvia. With waves of memory always came waves of renewed grief.

Brynn's father had passed away when she was only nineteen. He was an avid pilot and had his own plane. Brynn and Ben had both loved going up with their father and looking down over the area. They never ceased to be amazed at the sheer volume of water that surrounded them. The town of Blackwater was in southeast Texas near the Trinity River, and the view was incredible.

They were less than an hour from Houston. Anytime they were in the car, aside from a few bridges that stretched over bodies of water, much of the area seemed to be landlocked, with pastures, trees and rice farms as far as the eye could see. But from the air, their little town seemed to be adrift on miles of ocean. The Trinity River emptied into Galveston Bay, and then into the Gulf of Mexico. Brynn's father had loved to fly them over the water, pointing out the best fishing areas, and even the beach at Galveston.

When his plane crashed, it was over those very same waters he went down. Brynn missed him so much it hurt. His death had led Brynn's mother into a deep depression from which she never seemed to fully recover. Her health declined shortly afterward, and it was less than three years later that Brynn had found her in her bed, not breathing. The cause of death was determined to be an accidental overdose, but Brynn secretly knew her mother had lost her will to live long before. Not a single day passed that Brynn didn't think of her parents and how much she missed them.

She shivered, trying to ease out of the memories. The phone call from Sylvia had come out of nowhere and awakened memories she'd long ago stored neatly away. And now she had much to consider. She looked down at the wrinkled piece of paper where she'd scribbled Sylvia's number.

"What's wrong, Mom?" Blake's voice cut in.

"Oh, um, that phone call was from Aunt Sylvia." She stepped around him and opened the refrigerator, retrieving a bottle of water.

"I have an Aunt Sylvia? Why don't I remember her?"

"She's not really our aunt, I just always called her that." She relayed the story of how Sylvia and her mother had been such close friends. She shared with him stories of Piper, the bright but sometimes annoying little girl who had been such a present figure in her life.

"Sylvia just told me she has cancer," she told him. "She's been going through treatments at M.D. Anderson, but it doesn't look good for her. As of now, she's not going to go through any more chemotherapy." Blake's eyes glazed with tears. She loved that he was so sensitive. He cared for everyone in his life, even if he didn't know them directly. He was filled with so much compassion that he always had the extraordinary ability to empathize with others in a difficult place.

"She's at peace with this," she told him, brushing a tear from his eye. "She's known about it for quite a while and, after trying this one last round of chemo, she realized it was time to let things happen as they may." Blake seemed to take it all in and nodded, comfortable that his Mom was in acceptance of this news.

"I wish there was something I could do," he mumbled, clearly consumed with concern.

"Well, there just might be." She smiled when he popped his head up, eager to help.

"Her biggest concern is her daughter, Piper. When her Mom passes away, she'll be on her own."

"How old is she?"

"Oh, let's see, she's about five years younger than me, so that would make her…"

"Old!" he interrupted, then ducked when she threw a dish towel at him.

"What about her Dad?" he asked, a more serious expression etched on his face. He pulled a barstool out and climbed onto it, opening his backpack and retrieving books.

"She never really knew her Dad that well, Honey." She pulled out the stool next to him.

"Like me, huh?" She felt a tightening in her throat as she thought of his heartbreak over not having a father in his life.

"Yeah, in a way," she told him. "I think I remember that he was a long haul truck driver and wasn't around for very long. Sylvia never talked about him much."

"Well, what can we do to help?" he asked, his eyes wide as he waited for an answer.

"It is *just* like you to ask that question!" She gave him a reassuring smile.

"She doesn't really have anyone in her life, and once Sylvia's gone, well, she'll need someone to help her out. She said she had always wanted to be a nurse's aide. She's been watching the kind of care her Mom has been getting in the hospital, and now she thinks she might want to go into nursing eventually."

"So," she continued, "she's moving here to Blackwater. The hospital has a work learning program with the community college, and Piper signed up for a six week program."

"She's gonna live close to us?" he asked.

"I think so, we're going to start looking for an apartment for her in the area. If she does well with the nursing assistant program, and starts working regularly for the hospital, she'll consider starting school for her nursing license."

"I can help!" he offered. "I know where lots of places are." He gave a quick nod and flashed a confident smile.

She giggled and reached out to muss his hair, but he artfully dodged her hand. "I am sure you do."

It was less than a week before she heard from Piper. She had seemed hesitant to call, and said she didn't want to be an imposition. When Brynn encouraged her, she sounded a bit more confident, and the two of them set a date and time to meet. Blake was thrilled, and offered to go with them so he could be of help. He knew all the cool places in town, he assured his mother yet again.

Chapter 4

Brynn and Blake arrived at the Ladybird Cafe' before noon on Saturday. As soon as they found a table and took their seats, Blake was craning his neck and watching out the window for Piper's car.

"What does it look like?" he asked her for the third time that day.

"It's a Toyota, pretty old, I think, and it's blue," she told him. "Now, as much as I appreciate your willingness to be on the lookout, I'd like you to look up at the menu board and tell me what you want."

He perused the options quickly. "I already know!" he told her, with a silly grin.

"Cheeseburger and fries, right?" When he nodded, she told him he could resume his watch. Birdie, the café's owner, came and sat with them for a few minutes and chatted. Brynn's candle shop was only a few doors down from the café, and over the years Birdie and her crew had become pretty close friends with Brynn.

"How are Ludie and Ben?" Birdie asked.

"They're good, actually. Annie's a little doll." Birdie had been good friend to Ludie's late grandmother and was now spending a great deal of time with her grandfather. Ludie had even worked for Birdie in the café in the past. They were more like family than employer and employee.

"You tell them they better bring that little baby doll here to see me!" Birdie told her.

"I thought they were just here yesterday for lunch?" Brynn said, more a question than a statement.

"I know. But that was yesterday. I miss her already," she said with a laugh.

When they finally saw Piper's car pull up in front of the café a few moments later, they still hadn't placed their orders. Once inside, she peered around the room, looking for them. Piper Hampton was short in stature but what she lacked in height, she more than made up for in curves.

Her light-blonde, chin-length hair was styled in a short, reverse bob. Large, brown eyes peeped from beneath fluffy, light bangs. Large silver hoop earrings moved with her as she made her way toward them. She wore ultra-high stilettos with cropped tight jeans and a soft, filmy turquoise blouse. Her fashion sense was fearless and she radiated a confidence Brynn hadn't detected over the phone.

"Over here!" Blake shouted, waving his arm. When Piper reached the table, she leaned over and gave Brynn a hug and extended her hand to Blake, who promptly responded with a gentlemanly handshake and grinned while the introductions were made.

"Ooh," she said. "I like a man with a firm handshake!" Blake was beaming, glad to finally be recognized as more than just a little boy.

Taking her seat, Piper ignored the menu and took a sip from Blake's water glass. Clearly enamored of her, he didn't point out her mistake.

"How was your trip? Did you have a hard time finding us?" Brynn asked.

"Not at all," she replied, "once I took the Blackwater exit, the town square was easy. Everything's a lot smaller than I remembered it." She craned her neck and, glancing at the menu board, turned her attention back to Brynn and her son.

"So, have you ordered yet?"

"Not yet," Brynn answered. "I usually get the chicken salad, but Blake highly recommends the cheeseburger, so that's what I'm ordering today." She flashed a smile at him. "Their onion rings are huge, and really good."

"Mm, sounds good," Piper said. "Me too. Hamburger and onion rings." Her tanned skin was bedecked with silver and turquoise jewelry, and her arms were laden with bracelets that ranged from delicate silver chains to bangles. Her purse was gapped open on the seat next to her and Brynn couldn't help but notice the package of cigarettes and lighter inside. She wasn't enthusiastic about the influence it might have on Blake. Assuming Piper would be over to visit them at times, Brynn resolved to speak with her about the ground rules: no smoking inside the house.

"How's your Mom doing?" Brynn asked, her eyes softening in concern.

"She's going downhill pretty quickly." She was twisting a paper napkin in her hands.

"I'm so sorry."

"I didn't realize it would happen like this. Just a few days ago she was alert, talking to me. I just didn't expect everything to change this fast." Her downcast eyes filled with tears.

"That's the thing about hospice. Things change quickly, but I've seen the alternative," Brynn assured her. "I've seen this process drag out over an extended period of time, and it's always so much harder, both on the patient and the family."

"I don't know how we're gonna get through it." Piper looked down at the napkin in her hands.

"You will. On hospice care, they'll make it easier for her. They will keep her medicated."

"For the pain?"

"Yes. And even something for anxiety. Her heart rate will go up, her breathing could get very labored. The meds will help her pain, and also kinda help her breathe easier. It can even make the process go a little faster." She was careful to word it the right way.

Piper looked up quickly, her full pink lips pressed together. "Trust me, I'd *rather* it be this way. I don't want her to have to go through this for a long period of time." She looked back down, and Brynn felt a pang of sadness for her.

"No, of course not."

"Sometimes it just feels like time is running out so quickly. I don't want to leave anything unsaid. I even start to wonder if there is something important I will forget to ask her that I will regret later." For a few moments she remained quiet, and Brynn allowed her the time to reflect. Blake was wide-eyed, quietly taking it all in. He didn't speak, but rather waited for them to resume their conversation.

When the food arrived, Piper seemed glad she'd ordered what Blake had recommended, and she dug in hungrily. The pace of the conversation picked up, however, and they enjoyed the time recalling shared memories from childhood. Piper had an easy way with children and Brynn took note of her interactions with Blake. She was great with kids, she decided, and wondered if she would ever consider babysitting. Blake thought he was much too old for a babysitter, but Brynn refused to leave him alone. To placate him she told him it was because of his diabetes and how bad it could be if he was alone and had a hypoglycemic episode. There was truth to that statement. Only God knew how worried Brynn was over her son's condition.

After a relaxing lunch, Brynn suggested they leave Piper's car at her house while they hunted for apartments. They only found a couple that were in her price range, but they were in another little town nearby, but nowhere near the hospital and Piper expressed concern about living alone that far from town. She'd never lived alone, she told them. They found a few loft apartments across from the courthouse square. They were directly over a suite of law offices and also adjacent from there above a dry cleaner. They were all owned by the same man, a realtor, and he had agreed to show them both of the available units.

When they entered the real estate office, Mr. Wu stood from behind his desk and reached for a peg board to retrieve the keys. He was

Asian, had a slight build, and a professional air of confidence. He was most definitely all business.

Several family photos occupied his desk, all with embellished frames. A small-framed woman with a beautiful face and dark, exotic eyes was seated next to Mr. Wu on a porch swing in one of them, and Brynn assumed it was his wife. Two children who looked to be about preteen age stood over them both, smiling.

As if he'd read her mind, he gestured to the picture. "My wife, my son and daughter," he explained.

"They're lovely," Brynn told him. "You have a beautiful family. How old is your son?"

"He's going to be twelve soon."

"I know him!" Blake nearly shouted, a broad smile splitting his face. "His name is Jimmy! He's in my math class. I like him, he's cool."

Mr. Wu returned Blake's smile. "Yes, he is a good boy. You are welcome to our home to visit any time," he offered. "Now, as for this young lady," he turned to Piper.

"I believe I have the perfect apartment to show you," he said, opening the door for them.

"Thank you," Piper answered.

They merely had to walk half a block from his office to the courthouse square and climbed a flight of stairs to the first unit. Brynn was surprised to learn that not only was Mr. Wu a real estate agent, but he himself owned several small rental properties in town.

Piper squealed with delight when they opened the door and stepped inside. The granite countertops caught her eye first, then the stainless steel appliances. The living room was small, but she quickly assured them all that her preferred style was minimalist, anyway. She rushed from room to room, her heels clicking on the ceramic tile floors as she took in detail after detail. Brynn couldn't help but giggle over Piper's enthusiasm, figuring she would be signing paperwork before the day was over. The girl didn't seem to know how to contain her excitement, which would greatly reduce her power to negotiate.

When they returned to the office, Mr. Wu offered them a cup of coffee, which they both declined. Blake took a seat behind his Mom and Piper and began to chatter, asking Mr. Wu several questions about his son. Brynn was glad he was friends with a boy from such a nice family and made a mental note to invite him over some time. Focusing on the business at hand, she gave Blake a look to remind him to remain quiet so they could discuss business.

When Mr. Wu pushed a document across the desk towards Piper, she shriveled, her face registering a look of disappointment. "I can't, I mean…" she mumbled quietly. "I didn't realize it would be so expensive for a one bedroom." She lifted her eyes, hopeful when he began to speak.

"They are recently refurbished," he answered, obviously trying not to be defensive.

"I've just had the countertops done in granite, as you no doubt noticed, and the appliances are all new. I don't even have to remind you," he went on, "that the location is ideal." He softened a bit when he noticed the beginnings of tears forming in her eyes.

Piper sniffled and nodded. "I understand."

"Why don't you take some time to think about it, look over your budget, and get back with me tomorrow?"

Brynn stood, lifting her purse strap over her shoulder and gathering her keys. "That's a good idea, Piper. Why don't we go back to my place and work up a plan." Piper nodded reluctantly and stood. Mr. Wu handed her a business card and they left the office a great deal quieter and more reserved than when they started.

Blake was full of questions, asking Piper when she'd be moving and his mother when he could invite Jimmy over. A strong look from his mother encouraged him to keep his questions for later. Piper followed them to Brynn's house just a couple of blocks away.

"Blake, honey, why don't you go take Sarge for a walk so Piper and I can talk business?" Disappointment shone in his eyes, but he reluctantly complied.

Taking a seat at the table across from Piper, Brynn opened a legal pad and pushed it toward Piper. "Here. If you need to jot down some ideas for a budget, this might help." Piper shook her head slowly.

"There's really nothing to write down, or consider. I only have about five-hundred a month to work with until I finish the nurse's aid program."

"I'm sure it won't be long before you can begin working after you finish," Brynn encouraged her.

"It'll be a couple of months before I can start actually getting paid for my work." She swallowed hard and blinked back tears. Brynn understood completely that clinical rotations were unpaid internships.

"Now that Mama's in the hospital, we have to give up her apartment by the end of next month." Piper sniffled. A soft murmur of empathy from Brynn undid her, and the tears began flowing unchecked.

"What are you going to do? Do you have any backup plans for after that?"

"We did, I mean, her medical expenses took up the rest of the money she had. We thought we'd have the apartment for several more months."

"The truth is," Piper said, hesitantly, "I don't think I can stay in Houston much longer."

"The memories are too hard, aren't they?"

"What?" Piper looked up at her, a puzzled look on her face. "Oh, yeah, that's right. And the whole thing with Michael."

"Michael?" Brynn eyed her expectantly.

"Michael Lopez." Piper let out a long sigh. "He's my ex-boyfriend. He was too controlling, so I broke up with him. Only thing is, he wasn't ready to let go."

"That's awful! Did he ever hurt you, Piper?"

"A few times. I think he was just angry, and it got out of control. He never realized how strong he was."

Brynn cringed, hating to hear she'd been going through all that. "So, when did you speak to him last?"

"Nearly every day. He just keeps showing up. At the apartment, even the hospital." She kicked her heels off under the table and brought her foot up on the chair, her chin resting on her knee. She was picking at the seam of her jeans.

"I was at the store the other day, by the pharmacy section, and I walked around a corner to a different aisle. There he was."

"Did he say anything to you?"

"He grabbed me by my arm and started pushing me along telling me to come with him. I was so embarrassed."

"What did you do?"

"Well, I didn't want to make a scene, but I knew if he got me outside it would be bad. The pharmacist, Kimla, saw what was happening. She knows me because she fills all our prescriptions, mine, and especially Mom's since she's had so many lately."

Brynn took in a deep breath and waited.

"Well, Kimla saw what was happening and grabbed her intercom. She paged me on it. *Piper Hampton, your prescription is ready. Please come to the pharmacy.*"

"Thank God for her!" Brynn said.

"Yes. And she had one of her cashiers call security. When he showed up, Michael wandered off. The guard ended up walking me out to my car. I drove around for ages, checking to make sure he wasn't following me."

The impact of the situation registered with Brynn and, before she even had time to give it any thought, she knew what she had to do.

"You'll stay with me," she stated emphatically, her hand coming down on the legal pad. "That jerk would be very unlikely to find you here in Blackwater, especially at my house. Your program at school will only be a couple months and you should be on full-time with the hospital soon after that." She handed her friend a tissue.

With that, Piper looked up, her eyes wide and a smile trembling on her lips. "I don't want to impose".

Brynn interrupted her. "No, honey, you're not imposing! We were practically family when we were kids. Besides, it's only for a couple months, I think it'll be fun."

"I can never thank you enough." Piper stood and leaned over Brynn, embracing her.

"What's going on?" Blake stood in the doorway and both women looked up at him.

"What?" he asked, trying to look innocent. "I wasn't eavesdropping, I came back for Sarge's leash."

Piper left in the late evening, hoping to make it back to Houston before dark. She still needed to stop by the hospital and check on her mother once she got back. It would take her a few days to gather her things and, besides, she wouldn't be making any big changes while her mother was in hospice care. As she crossed the Trinity River bridge, her mind ran through all the recent events.

Her mom's cancer diagnosis had taken them both by surprise, and the ensuing battle had taken its toll on both of them. Watching her go through all the treatments, losing her hair, and becoming violently ill had almost been too much. This feeling took her by surprise. It wasn't often she felt such strong emotions.

She squinted against the setting sun as she made her way west toward Houston. She pulled the visor down at an angle to help filter the harsh rays but it only helped a little. She surveyed the bodies of water on both sides. There were a few bridges between Blackwater and Houston, and she loved driving past all the water. She knew, though, that if she took any of the nearby exit ramps, she'd find herself in small country towns that boasted pasture after pasture, with horses and cows as far as the eyes could see.

Brynn's generosity had touched her on a deeper level than she had imagined was possible. She had enough recollection to remember how much she had idolized Brynn when they were girls. Five years older than Piper, Brynn always seemed so sophisticated and beautiful with delicate features. Everything Piper wanted to be. She remembered wishing more than anything in the world that she had a big sister and that it would be Brynn. A bitter laugh rose up in her throat. How strange that it would take such sorrowful circumstances to reunite them. Better now than never, she accepted.

Chapter 5

Two days later, it was Brynn's next scheduled night to work. She arrived on the unit a few minutes before her shift was scheduled to begin and found herself looking around for Spencer. Standing at the desk, she pretended to flip through her report sheet, but kept secretly glancing up at the assignment board to see who was scheduled to cover the unit from respiratory therapy. She felt a warm glow when her eyes darted across the board to see Spencer's name. It would be good to see him, she told herself. They had a good rapport and worked well together. She admired the way he seemed to thrive under pressure. He was quick-thinking and his instincts were all but flawless in the midst of a code situation.

She'd made her first rounds and was just coming out of the medication room when she saw him. A smile lit his face when their eyes met and he stopped to greet her. Both hands full of clear plastic bags containing nasal cannulas and oxygen extension tubing, he leaned across her to set them down while they talked. She couldn't help but notice his strong arms and masculine hands, then let her eyes go quickly upward before he could notice her staring.

"How's your night going so far?" he asked, leaning against the medication room door.

"Great so far. I've got seven patients tonight, but we've got a good crew so it should go well. You?"

"Busy. Sabrina called out so I'm covering two units. Wanna help?" he asked. She secretly wished she could leave her patients and follow this gorgeous man around for the rest of the night. She could handle twelve hours of walking behind him, seeing his backside in those scrubs. Blushing, she caught herself and quickly spoke up before he noticed her deviant thoughts.

"I'd love to. But they'd be pressing those call lights before I could even get away from the unit." She flashed him a smile and wished him good luck. "I'll see you in a little while," she told him.

"Sounds good," he told her, picking up his cannulas and oxygen tubing.

"I'll probably be calling you as soon as I get the Ambien passed out," she said. "Wanna come set up the Bipaps for me? I only have two," she pleaded in a sing-song voice.

"Absolutely! I'm not too busy for that. Give me a buzz when you're ready and I'll even come sing them some lullabies."

"You're a doll." She cringed inwardly, wishing she'd have chosen a different term of endearment. *A doll? Seriously.*

* * *

The next few hours flew by, and when she finally had a few moments to catch up on some charting, her thoughts returned to Spencer. While she began trying to think of an excuse to call him to the unit, she saw Lindsey fly by. *Uh oh, this is not a good sign.* Sure enough, before she even got to her feet, she heard *"Code blue to Four West. Code blue to Four* West."

She jumped to her feet, sending the chair rolling back on its wheels against the opposite wall. Lindsey had already grabbed the crash cart and was in the room. *Good girl,* she thought when she arrived to see her already putting the oxygen on the patient. Mr. Arredondo. She sighed.

"Code blue to Four West."

His chronic obstructive pulmonary disease had been flaring and everyone on the unit knew his condition was worsening by the day. Sure enough, his lips were bluish gray and the pulse oximeter was reading 74%. It should've been at least 95%. Brynn was listening to the man's breath sounds when Spencer came rushing through the door, stethoscope in hand. He brushed past her and leaned over the patient. Brynn relaxed a little, knowing her patient was in good hands.

Having Spencer and Lindsey both working with the patient allowed Brynn to lead Mrs. Arredondo gently out into the hallway. She quickly murmured some soft words of encouragement and then simply pulled her in for a gentle embrace.

"His lungs are being squeezed with all the extra fluid that's accumulating in his pleural cavity, like we talked about before."

"I remember." She nodded, blinking back tears. Her eyes were wide with concern, and she hung on every word.

"The IV diuretics will alleviate some of the pressure, and of course we'll keep him oxygenated."

Mrs. Arredondo had her small trembling hands entangled together, wrapped with her delicate rosary beads. The tiny, frail woman had a transparently strong faith and was taking slow, deep breaths, almost visibly pulling on that strength even now.

"Do you have any questions for me?" Brynn asked her.

"No, honey, you told me everything I need to know." She forced a tremulous smile.

Thea, the charge nurse for the night, rushed past them to analyze the situation. Seeing that Spencer and Lindsey had the crisis well under control, she headed back down the hall, issuing orders to the unit clerk to contact the pulmonologist on call.

Brynn had a great deal of respect and a good working relationship with most of the nurses on the unit, but Thea was certainly not her favorite. She handled emergencies and stressful situations fairly well, but was not what most of the staff would consider a real "people person." She was from the Philippines and, like most of the Filipino nurses, was more than competent in all areas of nursing practice. In their home country, nurses were required to have a four year degree at the very minimum in order to practice and many of them studied further, developing specific areas of practice.

Thea was a bit snippy and wasn't always a favorite of the staff. She had been grumbling about retirement for several years, Brynn had been told, but she apparently never accepted the encouragement of other staff to go ahead and file her retirement paperwork. She was all business and seemed to frown upon the others when they shared moments of light-heartedness. Those moments were a life-saver. In Brynn's opinion, a sense of humor was necessary in order to keep from losing one's mind from all the stress. She suspected Thea had a good heart, judging by the affectionate way she spoke of her family, but her interaction with the nursing staff was strictly business and she rarely softened with any of them.

After things had settled down a bit in Mr. Arredondo's room, Brynn heard Lindsey calling report to ICU. He was being transferred there so he could be monitored more closely for the night. Not seeing his wife in the room, Brynn cast a glance in Spencer's direction. He shrugged, apparently also unaware of her location.

On a hunch, Brynn made her way down a flight of stairs and quickly into the chapel. Sure enough, there she was, kneeling at the altar, tears running down her cheeks. Brynn made her way to the altar and knelt beside her, draping a comforting arm over her shoulder. Mrs. Arredondo looked up at her, tears streaming down her face.

"Oh thank you, darling, you are my angel," she said in her broken English. Brynn helped her to her feet.

"They're moving him to ICU now."

"Is that better?" Her eyes were hopeful.

"They can keep a closer eye on him," Brynn explained. "And they can take actions a lot quicker there."

The small woman nearly crumpled, overwhelmed by a mixture of relief and fatigue.

"Thank you."

By the time they'd made it back onto the unit, the Arredondo's grown children were coming down the hall. Spencer, wonderful compassionate Spencer, was kindly explaining to them what was going on with their father's breathing. Brynn felt a warmth inside, touching her heart. Lately, she found herself growing more and more fond of this man.

When things had finally settled down, Brynn's vague awareness that her phone had been vibrating suddenly sharpened. Swiping the screen, she realized her friend, Roxy, had been trying to call her and had sent her a text message.

"In the emergency room, Love. Come and rescue me. Or better yet, send a gorgeous doctor."

Brynn asked another nurse to cover her patients for a few minutes and darted off to the emergency department.

Pulling the curtain across on its hooks, she took in the scene before her. There was Roxy, lying on a stretcher, checking emails on her tablet. IV fluids dripped by gravity from a pole into a site in her left arm. Her face, arms, and chest were covered with bright pink rashes and she was clawing at her skin with her elegantly manicured nails. She attempted to resume some work on her tablet for only a few seconds before scratching feverishly again. The woman was a powerhouse, and her air of authority and elegance combined to create attention wherever she went. Her exotic accent didn't hurt. But *this*, Brynn thought, *this side of Roxy, was unlike anything she'd ever seen.*

"What's going on?" Brynn asked her.

Dennis Cunningham was at her bedside and Brynn knew just by looking at him that he was absolutely smitten with Roxy. His tall figure gave an aura of ruggedness, and his dark brown moustache only added to it. He was a man's man, firefighter, cowboy. And Roxy simply adored him. He gave a polite nod to Brynn before excusing himself.

"I'll let her fill you in," he said, "while I go for coffee." Turning to Roxy, he asked if she'd like a cup.

"No, I'm all right, *ta*," she said, falling into her casual Australian lingo to thank him. Once he'd stepped out, she began, "That bloke is so in love with the outdoors! I'm happy to see the beach, maybe spend a bit of time outdoors, but he wanted to hike!" She dug into her bag and retrieved a hairbrush, which she immediately began using to scratch her skin. "Poison ivy!"

Brynn grabbed the brush from her. "No! You'll damage your skin!" she shouted.

"I don't care! My nails don't have sharp enough edges and I'm bloody miserable!"

It didn't go unnoticed by Brynn that although Roxy had joked about sending a gorgeous doctor to her bedside, she was all about Dennis. The woman never took her eyes off him when he was in the room.

Brynn told her she'd be right back and left to find her nurse. They'd already begun cortisone injections to calm the inflammation in her skin. Brynn returned shortly, informing Roxy they'd be bringing her a big dose of Benadryl to help with the itching. IV fluids infused from a pump at the bedside in effort to rehydrate her. The outdoors and Roxy weren't a great match.

"Well it's about bloody time! I'm miserable!"

* * *

The rest of the shift flew by. Just before the end of it, the sun had come up and patients were beginning to stir. Lindsey let everyone on her unit know she'd just spoken with ICU and that Mr. Arredondo was holding his own. The aroma of fresh coffee brewing traveled throughout the hallway and the lights that had been dimmed throughout the night were coming to full brightness. The nurses were getting their second wind and preparing to make final rounds before the morning nurses arrived. Brynn sighed in disappointment. She had hoped she would have the opportunity to see Spencer once more before the shift ended.

Just as she closed the last chart, she heard a voice behind her. "Good morning, gorgeous." It was Spencer. She fought to mask her excitement and forced a calm smile on the exterior.

"Good morning!" she breathed. "We made it through another one, didn't we?"

"Yep. Good work. We make a good team." He smiled down at her and set her emotions on edge. Did he have to be so damned irresistible, she wondered?

"Will you be back for another shift tonight?" she asked. Not pausing to allow him to answer, she went on. "Because if you are, I was thinking we could order out tonight. I mean, all of us on the unit. We could get our orders together and call it in, then maybe one of us can go get it, and if, well, I mean if you get time, maybe you can come over to our lounge and have dinner with us?" She could kick herself. *Stop that!* she chided herself. *You're rambling.*

"Are you asking me for a date?" he laughed, not knowing how closely he'd read her mind.

"I just meant, I don't want you eating all alone in your office when we're all down here together, that's all." Her face colored.

"Actually, that sounds pretty good. I'm on the schedule to come back tonight, so let me know when y'all call in the orders." He pulled his phone out and handed it to her. "Put your number in for me. And I'll save mine on your phone."

Her hands trembled while she entered the digits. He wanted her number! She handed him her phone. "Any preferences?" she asked. "Hamburgers? Mexican? Pizza?"

"Any or all of the above." He looked up from the phone. "I'm always starving when I get to work after the cafeteria's already closed."

They switched back to their own phones, and she promised to text him as soon as they were ready to order.

On her way home from work she felt a delicious tingle every time she thought of Spencer having dinner with her. *Relax, Brynn,* she told herself. *It's not a date, it's a lunch break.*

The next night when the other nurses were ready to start talking about ordering dinner, she texted Spencer to get his order just as promised.

When one of the nurses returned with the food later, Brynn texted him again to let him know. He joined them a few minutes later and they sorted out everyone's orders from the bags.

Brynn found Spencer to be an easy conversationalist with a quick, witty sense of humor. She knew she would want to spend more time with him, and it looked to be mutual. There were several people in the lounge, but his comments were directed to her more than the others. She caught him looking at her on more than one occasion, and felt her cheeks coloring each time. Rather than being awkward, he responded with a warm smile.

Chapter 6

Spencer caught Brynn completely by surprise when he texted her a few days later to ask how her week was going. She replied and, after exchanging a few comments and replies by text, her phone rang.

His voice was warm and rich like honey on the other end of the line. "Hey. Thanks for including me for dinner the other night."

"Anytime," she told him. "It was fun." She grew a bit nervous when the line grew silent. They both spoke at once to fill the silence, then laughed. "You go first," she said.

"I was just wondering if you might want to go out and have dinner sometime, when we can eat dinner without being interrupted by call lights."

"Sure, that sounds fun. When?" She felt her heart do a little flip-flop in her chest. Or was it her throat?

"I'm off tomorrow night... if you're free?"

"Actually, I am. I just need to make arrangements for Blake. My son."

"Oh, you have a son?" he asked her.

"He's twelve. He stays with my brother and sister-in-law when I'm working. They have a little girl. Annie. She's a tiny little thing, not quite two years old yet. Blake adores her."

"That's great. Cousins are wonderful. I'm glad he has one. Did you grow up with a big family?"

"No, it was just me and my brother, Ben. We had some cousins but they didn't live very close. We tried to get together as much as we could, just to have someone to play with."

"There's nothing like having other kids to play with growing up. I'm glad you had your brother. I have an older sister." Brynn couldn't help but think of Piper and their childhoods together.

She and Spencer chatted a few more minutes, then agreed on a time for the following night.

* * *

The next morning, Brynn found herself struggling to focus on tasks for any length of time. Every time she thought of Spencer, she got distracted. She was in the midst of putting clothes in the dryer when her phone rang. She pounced on it, then chided herself for being overly eager. It was Piper. She was calling to fill her in on her mother's condition.

"She's gotten a lot weaker. They're putting some kind of liquid medicine under her tongue every hour or two to help with the pain and keep her heart rate under control. From what the nurse told me a little while ago, it doesn't look like it will be very long."

"Oh, Sweetie, I know they'll keep her comfortable. They don't want to see her go through any additional suffering either." Brynn spoke with her a few moments longer, trying to reassure her. "I'm so sorry."

They spoke only a few more minutes before Piper said she needed to get going and get back to the apartment to start packing. She'd been at the hospice most all morning. Piper told her she'd more than likely be bringing a few of her things over before the weekend. Brynn encouraged her to call any time if she needed help with anything.

Glancing at the clock, Brynn wondered if she'd have time to go into Houston and see Aunt Sylvia before Blake got out of school. Even though she hadn't seen her in years, she *had* been an important person in her childhood. And in her mother's life. She grabbed her cellphone, purse and keys and headed out the door, dialing Ludie's number to let her know what was going on.

* * *

Just over an hour later, Brynn pulled into the parking lot of the hospice facility. It was a gorgeous brick-red rambling building that looked like a very large home, complete with peaks and dormers, and dollhouse shudders; it was very charming. It was on a tree-covered lot within the Texas Medical Center in downtown Houston. Looking at the building from the road, you could see the tall buildings looming behind it, but from anywhere on the lot, you'd never know you were in the city just by looking. She was grateful that Sylvia had been moved from M.D. Anderson. Not that it wasn't a wonderful hospital because it was, in reality, one of the most prestigious cancer care hospitals in the world. But a hospice facility, this one in particular, was an environment more like home. It lacked the pristine, bleached-white hallways and the medicinal smell of most hospitals. Everything here was centered around the patient, and the environment was conducive to comfort and family togetherness. The warmth of the atmosphere made it much easier on both the patients and their loved ones in the final stages.

She inquired at the front desk and was greeted by a short, middle-aged woman with a broad, warm smile.

"Sylvia Hampton's room, please?" Brynn asked her.

The woman promptly directed her to Sylvia's room. When Brynn walked in, she was stunned to see her looking so small, so frail. Even given the fact that Brynn was a nurse and had experienced end-of-life situations, she couldn't help but be shocked at Sylvia's appearance. As far as she could recall, Sylvia had always been the self-labeled "master of her existence." She carried herself well, and her confidence led you to believe she had it all and, whatever "it" may be, you wished you had some, too.

But now, she seemed so tiny, swallowed by the immense softness of the bed, the linens that seemed to swell around her. Although Piper had described for Brynn in detail what Sylvia's condition was, it was still a shock. Reminding herself it had been many, many years since she'd seen her, she was nonetheless surprised by the changes. The emaciated look, the paleness of her skin, the hollow, open eyes staring at the ceiling... none of that surprised her. It was her *aura* that was gone. The almost visible border that had always surrounded Aunt Sylvia and defined her nature was no longer there.

Forever the nurse, Brynn rummaged in the drawer for glycerin swabs. Sylvia's mouth was gaped open, lips chapped and dry with gunk growing all around the corners. She made quick work of cleaning them with a spongy swab and then applied a moisturizer that could be used not only on the lips but inside the mouth as well. Sylvia barely responded with a quiet whimper, until Brynn spoke to her.

"Aunt Sylvia, it's me, Brynn," she whispered softly, close enough for her to hear. "Piper told me you were here, and I wanted to see you." The older woman's eyes immediately moved to focus on her, her brows furrowing as she registered recognition. Brynn was surprised her mouth could even close, as the prominent sharpness of her cheekbones seemed welded into place like cold concrete. Brynn was taken aback when she attempted to speak. She appeared troubled, but not simply with the look of pain that was so characteristic of end-stage hospice patients. It was clearly something more.

"Br..." she mouthed, then sacrificed what seemed to be the majority of her strength to make a sound. "Brynn." She shook her head in small, rapid motions that were barely perceptible, her eyes wide with focused tension. Her mouth continued to open and close rapidly but only slight, imperceptible sounds were emitted. "I have to tell you…" What was she trying to say?

"Shhh, it's okay. Don't wear yourself out."

"But, Piper, she…" Sylvia slurred. "I…"

Leaning in closer, Brynn planted a gentle kiss on Sylvia's forehead. "Save your strength. Now, I want you to do something for me. I'm gonna hold your hand, and I want you to squeeze my fingers if you are in pain." She placed her index and middle fingers firmly in Sylvia's palm and felt two strong contractions. "All right. I understand. Let me get your nurse."

Again, Sylvia began struggling to speak, a worried, even frantic, expression in her eyes. She was trying to tell her something about Piper, and it seemed to be the thing that troubled her most at the time. She was clearly agitated.

"Aunt Sylvia, I know you're worried about Piper, but I can assure you I'm going to help her. Try not to worry," she whispered. In response, Sylvia shook her head and continued trying to speak.

Within moments of pressing the call light, a nurse came in with her medication and squeezed liquids from two different syringes beneath her tongue. "It will only take a few moments to work," she said while she adjusted the pillow slightly beneath her head. "Call if you need anything."

Brynn sat back in the overstuffed chair nearest the bed and observed her mother's oldest, dearest friend. The room was very nice, and she was glad Sylvia was surrounded by beauty. The walls were a soft, muted pink, with cream-colored accents. A lovely moss-green vase stood on a half-circle drop-front table near the door. It contained silk, ivory roses with soft greenery. Beneath the flowers next to the vase stood a mantle clock that kept the time, only a few minutes slow. Tick, tick, tick. It lent an air of home to the room. The draperies were merely ivory sheers in front of natural-colored room darkening shades, allowing in only a small amount of filtered light to peep through the edges and stretch across the floor in straight lines. Tiny fragments of dust glittered and danced in the air along the entire streak.

Brynn returned her attention to Sylvia, watching her closely, monitoring her movements and respirations as much out of habit as of concern. Within a few short minutes it seemed Sylvia was calmer. Her eyes returned to the glazed-over blank stare Brynn had seen when she had first arrived. She was finally getting comfortable. But what on earth had gotten her upset on learning Brynn was there? What had she been trying so hard to tell her?

Sighing, Brynn reflected on her memories of Sylvia and Piper and what they had meant to her family's lives so many years ago. Brynn had never fully understood what had made them leave so abruptly. A job in Houston couldn't have been the only reason. After all, Sylvia had been teaching with the Blackwater Independent School District for as long as she could remember. Surely she had her retirement there solidly in place. Maybe the district in Houston paid more, had more to offer in the way of benefits. The sudden move certainly wasn't to be nearer to family as she knew Sylvia and Piper had no close family, not anywhere in Texas, at least. Any time Brynn had asked her mother about it, she had quickly changed the subject and it was clear by her reaction she didn't want to discuss it.

Noticing the time, Brynn bent over and kissed her once more and told her she must get going. This time, she didn't respond. On the drive back, she began anticipating her date with Spencer. It was only a few short hours away. What would she wear? She smiled with the realization that she really enjoyed Spencer's company. It wasn't just the excitement of a hot date with a gorgeous guy, although that was certainly a big factor. But there was more. She genuinely admired this man, and as soon as she could learn to control the numerous butterflies doing gymnastics in her belly, she knew she would thoroughly enjoy her time with him.

As she made the drive home, her thoughts returned to Aunt Sylvia and the unanswered questions that surrounded her visit this morning. What was she trying to tell her and why did she struggle so hard to say the words? As she pulled into her driveway, she made a mental note to ask Piper more about it later.

Chapter 7

Brynn stood in her closet sorting through her wardrobe and found it sorely lacking. *What look is best for a date?* she pondered. *Feminine,* she decided. *Romantic and feminine.* She finally decided on a shell pink blouse with three-quarter sleeves and a soft, filmy floral skirt that flowed delicately from her hips and ended just above the knees. Strappy sandals and a thin anklet finished the look. She decided to wear her hair down, letting it fall in dark, soft waves to rest on her shoulders.

A little while later, Spencer stood on her front porch, one hand bracing him against a column, the other clutching a bouquet of flowers.

"As impossible as it is, I think you look even better *without* your scrubs on," he said.

"Did you rehearse that all the way over here?" she asked him, smiling, a hint of humor in her eyes. She took the bouquet from him and smelled the flowers.

"You're on to me." He gave a sheepish grin.

"They're lovely. Come on in."

He followed her in to the kitchen and watched while she searched the cabinet beneath the sink for a vase. "I like your house," he told her. "You've done a good job making it look nice. I just hung a few pictures on my walls and called it a day." His eyes moved across the dining room to the living room, surveying the décor.

"Thanks. "I've been planning to redo my living room for ages, just haven't gotten around to it yet. I've lived here ever since Blake was a baby. I wanted him to have a place to call home, so when he's older maybe he'll be sentimental enough to visit his old mother often." She looked up, revealing a smile of gratitude.

"I think it would be impossible for him not to," Spencer replied. "And not just because of the house, either. You're his Mom, his home will always be wherever you are."

He was watching her intently, and she felt her face flush with pleasure. She busied herself filling the vase and arranging the flowers in it, but managed to study him out of the corner of her eyes when she thought he wasn't looking. She couldn't help but admire the way he was built. His white, open-collared shirt revealed just a hint of the broad, muscled chest it covered. His masculine build was accented by his short, military type haircut. He looked pretty damned fine without *his* scrubs, too. The jeans he wore, well, she was just grateful he didn't wear them at work. If she were following him down the hall on the way to a patient in crisis, she was afraid she wouldn't remember the first thing to do once she caught up with him… with the patient, anyway.

"Are you ready to go?" he asked. "I'm getting a little hungry."

"Sure, let me get my purse."

"What are you in the mood for?"

She nearly bit her lip to keep from answering too honestly. *Down, girl.*

"Oh, I'm not picky."

"Seafood?"

"I love seafood." She grabbed her purse and followed him out to his car, where he opened the door for her. They headed south on the freeway towards Galveston county, chatting comfortably the entire way. She felt a warmth and comfort inside she hadn't felt in a very long time.

He had very little in common with the guys she'd dated in recent years. She didn't really go out much, mostly just an occasional drink and a couple of rounds of darts or shooting pool with the hospital staff over at Star Bar. She could get used to dates like this. The motives of some guys were so transparently lewd, with some of them almost visibly panting when the evening was coming to an end.. Spencer, however, seemed content and happy just to be with her, talking and laughing.

She couldn't help but look over at him often, hoping his driving kept him unaware of her intense appraisal of him. His profile, dark against the moonlight, was strong, handsome. His jaw was working in rhythm to the music and she wondered if he was chewing something. Just then, he picked up a cup from the console, spit into it and set it back down in the cup holder. *What on earth? Tobacco?* she wondered.

"What are you spitting?" she asked, picking up the cup and daring to look into it. There were mounds of wet black and white pieces that glistened in the scant lighting of the dashboard.

"Sunflower seeds." He chomped down and reached for the cup again.

"At least it's not tobacco," she said, relieved.

"No way. That stuff causes cancer," he told her, spitting into the cup once again.

She sighed, almost relieved to discover that the only flaw she'd seen in him was minimal. Getting to know him so far, she kept wondering if he was too good to be true. He had to have a flaw or two, she knew, but up until now she hadn't known what it was. *Could be worse,* she knew.

He flicked his turn signal on just on the other side of the bridge. The Kemah Boardwalk was one of her favorite fun spots on the Galveston Bay. In the daytime, it was a great place to visit all the little shops that lined the boardwalk, or to have lunch with a friend, or a cappuccino. There were amusement park rides along the waterfront, making it one of Blake's favorite spots as well.

Spencer laughed when she told him how hard it was to get on a roller coaster with a twelve-year-old boy when you've got a belly full of king crab and lemon butter sauce. He even mentioned that he'd like to come back sometime and bring Blake.

At night, the Kemah Boardwalk was also a great place to bring a date. Something about the lights on the water, being inside a restaurant with floor-to-ceiling windows, being able to look out on the bay. There were always a few stragglers, boats coming in after dark, that added to the atmosphere.

When they arrived at the restaurant, they were seated at a table on the patio and enjoyed the view of the sun setting on the bay. There were pleasure boats and dinner cruises going by, close enough for the people on board to smile and wave at the diners on the terrace. Brynn ordered a Grey Goose Martini, and Spencer got the same. Soft piano music tinkled in the background, but not loud enough to deter intimate conversation.

The evening was easy, lazy somehow. It was tranquil, but in no way boring. It was simply the unique feeling a couple gets when they've so thoroughly enjoyed each other's company. That moment that rarely occurs on a first date that tells you "this could possibly be the one." It caught Brynn completely off guard, and she wasn't sure what to make of it. She'd barely finished her drink by the time their meals arrived. They were in no hurry and the waiter sensed that, allowing for a leisurely gap between drinks, appetizers, and the meal.

Brynn couldn't stop herself from stealing glances at Spencer, drinking in his presence with her eyes. His cologne, the way he moved, his handsome face. She couldn't even choose a characteristic that attracted her most. It had been quite a while since she'd dated, so this feeling was probably one of those things where all those separate facts combined and made it seem like this was something it was not. She made up her mind to try to keep things in perspective and just enjoy his company and see where things would go. She took a big sip of her iced water and vowed to stick with that for the rest of the evening.

Besides, she realized she was already quite at ease with him.

When their meals arrived, she laughed when Spencer eyed her plate hungrily, vowing to taste a bite of nearly everything she'd ordered. Normally she would have chastised her son for that and told him to use his manners, but the way Spencer did it was charming, intimate even. She disliked her double standard, but not enough to keep from picking up a stuffed shrimp and putting it up to Spencer's mouth. "Mmm... try this!"

Their chairs had somehow pushed themselves gradually closer together. She had ordered crab claws and shared them with him. He convinced her to try shark meat, and she was surprised it wasn't half-bad.

By the time they had finished eating, both were so at ease and thoroughly enjoying every moment. She couldn't recall ever being on a date that was so utterly perfect.

After Spencer paid the check they strolled along the boardwalk, looking into various shops. The theme for tonight appeared to be a nod to Texas's neighbor to the east, Louisiana. Live Cajun and Creole bands played alternately, sending beautiful, meaningful, and mostly just fun strains of music out into the air. A few people even got out in the middle of the expansive tiles and started dancing. Some of them were true Cajuns and Creoles and their dancing reflected the love they had for their heritage. Some people, on the other hand, weren't Cajun or Creole at all, they were more like drunken rednecks.

Spencer grabbed Brynn's hand and led her out onto the paved stones of the boardwalk and they danced as well, trying to ramp up their Texas steps to the quick beat of zydeco. The Louisiana border was less than an hour and a half away, depending on who was driving and which route they took. The Cajun people's style of dance was fun to watch, and even more fun to join in.

The sounds of boat motors and the splashes from the wakes they made faded in the background, enhancing the mood. The music and laughter took center stage throughout the boardwalk, marina and shops. Stopping on the sidewalk next to a small gazebo to listen to another band, Spencer reached out and took Brynn's hand in his. Small, pleasant sparks of electricity worked their way up her arms and into her chest. Her hand felt small in his stronger, masculine one. Their arms brushed a few times, once when they were turning to walk in another direction and then again when they sat down on a park bench for a few minutes.

The chemistry was there, Brynn realized… unless she was so date-deprived that she was overly responsive to every little touch. Regardless, she was loving every moment of this date and hoping that Spencer was feeling the same way.

As the evening was wearing down, her mind was racing with the possibilities. *Do I invite him in?* she wondered. *Would it seem too forward?* She wanted more time with him, to see him smile more, to laugh at more of his funny jokes. She wanted to experience more of that feeling she got when his arm brushed up against hers.

But what she did not want was what might happen if she invited him in for a drink and they continued to feel that spark. *What if they gave in to it? How many dates before it would be okay?* No, she settled firmly. She wouldn't be inviting him in tonight, she needed him to respect her, to spend more time with her and learn to know her. As intoxicating as his glances were, and as full and sensual as his lips were under that dark moustache, and as much as she wanted to invite him in, she knew it would be better to wait. Inwardly she scolded herself for allowing herself to think that way, even for a moment.

His eyes traveled over her body, but always returned promptly to her eyes, her face, to let her know he was interested in *her*, and not just her body. In spite of his smoldering gazes, there was something in his manner that soothed her, something that let her know that in spite of how much he clearly desired her, she was safe with him. She could already tell that there was a spiritual intimacy he desired as much as the physical. *What are you doing?* she asked herself. *First date, and you've already got his feelings all figured out? Just by the way he's looking at you?* She shook her head and looked up, the beginning of a smile tipping the corner of her lips.

When they stood at her doorstep later, Spencer took both her hands in his and raised them to his mouth, pressing the backs of them to his lips for a fleeting moment.

"I enjoyed being with you tonight," he murmured against them.

"Me too. Thank you for this," she told him. "I needed this. I love my job, and taking care of

Blake, but... I really needed this change of pace." She narrowed her eyes, letting him know how sincere her statement was.

"I hope we can get together again sometime." There. She'd said it.

With that, he straightened his stance and broke into a wide grin. "I would really like that a lot. And soon." He smiled, and asked about her plans for the following weekend. After verifying that she should have at least one evening free next weekend, they said good night and planned to touch base during the week to finalize the plans.

She reached out and took his hand, playing with his fingers while she spoke, slightly surprised at her ease with him. "You know where to find me at work and, well, you have my number." When she looked back up into his eyes, he leaned forward and kissed her. It was worth the waiting and wondering and stressing of "would he or wouldn't he?" It was the most wonderful kiss, with his lips so warm and soft and yet firm at the same time, and sweet. Again, it felt as though his lips were melting into hers and her mind was instantly muddled and drained of any coherent thought to speak.

When he pulled away, it was only to say goodnight, but the way he looked into her eyes reached her to her very core.

"Thank you, Spencer," she whispered. "I'll see you soon, okay?"

"Absolutely. We'll talk soon." As she watched him walk away, she felt herself tempted to call him back, and to invite him in. Instead, she watched as he got into his car. Inside the house, she closed the front door and secured the latch. Turning around, she leaned her back into it, and nearly slid down the door. Spencer Evans was incredible!

Chapter 8

The next morning, Brynn popped over to Ben and Ludie's for a visit. It was great having them just across the street and down a little, caddy-corner but close enough to see their home from her front sidewalk. Ludie had been her long-time friend and had come to work in her candle shop a few years back. After a really difficult and abusive relationship, Ludie had begun seeing Ben. Brynn couldn't have been happier and was delighted to welcome her into the family. She and Ludie had managed to maintain their closeness, and it was mornings such as this that she enjoyed a break from her busy routine.

Pouring a cup of coffee she took a seat in the living room where Annie was on the floor playing with her toys. Ludie came into the living room, snapping the lid on Annie's juice cup.

"So what's new with you?" Ludie asked.

"I had a date last night."

"Oh, really?" she drawled out. "Ben just said you had plans but we didn't know it was a date." With an invigorated interest, she pressed her for details.

"His name's Spencer." She wrapped her hands around the mug, smiling as she brought it to her lips. "He works at the hospital, he's a respiratory therapist."

They spent a little while catching up when Ben came into the living room.

"Hey, how's it going?" he greeted her.

"Good," Brynn said. "Oh! I meant to ask you... do you remember Aunt Sylvia and Piper?"

He lifted his eyebrow in response. "Of course. Wow. I haven't heard those names in years. Whatever happened to them?" He bent down and scooped Annie up into his arms.

"Well, remember they moved to Houston? Sylvia was going to teach there."

"Yeah, I guess so. I don't remember much about that part. I just knew we didn't see them again much after that."

"We didn't see them at *all* after that," she corrected him. "It was really weird. Anyway, Sylvia called me. She's sick." She set down her mug, her expression growing more serious.

"It's cancer. She never remarried, it's always just been her and Piper."

"How bad is the cancer?" he asked.

"Pretty bad. They've tried chemo and basically she's out of options."

He nodded, taking it all in, before bringing Ludie up to speed on his and Brynn's childhood and Piper and her mother being such a big part of it.

"So how's Piper taking all this?" He sat next to Brynn on the couch. Annie had clutched his hands and was bringing them together, trying to get her daddy to play patty-cake.

"Not great, I'm sure. But Sylvia asked me a favor. She wants me to help Piper get through all this."

"Why?" he asked. "We haven't heard from them in years."

"I know. Apparently they don't have anyone else. Piper wants to be a nurse's aide, maybe even become a nurse eventually. Sylvia helped her get enrolled in the program here in Blackwater. She'd heard through the grapevine I became a nurse and was hoping I could take her under my wing. At least until she can get on her feet."

Annie thrust herself across her Daddy's lap and toward Brynn, who grabbed her up, greedily stealing kisses from her soft cheeks.

"Are you going to help her?" Ludie asked.

"Yeah, I think I have to," Brynn told her. "In fact, I've already given Sylvia my word. They were like family."

Ben nodded in agreement. "They were."

* * *

That afternoon Piper began moving her things into Brynn's house. She didn't bring much, it seemed, and most of what she brought reminded Brynn of things a college student would bring for her dorm room. She had her own brightly-flowered comforter, throw pillows, and decorative memo board. She brought a few books, her laptop and even a goldfish in a bowl that looked like a martini glass. Her clothes fit in the guest room closet with a little creative maneuvering. Once she'd arranged her shoes neatly in the bottom of the closet and put her folded items into the drawer, she came into the living room and announced her presence.

"Honey, I'm home!"

Brynn chuckled and told her that was exactly how she wanted her to feel.

Piper's smile quickly faded and she blurted, "Oh, I didn't mean to imply that this was my home, forever!"

"Relax, I didn't take it that way at all. You've got enough to worry about with your Mom's health and trying to get through your program in school. Not to mention getting away from the ex-boyfriend. Just make yourself at home here, and we'll find you a place when things settle down a bit." She patted the cushion next to her on the couch and told her to sit down.

With that, Piper visibly relaxed. "Wanna watch a movie tonight? I can order us a pizza."

"Sure," Brynn replied. "As long as it's a family-friendly movie. Blake will be home. In fact, I need to go make sure he didn't go far." With that, she stood and made her way out front where she found Blake shooting hoops with one of the neighbor boys. Sarge laid at the edge of the driveway, watching, as always.

"Blake!" she called. "It's getting dark. Five or ten more minutes and then you need to come in and shower." He rolled his eyes and mumbled under his breath.

When she reminded him Piper would be staying tonight and ordering pizza, he said goodbye to his friend and made it inside a few seconds after his Mom did. *That's a quick change of attitude.* They called in their pizza and had just started the movie when Brynn's phone lit up. It was Spencer. "Let me just tell him we're busy right quick and that I can call him later."

"Absolutely not!" Piper ordered, grabbing Blake by the hand. "Come on, Blake, show me your room," she said, leading him out of the living room. "We'll start the movie over again after you're finished with your phone call."

"Hello," she answered. She sat in the corner of the couch and sunk into the soft, fluffy cushions. Sarge followed Piper and Blake from the room, then returned and laid at her feet. She bent down to stroke him behind the ears.

"Hi," Spencer said. "I just wanted to tell you again how much I enjoyed your company last night." He had no idea how sensuous his voice sounded in her ear.

"So did I. Are you working tonight?"

"Yes. I'm just about to jump in the shower and get ready. I slept a few hours this afternoon so I should manage to stay awake. For most of the shift anyway," he chuckled. "What about you?"

"I'm off tonight." She could almost make out a small sigh of disappointment on his end. "We just ordered pizza and we're going to watch a movie with my son." He suddenly grew quiet. She had said *we,* she realized.

When he finally spoke, she picked up a hint of jealousy in his voice. "I'm sorry, I didn't mean to interrupt anything."

She was quick to correct. "I have a new roommate," she blurted. "Her name is Piper, and she just finished moving her things in today." This time the sigh she heard was a sigh of relief.

"That's right! You mentioned her! I have to admit, I'm greatly relieved to hear that." He laughed. His voice was like honey to her. She felt a smile tugging at the corner of her mouth.

"Did you think I had a boyfriend?" she asked playfully. "That I went out with you last night and then tonight I'm sharing a quiet, intimate evening at home with my boyfriend?" She was clearly having fun with this.

"You did make me wonder a bit," he said. "And on that note, I'll let you go and get back to your evening. Your evening with your roommate. Who is a girl. And not your boyfriend," his voice teased. "I hope to meet both her and your son soon. You have fun. I'm going to help people breath for a while. Um, call me if you need anything."

She found a note of fearlessness within herself and said, "If I become short of breath, you will be the *first* one I call." *Look at you flirting shamelessly!* she told herself, and hung up with a smile.

She walked down the hallway with Sarge trailing closely behind. She found Piper and Blake in his room, sitting cross-legged on the foot of the bed playing a video game. They were racing cars and Blake was winning, although Piper was clearly giving him a run for his money.

"All right, you two. Time to get cleaned up for dinner and get ready to start the movie."

"Aww, Mom!" he protested. "We just got started!"

"Yes, you did, but the pizza will be here soon and Piper's waiting for us."

Puffing out his chest, he told her, "I'll turn it off when the pizza comes."

"You'll turn it off now."

With a loud groan, he begrudgingly turned off the game and started winding up the cords to the controls. When the doorbell rang, Piper offered to pay and left the two of them in Blake's room. Brynn sat on the edge of Blake's bed.

Not wanting to alienate her moody preteen with a new roommate moving in, she decided to take a different approach. "You and Piper seem to be hitting it off well," she told him. Sometimes she could so easily see the little boy in him. Other times, he seemed so grown up. He'd been going through some of the most awkward stages, tall and lanky and not sure how to carry himself.

"I like her, she's cool." That was a glowing report, coming from a twelve year old boy.

"Yeah, she *is* cool, isn't she? Now let's go eat pizza and watch the movie with our cool new roommate."

Chapter 9

The next morning after seeing Blake off to school, Brynn and Piper were walking into the coffee shop just as Spencer was leaving.

"Good morning," he told her, a warm smile playing on his lips. "How was your movie and pizza?"

"It was great! Spencer, this is my old friend and new roommate, Piper. Piper, meet Spencer." Spencer extended his hand, and Piper shook it firmly. A slow smile spread across her face as she took in his features.

"It's very nice to meet you. You work in the hospital with Brynn, then, right?" Brynn wasn't surprised at Piper's response. Spencer's eyes were warm and friendly and they drew people in to conversation easily.

"Yes, we work the same unit most of the time. I'd have to say she's my favorite nurse."

"Mine, too. I'll hopefully be working with her soon. I'm going to school to become a certified nursing assistant." She grinned proudly.

"That's great!" Casting a glance at Brynn, he told her, "You're in great hands. I can't imagine a better mentor than Brynn."

"Thank you." Brynn said, breaking in to the conversation. "So, how did last night go?" she asked him.

"Busy. I came by for a coffee just to help me stay awake long enough to make it home. It's usually either coffee or crunching on sunflower seeds that keeps me awake."

"Um, you live only a mile away."

"Told you we were busy," he said with a wink. "I didn't even get a power nap last night! If you're planning on working tonight, you better plan on stopping by here for a double shot espresso on your way to the hospital."

"I actually *am* on the schedule for tonight, and I will take that under advisement. In fact, I'll probably be here around 6:00. Meet me here? It's *my* treat." She lifted a brow, awaiting his response.

"It's a date. See you then." With that, he leaned over and gave her a quick kiss on the cheek and headed out the door.

"Whoa!" said Piper. "You didn't tell me there were guys like *that* working at the hospital. I would've started much sooner!"

"Spencer is one of a kind," she answered proudly. "But we'll have to see if we can find you a nice guy. We do have some great male nurses."

"If all the male nurses aren't taken or gay, count me in! Now, let's get a cappuccino."

Brynn rolled her eyes at Piper's comment. *Really?*

"No way, I need to stick with a decaf latte so I can get some sleep. I've got a date at 6:00, remember?"

"Yeah, yeah, fine." Piper moved toward the counter. "I'm going to be driving to Houston to see Mom. I'm getting cappuccino."

* * *

Exactly ten hours later, Brynn sat at a small, raised round table across from Spencer, sipping on a cappuccino with an extra shot of espresso.

"So, tell me about Piper," he told her. "You knew her before, right? Old friends?"

"Yea, she was my childhood friend. Actually, our mothers were best friends, and we spent most of our time together. I called her Mom "Aunt Sylvia" because they were like sisters. They moved away when I was fifteen and we lost touch. I was never really sure why."

"I guess the important thing is, they're back in your life now."

She filled him in on the details, explaining the recent events that had led Sylvia to contact her, and how she was in the end stages of cancer.

"I'm so sorry you had to be reunited under such horrible circumstances." His voice held a note of compassion. "It says a lot about you, you know." He fiddled with the lid of his cup.

"You're very kind to say so." She looked up at him, her blue-green eyes expectant.

"It's true. It means you have an incredibly warm heart, and that you're a good friend, for them to turn to you in such a time." She warmed at his kindness.

"I only hope I can make a difference." She told him about her visit with Sylvia the day before and how she wasn't sure whether or not she'd been able to really reach her. "I'm not even sure if she knew who I was at first," she told him. "But it did seem she responded when I told her my name. She got almost agitated, even, like she was desperate to tell me something but she couldn't." A shadow of sadness touched her face. At the sound of his voice, she looked up and listened.

"You're already making a difference. You've brought her daughter back into your life, your home, even, so she can make it through school and get a job. She can go in peace knowing that you've got her daughter's back and that she's not all alone in this world. What more could any mother ask?"

He has a way with words, she thought. *No, he has a way with me.* She looked up at him over her foaming cup of cappuccino and smiled. Spencer was definitely one of the good people in the world. And she was one of the lucky people.

* * *

Shortly thereafter, they pulled into the hospital parking lot and parked next to each other. Together, they walked inside. No one seemed to notice, which was fine with Brynn, because hospitals were known for gossip as it was, they didn't need to add to it. She supposed if she kept seeing Spencer that in time people would start to notice and ask her about it, but for now, she had enough on her mind without having to answer a lot of questions.

They said goodbye at the time clock in the main lobby, knowing they'd likely see each other several times before the shift ended. "Thank you for the coffee," he said.

"My pleasure. It was the least I could do, since it *was* my idea." She flashed him a flirty grin.

"Yes it was, wasn't it?" he teased. "And I'm glad you thought of it. If I wasn't certain that there are eyes all over us, I'd give you a thank you kiss right now." Her mind thrilled at the thought of it, but he was right. It would draw too much attention. There would be time for that later.

"Have a good shift. I'll see you soon." He gave a little wave as he walked away, disappearing quickly down the hallway toward the respiratory department.

Her shift would be heavy, she knew. The assignment board gave each nurse seven patients, and they were short one nurse's aide. That would make a big difference in how the patients would be managed. Each nurse's aide, or tech, as they were called, would be assigned a certain number of patient baths and would be trying to equally share the number of call lights answered. Quite a few of the patients on the unit right now were of a higher acuity than usual which meant closer monitoring. Brynn sighed, glad she had the extra jolt of caffeine before work.

Brynn and Lindsey were on the same hall tonight, which was a good thing since they worked well together. Lindsey had apparently seen her friend walking across the parking lot with Spencer and was full of questions.

"Just because we're busy doesn't mean you don't have to talk," she teased. "It just gives you a little extra time before you have to spill it." She ducked into a room and Brynn laughed, knowing she would end up revealing all before the night was over.

As of right now, Brynn needed to make a quick set of rounds to briefly introduce herself to each patient, make sure their IV lines were dripping as ordered and that no one was in acute distress. She would have to hurry since it wouldn't be long before she would need to start giving medications and needed to go out and get a plan of action going first. Her assignments started in room 415. Mrs. Casey lifted her head from the pillow when Brynn walked in.

"Come on in, honey, I've got a list to go over with you." She reached for her bed control and raised her bed to an upright position. She grabbed a notepad from her bedside table and started at point one.

"First of all, my dinner tray had peas on it, and I've told them I can't have peas. Second, my doctor told me these antibiotics would be finished today, but they're not. Third..." she trailed off when Brynn stood near the bed, examining the labels on the IV bags infusing through the pump.

"Mrs. Casey, you don't have any antibiotics going right now. If you'll give me a little time to go and check my medication orders, I can let you know where we stand on that when I come back in a little while." She gave her a reassuring glance and jotted a note on the report sheet regarding her medication orders.

"Well, just see you do," Mrs. Casey pouted. "I don't want one more dose of those things than I absolutely have to have. Now, as for number three, I want to take a shower but they won't let me get my bandages wet. How are we supposed to do that?"

Brynn forced a smile and promised her patient that she would work on that just as soon as she could get caught up. She heard her name over the intercom and had to excuse herself quickly. She had made it just a few steps outside of room 415 when she could have sworn she heard Mrs. Casey say "and fourth…"

Fortunately, three of her patients were sound asleep when she made her initial rounds, allowing her to do a quick visual assessment and leave quickly for the next room. Sometimes it worked out that way, where she would have quiet, easy patients to even out the demands on her time made by the more challenging ones.

Just as Brynn had organized her medications and was ready to get started, she was called to the phone. "Pharmacy? Doctor?" she asked the unit secretary.

"I'm not sure," Shannon answered. "It sounded personal. And urgent."

She picked up the phone and pressed the flashing line. "4 West, Brynn." She immediately heard stifled sobs on the line. "Piper? What's wrong?"

"It's my Mom," she cried. "She's at the very end. They told me to come down there now."

"Oh, Sweetie, I'm so sorry." She knew how it felt to lose someone, and the memories of her own mother's death resurfaced. "Is there anything I can do?"

"No," Piper sniffed. "I just have to go there, I'm leaving now. They said there's not much time. I just need to, I dunno... I need her to know I'm there. I need to say goodbye."

"Please, take your time, don't get in too much of a rush and risk your safety. She wouldn't want that. Remember, you were just there today, and she knew you were there."

"I know. They said it wasn't long after I left before she started going downhill. I'm getting my things together, I'm not coming home until, well, you know."

"Are you okay to drive? Why don't you let me see if I can get someone to relieve me so I can take you?" She glanced up to see a stern look of disapproval from Thea, her charge nurse for the night.

"No, it's okay," Piper said. "I'll be careful, I promise. You finish your shift, I need to be leaving now, anyway. I'll call you later, okay?"

"Piper, have they explained to you what the final stages look like? Because if not, don't be afraid to ask what to expect. When I saw her day before yesterday, she looked like she was nearing the final stages, and I know there are no two patients exactly alike, but.."

"What?" Piper interrupted. Her voice had quickly turned to ice. "You went to see my mother?"

"Yea, I'm sorry I didn't mention it. When I got back, I was racing to get ready for my date, and then everything's been so hectic. I'm sorry."

"Did she say anything to you?" Piper asked coldly.

"No, I mean, she said my name, but it's not like she was able to really talk or anything."

"I just wish you would've told me." There was still an edge to her voice.

"Oh, honey I'm sorry, I didn't even think to ask if you'd want to come along. You were busy in registration and getting your books and things ready for school."

"It's okay," Piper responded quickly. "I'm sorry. I guess I'm just a little tense."

"Of course, honey. I understand. Be careful driving into Houston. Let me know something. And Piper?"

"Yea?"

"I'll be praying every chance I get."

"Thank you."

She heard sniffling, and then a click. Before she could place the phone in the receiver, Thea was in front of her, insisting that the unit was short-staffed as it was and that being down one nurse at this point would be a complete disaster for the unit. Apparently she had overheard Brynn's end of the conversation and was afraid she'd be asking to leave early.

"I'm not going anywhere, Thea. I'm here for the rest of the shift." Brynn took off with a worried look on her face, leaving Thea behind, looking almost disappointed that she didn't get an argument out of her.

Brynn was vaguely disturbed by her conversation with Piper. She hadn't meant to offend her, and she would've been glad to take her along. It just never occurred to her that it would be a problem. *Why on earth would she have not wanted me to visit her mother?* Brynn dismissed her concerns and refocused her attention on her patients.

The night went by quickly, as there was very little time between call lights. Several times she found herself racing from room to room, wishing she could be in more than one place at one time.

She saw Spencer several times, mostly from a distance, as he raced about, administering nebulizer treatments and responding to patients in various forms of respiratory distress. Twice she was in a room with Spencer, but they didn't have the opportunity to speak. They did exchange glances over a patient. When she would see him at a distance she would flash him a shy smile and return his wave. As busy as she was, each time she saw him she felt herself responding to his presence with a little flutter of butterflies in her tummy. *Oh for heaven's sake. You're not sixteen,* she thought, but secretly delighted in the feeling.

It was nearly 4:00 am when she finally heard from Piper again. She was angry with herself for not finding the time to call her friend before then, but was glad to hear from her now. Aunt Sylvia's battle had ended just moments ago, and Piper was waiting for the hospice staff and funeral home to prepare her for the next step. She said she should be home by the time Brynn got home from work.

When they hung up, Brynn went ahead and contacted the nursing supervisor to ensure she'd have someone to cover her shift the next night. Thea could protest all she wanted, but once she'd explained to the higher supervisor, there wasn't much she could say. Besides, Sylvia and Piper were like family. Brynn had promised Sylvia she would look out for her daughter and that's what she was going to do.

When Spencer came to the unit to give his last set of treatments, he knew Brynn was upset.

"What's going on?" he asked her. She briefly filled him in on what had happened and told him she was taking tonight off to be with Piper.

"I don't think so," snapped Thea, who was standing behind Brynn, listening to her conversation. "We're supposed to have a pretty high patient census tonight, we've got hardly any discharges on the schedule. This is not a good time for you to be taking off." Thea pursed her thin lips and crossed her arms.

"I'm sorry, but I just can't be here tonight. I have a family emergency." Apparently Thea hadn't been there for the whole conversation. "I've already cleared it with the house supervisor."

Thea slammed shut the chart she was holding and stormed off. Brynn knew she wasn't alone in her feelings toward Thea. The woman was on a massive authority kick and loved to put people in their places. She was all business, unless it suited her not to be. She had an inflated sense of power, unlike the other charge nurses on the unit who, for the most part, fostered an environment of cohesiveness.

Spencer looked Brynn in the eyes and placed a hand on each of her shoulders.

"Listen, you do what you need to do. Don't worry about Thea. I'm sure the scorpion that crawled up her butt will die soon and things will ease up around here." He gave her a wink and a quick kiss on the cheek. Brynn loved his sense of humor and his ability to make her laugh under even the worst of circumstances.

Chapter 10

When Brynn got home from work, Piper still wasn't home so she showered and waited up for her. She was curled up on the couch in her bathrobe when she heard keys in the door. Jumping up, Brynn met her near the door and wrapped her arms around her. Piper's eyes were rimmed with red and it was clear she'd been crying, but as soon as she laid her head on Brynn's shoulder she melted into a series of sobs.

Brynn led her to the sofa and just held her while she cried. She periodically offered tissues from a box next to her and just waited and allowed her to cry.

Piper's sobs finally subsided and she drew in some deep breaths. When she was finally able to speak, it was like the bursting of a dam. Piper told story after story of her mother and of their lives together. Brynn's heart felt crushed for her friend. She knew what it was like to lose a parent, it had happened to her twice. The difference was that Brynn had her brother, Ben, to help her through it. Piper was an only child and would be grieving alone if it weren't for Brynn.

After Piper had talked until her voice was hoarse, Brynn told a few stories about Sylvia that she remembered fondly. Piper appeared to cheer a little at the happy memories. They were simple memories, mostly of days well spent at the beach or shopping together when they were young, and the way their mothers had laughed together so much.

Piper likely had many of the same memories but being five years younger than Brynn she would've been roughly ten years old at the time they moved away. Brynn was more than happy to share with her what memories she had. Piper told her she would be meeting with the funeral director later in the afternoon. She would have a small memorial service and a simple burial. She explained that it was mostly just the two of them in recent years and that they had kept to themselves most of the time, especially when Sylvia had been diagnosed with cancer. Brynn understood and offered to accompany her to the funeral home.

"Would you?" she sniffed, blowing into a worn tissue.

"Of course. C'mere." She pulled her into a gentle hug.

* * *

The next couple of days went by quickly. The service and burial were very intimate and unassuming. A few people Sylvia had taught with came by, the principal and librarian as well. Aside from the school district, Sylvia and Piper didn't really have anyone else.

There were a few other people who appeared to be casual acquaintances there, but

Piper merely introduced them by name. Brynn didn't press for details. She was just relieved that Michael, Piper's ex, didn't show up.

Brynn considered the small, unpretentious funeral and wondered about the expense. Brynn didn't question Piper about it, but guessed that finances were limited.

Once they left the cemetery after the graveside service, Brynn drove them home. "What would you like for dinner? It's my treat."

Piper was staring down at the crumpled tissues she was working between her fingers. She looked up and smiled sadly.

"You're so good to me, Brynn. Why?" Her brows pulled together in question.

Brynn reached across and patted her on the leg. "Sweetie, we were practically family. I never knew why our Moms parted ways, but you were always such a big part of my life back then and I've thought of you often over the years. I'm just glad you're here now and we can be friends."

At that, Piper began to cry again, choking back sobs. "Thank you, Brynn. I'll never forget your kindness."

* * *

When things had settled down a bit in the days after the funeral, Brynn made a concerted effort to include Piper in as many things as she could, including Blake's activities, shopping, and dinners. Brynn loved to cook and loved trying new recipes. Involving Piper might help her feel more connected. One morning Piper knocked on her bedroom door.

"Come in."

Piper approached tentatively. "Got a minute?"

"Sure. Sit down." She patted the bed beside her.

"I was just thinking…" Piper swallowed hard, and Brynn couldn't help but wonder if she was trying to choke back tears.

"Talk to me."

"It might help me to see some of the places I remember. From when we lived here before."

"That's a great idea!" Brynn encouraged her. "Maybe see where we lived back then and where you and your Mom lived. Yeah, let's do it."

Piper exhaled as if she'd been holding her breath for a very long time. "Thank you."

"My pleasure. In fact, I think it would actually be very therapeutic."

* * *

A few days later they loaded up Blake and Sarge and made a day of it.

Piper seemed to really light up at the sight of some of the old familiar places. Seeing her old house brought tears to her eyes, which upset Blake. *Such a tender heart,* Brynn thought.

"Happy tears," she told him. "When they lived here, it was a good time in Piper's life and it's nice for her to experience the good memories."

"Exactly," Piper added. "This helps me."

They also drove by Brynn and Ben's childhood home, which was only a block away from Piper's. After a brief stop at the dog park to give Sarge a break, they went through a drive-thru and got hamburgers and drinks.

"Brynn," Piper asked. "Do you think we could go one more place?" She played with her straw in the cup, looking back up to await her response.

"Of course! Where do you want to go?"

"The air strip? I remember when your Dad took us up with him. It was even fun being on the ground and watching them take off and land."

Brynn was a bit surprised, since she didn't really recall Piper having spent much time there. Brynn's father had owned a warehouse/hangar on his property bordering the airstrip. Back when he'd owned a small business, he used his hangar as an office space as well. He ran deliveries throughout various areas in Texas and Louisiana.

On a typical day, he might make a trip to Dallas, or Austin or New Orleans to pick up a delivery for Houston or vice versa. It had been fairly lucrative and he'd always said he preferred it to being tied up somewhere in a concrete jungle.

There were many occasions on days when he didn't have any deliveries to make that he'd take Brynn and her brother up for a flight. She'd loved every single minute of it, him pointing out his favorite sites and explaining to her and Ben where everything was. She remembered thinking how interesting it was that so many pastures looked like squares and other geometric shapes. It was almost like a patchwork quilt; some of the squares were a brownish color, while others were lush and green. Some areas were so heavily covered with trees you couldn't see the ground for miles.

Although those flights and hanging out at the hangar had been fun for Brynn and her brother, she found it slightly puzzling that Piper had given it so much thought she wanted to visit it.

"Are you sure?" she asked her. "I mean, I didn't realize you had been there much?"

Piper managed a tremulous smile. "Of course I've spent time there," she answered defensively. "With you."

"I'm sorry, I had forgotten."

"I didn't have a Dad like you and Ben to take me places. Getting to come with you those times was a real treat for me." She looked down at her hands in her lap. "If you don't want to take me, I understand."

Brynn shook her head, still a bit puzzled, but sorry she'd made her feel excluded from the pleasant memories. "No, that's not it at all. I guess I just didn't realize you'd come with us more than a couple times."

Chapter 11

They drove out to the airstrip and found the hangar. Waves of nostalgia spread over Brynn, and the pain of losing her father hit her all over again. Blake's enthusiasm, however, not only eased the awkward moment but helped soothe the painful sadness she felt at the loss. Sarge bounded along with them as they explored the area.

The hangar itself was in poor repair. It had been years since Brynn had visited and it suddenly occurred to her to wonder why she and Ben hadn't been informed of its disposition when the will was probated.

Piper seemed to enjoy the visit, running her hand across the worn and scarred desk that still sat in the office. An open file cabinet sat in the corner, the top drawer slightly open with a few papers stuffed in haphazardly. A travel mug sat atop the desk and, had it not been for the layers of dust, it might look as though her Dad had just left his coffee there this morning and might return for it.

Wandering into the hangar itself, Brynn was surprised at how small it seemed now. When she was a little girl, it felt like the biggest place in the world, with lots of room to run across the concrete floors and play. Even when he'd stored his plane in there, there was adequate space for even a couple of cars to park inside. Brynn made a mental note to come back sometime when she was alone and sort through some of the papers and other items that had been left behind. She wondered if she could check with the county to inquire about the ownership of the building and its property, again vaguely wondering why it had never been discussed.

It was one of many days Brynn went to the effort of including Piper in her activities. She hoped there would be more. She couldn't erase the memory of Aunt Sylvia and the promise she'd made to her the day she'd visited her in the hospital.

One of Brynn's most recent ideas for shopping projects was to redecorate her living room. She had long since tired of the black wrought iron designs and glass-topped tables. It was time for something new. Most everyone on her unit at the hospital was aware of Brynn's desires for the perfect living room since she used her rare free moments, searching magazines and online for ideas. She knew for the most part what type of curtains she wanted, had already picked out wall colors and throw pillows, and had all of her ideas bookmarked on her computer.

One afternoon when Piper came home early from her classes, Brynn caught her before she got too comfortable. "Come shopping with me," she said.

"Where? What are we shopping for?" Her interest was piqued, and she stopped before putting her keys down.

"I am going to redecorate this hum-drum living room into something fabulous!" she announced, moving her arms across her in a sweeping motion. "Come help me. We can go to Houston. It'll be fun."

Piper laughed. "Sure, why not?"

When they arrived at the first home décor shop, they must have looked through dozens of curtains and draperies. The one thing Brynn liked least was black and white, since she'd had so many black accents in the room in the past. "A soft tranquil pallet is what I need. Ocean colors, like light blue, and sand and seashell.

"I know you're not wild about black and white," Piper drawled, holding up a package and pointing to the photo on the front, "but look at this! Isn't it gorgeous?"

Brynn studied the picture and made a face. "It might be pretty somewhere, but it's not what I had in mind." It was heavy black brocade with white fleur de lis designs on it. "I've just never been wild about fleur de lis."

Piper gave a slight eye roll and put it back. "Well, *I* think it's pretty," she huffed. "And I think you're pretty picky!" She stuck out her tongue and they both laughed.

"Come on, let's keep looking." Brynn found the softest shade of blue as her foundation color and picked out beautiful draperies in soft sea-mist green and sand. The throw pillows she loved the most had soft beige with pink shells and an aqua-colored border. When combined, they really were breathtaking. "I'm going for the beachside cottage look, tranquil and serene."

Piper pointed out some wallpaper in bold, graphic print designs, and Brynn told her it was pretty, but she really had her heart set on mostly solids. If she was going with her breezy, shabby-chic cottage look, she needed to stay completely away from prints and stay with a minimalist style when it came to accessories. A few seashells and natural-colored candles would complete the look.

She ended up deciding not to make any purchases yet but did pick out some paint sample cards in the color she wanted to paint the walls as well as samples of each of the colors she wanted to use in her overall design. Piper found a few things for herself. She bought an alarm clock and throw pillows for her bed.

Even though they hadn't bought anything for the living room yet, Brynn was satisfied that she'd solidified her plans a little better and was looking forward to pulling it all together. She loved the idea of a wall decal with a positive saying or Bible verse to apply to one wall. Piper kept choosing large, bold designs in bright colors for the decals until Brynn reminded her of her plans to stay simple and elegant.

"You'll see," Brynn promised. "You'll love it when it's done."

For dinner, they decided on a little bistro for soup and salads. Piper attempted to make up for her overly eager suggestions by encouraging Brynn to stay with her heart and go for the designs she wanted most. When the waitress brought their salads, Brynn closed the brochures she had opened up in front of her.

Piper gave a quick nod toward the brochures.

"You might as well have it exactly like you want it, since it will probably be quite a while before you're ready to redecorate again." She popped a crouton in her mouth and continued.

"You work hard. You make good money. I say go for it," she said, pointing at her plate with the tines of her fork. "This salad is so good!"

Brynn picked up her fork and gave a confident smile. "You know you're right. I'm gonna do it. And I'm gonna do it exactly how I've always envisioned." She took a few bites of salad, apparently deep in thought.

"What's wrong?"

"Ah, nothing really. I was just thinking, you must think I'm terribly over-picky."

"Nooo!" Piper said. "Designing your living space is a personal thing. No one can tell you how you want it."

"I suppose you're right."

"Of course I'm right. Besides, you are the one who will have to look at it for the next however many years."

"You've talked me into it," Brynn replied. "Now, talk me into some dessert."

Chapter 12

Over the next couple of weeks, Spencer was a more present figure in Brynn's life and had finally met Blake. It went surprisingly well, and Brynn had then invited him to come over for dinner one night. Piper helped her prepare the ingredients, while she mixed the marinade for the shrimp.

"What can I do to help?" Piper asked, taking a sip of the moscato wine Brynn had opened.

"Chop the salad veggies for me. We've got another half hour before Spencer gets here. I'm gonna call Blake in to wash up and put on a clean shirt. He invited his friend, Jimmy Wu, to come have dinner with us. His Mom's gonna drop him off here in a little while." She crossed the kitchen to the back door and opened it.

"Blake!" she called, and came back into the kitchen.

Piper looked up from her cutting board. "You really like this guy, don't you? Cooking this nice dinner from scratch, a very nice bottle of wine, might I add, and a clean shirt for Blake." She wiggled her eyebrows up and down, and Brynn couldn't help but giggle.

"Yeah, I like him. A lot. We'll see how it goes." Brynn dried her hands on a kitchen towel and went back to the back door to call for Blake again.

"C'mon, Son. Jimmy will be here, soon. Come get cleaned up." When she came back in, she took a seat at the bar and became quickly lost in a daydream, her chin in her hand.

Spencer arrived right on time, and with a bottle of wine. Stepping into the kitchen, he eyed the half-full glasses on the bar. "I guess my idea wasn't too original. I figured you might like a nice wine tonight, you said you were making pasta." Piper and Brynn exchanged glances.

"Moscato is perfect," they said in unison.

"All righty then," Spencer breathed a relieved sigh. "I guess I got it right."

Brynn glanced around to the back. Blake still hadn't come back in yet. "Excuse me, I'll be right back." She opened the back door and called out to him. He didn't answer.

"What are you doing?"

"Nothing, playing with Sarge." He appeared from the corner beside the garage.

"I told you to come in and get ready for dinner."

"Dinner's not even ready yet, is it?"

His back-talk didn't set well with her. She had been looking forward to having a nice dinner and seeing how things went with Spencer there. It was so important to her that they all get along well.

"I didn't ask you if dinner was ready. I asked you to come in and get cleaned up."

"I'm not dirty," he retorted, walking toward her. Sarge came bounding up beside him, eager to please, as always. *Why couldn't Blake be more agreeable?* She wondered.

"Well. You smell like a wet dog. Do you want to smell like that when your friend gets here?"

"Mom, that is so harsh." He brushed past her, and she caught a whiff of him.

"Take a shower. Now." Brynn followed them into the house.

"That's a great dog," Spencer said, coming up behind her. He stepped forward slowly and knelt down to let the dog sniff his hand. Blake hesitated, looking at his Mom for approval for the delay.

"I love German shepherds," Spencer said. Sarge sniffed him out and licked his hand, confirming his approval. Blake hesitated, waiting for Sarge.

"He's been wonderful," Brynn offered. "He's very protective." She and her son exchanged glances, sharing a warm, conciliatory smile. *If only the others knew,* the smile said.

She couldn't help but notice Piper had backed away from the dog a little, apparently a bit uneasy. "He's a good companion for Blake."

"He won't hurt you, Piper," Blake said with confidence. "He knows you belong here." As they headed into the kitchen to chill the wine, Brynn could've sworn she heard a low growl from Sarge when Piper passed him.

"Come on, boy," Blake said, calling Sarge to follow him to get his clothes ready for his shower.

When he appeared, fresh and clean a few moments later, there was no further trace of attitude. Or the stench of a sweaty boy.

The conversation over dinner was easy, relaxed. Spencer complimented Brynn on her cooking skills several times. He finished everything he had started with and added just a bit more shrimp and pasta to his plate. Brynn couldn't help but notice how Blake and Spencer seemed to get along so well. They talked about the dog, and about the latest video games. Apparently Spencer was still part boy inside as he didn't have to pretend to be interested in the games Blake liked most. Jimmy seemed to be a very polite young man, and Brynn was glad she had let Blake invite him over.

After dinner, Blake and Jimmy went outside for a while and the adults stayed around in the kitchen to clean up. Brynn put some music on, and they began putting things away.

Piper had already had a couple of glasses of wine since dinner and was a little more talkative than Brynn had noticed before. She followed Piper's eyes and the realization hit her.

Why didn't I notice it before? she wondered. *Piper has a little crush.* It was nothing to be concerned about, Brynn assured herself; in fact it was a little cute. She did want to have a little time alone with Spencer, however, so she sent Piper outside for a few minutes.

"Piper, would you do me a favor, please?"

"Sure." She looked up from her wine glass, her eyes wide.

"Would you go in the backyard and check on the boys for me, please? I don't want Blake getting all sweaty tonight. He already had his bath."

"No problem." She stepped into her flip-flops and went out the back door.

Brynn and Spencer moved into the living room and sat together on the sofa. They each had some wine remaining in their glasses and sipped as they talked. Moments later, Blake burst through the back door, shouting.

"Mom! Mom! Piper's hurt!" he yelled, then raced back outside. Spencer and Brynn were right behind him. When they got into the backyard, Piper was sitting in the grass, with one knee bent up and holding her ankle.

"What happened?" Brynn bent to check her ankle.

"I was running. That dog was coming at me, and I was trying to get away. I stepped in a hole or something and twisted my ankle." She cast a glare at Sarge, biting her lip. "It hurts."

"He wasn't gonna hurt you," Blake protested. "He didn't even really growl!" He was walking around in circles, inspecting the ground for holes. Jimmy stood beside him, nodding in agreement.

"He looked at me like, I don't know, like I was some kind of intruder, and then he just charged me." Her bottom lip protruded slightly.

"It looks okay, but it might be starting to swell a little bit. I'll go get some ice to put on it," Brynn offered, heading into the kitchen. Spencer bent to help Piper to her feet, but as soon as she put any weight on it, she grimaced and buckled at the knees, almost going back down.

Glancing up at Spencer, she asked innocently, "Will you help me?"

Reluctantly, he bent down and put one arm around her waist, scooping her upward, and helping her as she limped across the yard and through the back door.

Brynn looked up just as they made it into the kitchen. She swallowed hard, biting back words. She could've sworn she caught a quick glimpse of triumph on Piper's face. Surely not, she told herself. Piper had, after all, hurt herself in *her* yard, and while being chased by *her* dog. And here Brynn was being suspicious of Piper.

She glanced over at Sarge, who lay on the patio just beyond the kitchen door with his chin on his paws. His expression was soulful, almost remorseful. She couldn't imagine him being remotely aggressive toward anyone he knew, especially if they hadn't posed a threat.

"Here's some ice," she said, offering an ice pack to Piper, who was just settling into the couch cushions. Blake came running back from Piper's room with a pillow to put beneath her ankle. *He had certainly forgiven her quickly,* Brynn thought. She retrieved a bottle from her purse and took two ibuprofen tabs from it, then returned it.

"These should help keep the swelling and inflammation down."

Spencer had gone back into the kitchen after helping Piper to the couch. When Brynn returned she detected a hint of awkwardness on Spencer's face.

"I'm sorry," she whispered. "I never expected any of that to happen."

"No, it's not your fault."   Looking behind him quickly to make sure they were out of earshot, he mouthed, "I'll tell you later."

They walked together into the living room to check on Piper. "You okay?" she asked her.

"Yea. I think I just maybe sprained it a little. Nothing too serious, though, I'll be okay." She turned her eyes down, pouting. "I don't know what you're thinking as far as what to do with that dog, but I don't think you should put him down or anything," she said. "He just needs to be taught how to behave or maybe sent somewhere. Don't they have shelters for things like that, dogs that turn on humans?"

Brynn inhaled deeply, ready to launch into her, but then checked herself and waited a second or two to get control over her emotions before speaking.

"Sarge is a very well-behaved dog, he went through extensive training as a service dog before he came to us. He had a slight hip injury that prevented him from being assigned, but he's a great dog." She wisely bit back a comment about Piper's behavior. "They evaluate them carefully."

"I'm sorry, I wasn't implying he's a bad dog," she drawled. "I don't know why he did that. Please, I hope you aren't thinking I provoked him?" She bit her lip and looked up at Brynn.

"I wasn't there. I didn't see."

"I'm sorry, I didn't mean anything by it, I guess it just startled me and I'm not thinking straight. Please forgive me." A look of sincerity swept over her face.

"Whatever." Brynn took a breath, then softened. "I guess it *was* a good scare. Just try to rest and stay off it as much as possible till morning. If it's swollen or still inflamed I'll take you to get it checked out."

Piper nodded, apparently satisfied. She was holding the ice pack and sliding it to the other side of her ankle. Spencer came up behind the couch just then.

"Well, while you're resting there, I was thinking about stealing Brynn away for a few minutes for a walk," Spencer said. He cast a look Brynn's way, an expectant expression on his face.

"Sure, I'd like that," she answered. She gave Blake and Jimmy quick instructions to keep an eye on Piper. Looking back at Spencer, she asked him, "Do you mind if Sarge comes with us?"

"Not at all," he said. "Where's his leash?"
"I'll show you, let's go." Reaching to a shelf just inside the foyer, she grabbed the leash, handing it to Spencer. "You'll have a friend for life, now," she laughed. As soon as he saw the leash, Sarge came running.

Piper looked up and flashed a suggestive smile. "You two don't do anything I wouldn't do!" she called after them as they headed out the door.

Just as they reached the threshold, Sarge came to a stop. Brynn gave his leash a gentle tug. Nothing. He dug his paws in.

"Sarge *loves* to go on walks," Brynn said, puzzled. "I guess he just doesn't want to go tonight. That's weird." She unfastened his leash, and he immediately went to the hallway, turned around and sat, facing Piper.

As soon as they were outside and the door closed securely behind them, she asked, "What do you think that was all about? I'm so sorry you had to witness that."

"No worries." He smiled down at her. "Dogs have minds of their own."

"Not about Sarge," she breathed. "I meant about Piper. What were you going to tell me, earlier?" she asked him.

"Oh. Maybe it's just me, but, well, it seemed like she was limping on the wrong foot for a minute there." He stepped away from the porch and she followed.

"I probably wouldn't even have noticed," he added," but since my own injury and all the physical therapy I guess I'm more apt to notice things like that."

"Really? I'm not sure *what* she's all about," she confessed.

"I thought you two were close?"

"We were. As kids. But that's been years ago, and she's really different now. Or maybe I am, who knows? Sometimes I get a little frustrated with her, then I remember she's had a pretty rough go of it, and then losing her Mom..." her voice trailed off. She looked down as she walked. "I know what that's like," she continued. "I just want to help her get through this rough time. I'm sure she'll be back to her real self as time passes. Time heals all wounds, they say, right?"

"There's something else," she told him. "She has this ex-boyfriend, Michael something. Apparently, he was controlling and abusive, and when she broke it off, he didn't get the message."

"That's not good," he said.

"No. That's why I thought it would be good here. Michael Lopez, that's it. But now, she keeps checking out the window, telling me she's afraid he'll find her."

"Are you worried?" His jaw clenched.

"Not really. I think that's premature at this point. There's been no sign of him, she just says she feels like someone might be watching her."

He listened, smiling, then paused a moment before speaking.

"If you have any problems with this guy, you let me know."

"I will, but I don't think it'll be a problem. He doesn't even know where she moved. I think he lives in Houston."

"I mean it, though. Although, I'd like to see him try to get past Sarge. That won't be pretty."

"You are correct there, my friend," she said with a chuckle.

"Still," he re-emphasized, "Don't hesitate to call me if you have a problem. Sounds like you and Piper have a few issues. I think maybe you both just need some time to adjust. It always takes roommates a while to settle in and get used to each other. I'm sure that's all it is. Besides, if it means me getting to spend time with you, I can put up with her." He gave a wink and she laughed. Before they reached the sidewalk that ran alongside the street, he reached for her hand.

"It's a nice night, isn't it?" he asked.

"It is. The moon is full." He followed her gaze to the bright, white moon that hung in the sky, full and ripe. "It's a good thing we're not working tonight."

"That's the truth," he said. "You can always tell it's a full moon when you work at a hospital."

Glancing back up at it, he spoke again, more seriously this time. "It's beautiful. Like you," he breathed. He pulled her closer to him and slipped his arm around her waist. "Dinner was wonderful. And Blake is a great kid."

"Thanks. I'm really proud of him." She looked down at the sidewalk as they walked, deep in thought. "You know, sometimes I worry about him. Not having had a father, and all."

"Hey, don't question that. He's got a great Mom, and he's so bright. He's a totally well-adjusted kid." His expression grew serious. "You've done a great job."

"Thanks," she breathed. "Ben was a huge part of that. And now Ludie, well, she's a wonderful aunt."

"You're lucky to have them."

"I know. They're such a blessing." She paused, biting her lip. "It's just..." she trailed off.

"What is it?"

"Sometimes I really do worry. He's gotten to where he smarts off to me. Out of nowhere."

"He's a twelve-year-old boy. It's what they do. I speak from experience."

"He wasn't always like that. I remember when he was so easy to be around. He seemed to trust me so much back then. Whatever I said, he did it. No questions asked."

"It's his age." He shrugged. "I really don't think it's anything you did or didn't do. I can barely stand to think of how I talked to my mother at that age."

"Really?" she asked, almost hopefully.

"Really. I'm lucky she even speaks to me."

"But you seem so polite now, so respectful." She almost looked surprised.

"I had to be. She put up with a lot from me, but when she gave me a certain look, I knew it was time to back down."

She laughed. "I know that look."

"I'll just bet you do."

They continued on in silence for a bit, both of them reflecting on the night, and their ease with each other. Brynn had a great feeling about the way things had been going, and with each date she felt closer to him. It was apparently mutual, considering the plans Spencer had for them next. Stopping a few houses down, he turned to her.

"I was just wondering," he started, then took a deep breath.

"Wondering what?" she teased, looking into his eyes.

"Well, I was just thinking about taking a weekend trip. Do you like San Antonio?" His eyes glowed with a shine of purpose, hopeful. Their last few weeks had gone so well, it sometimes felt to her like they'd known each other for years.

The heavy lashes that shaded her face flew upward and she gave him an encouraging smile. "I love San Antonio. The River Walk is so romantic."

"Good," he let out a heavy breath, and she realized he'd been holding it. "I was thinking about finding a hotel right on the river, and we could have dinner there, shop during the day at the market square, whatever you want to do."

A swell of excitement rushed through her. "Let's do it!" she answered. He gave her a quick hug, lifting her slightly and spinning her around.

They prolonged their walk, one minute talking excitedly about their upcoming trip, then the next simply enjoying each other's company in silence. When they'd reached Brynn's front porch, she opened the door and Sarge came rushing out.

Brynn grabbed two cold bottles of beer from the fridge and returned with them, taking a seat on the porch swing. Spencer joined her, taking a package from his pocket before taking a seat. Of course. Sunflower seeds. Their conversation was easy, comfortable. The sound of crickets chirping provided the perfect background for the symphony that was their joined laughter. Occasionally a car would drive by, and faint music drifted on the air from a house down the road. A night like this was just what Brynn had needed.

Chapter 13

The next morning Brynn sat in Ben and Ludie's kitchen. She and her sister-in-law chatted over coffee while her niece, Annie, sat in her high chair between them. A line of Cheerios made an impressive formation across the tray. Instead of being poured on the cereal, in a bowl, the milk was in a sippy cup.

"Trust me, it's a lot less messy that way," Ludie laughed.

Brynn's phone rang, and she fished it out of her pocket. "Hello."

"Hey, it's me."

"Piper? I didn't recognize the number."

"Yea, I had to change it, that's why I'm calling you, so you'll have my new number."

"What happened?"

"Michael. I told him to stop calling, but he wouldn't."

"I'm glad you changed it, then. Are you okay?"

"Yeah. Just a little rattled."

"I know." She looked up at Ludie. "Hey, Piper? I'm with someone, can I talk to you later?"

"Sure."

"What was *that* all about?" Ludie asked.

Brynn filled her in on Piper and the whole sordid story.

"Just be careful, Brynn. Don't take any chances. I don't want something to happen to you and Blake just for helping her out."

Brynn felt a laugh bubbling up in her throat. "Hey, no good deed goes unpunished, right?"

"So, talk to me. It seems like you and Spencer have gotten pretty close over the past few weeks." Ludie blew her coffee to cool it. "You think it could be serious?"

"That's what I wanted to talk to you about. He asked me to go out of town with him this weekend," Brynn said.

Ludie's face spread into a smile. "Oh my gosh! What did you tell him?"

"I said "yes," of course! We're going to San Antonio." She quickly corrected herself, "I mean, if you and Ben don't mind..."

"Of course Blake can stay with us, are you kidding? Tell me more..." Ludie's expression showed her enthusiasm, and it was clear she wouldn't give up until she had coaxed all the juicy details.

Annie responded to her mother's enthusiasm by mimicking her mother's words. She stuck her index finger into the hole of a Cheerio and pushed it to the other side of her tray.

Getting up to pour some more coffee, Brynn asked Ludie if she'd heard from Roxy.

"Is this your way of changing the subject?"

"Maybe."

"Fine. Yeah, I forgot to tell you. I saw them walking across the square a couple of days ago.

Her and Dennis. They were so cute, holding hands. Totally unreserved affection."

"Really?" Brynn answered. "Wow, that's not like her."

"Nope." Ludie set her mug down. And do you know what was conspicuously missing from her hands?" She paused for dramatic affect. "Shopping bags!"

"Whoa," Brynn said, turning around, her back to the countertop. "Who would've thought? I've never heard her talk about a serious relationship before, have you?"

"No, never. I mean, she talks a good game about the men in her life and the standards they'd have to uphold, but I've never actually heard her speak of anyone in particular, until Dennis."

"If I tell you something, you've got to swear you'll never breath a word," Brynn whispered, a conspiratorial glint in her eyes.

Ludie crossed her heart and leaned forward expectantly.

"Roxy was in the ER last night."

"What?"

"Yep. Poison ivy." She flashed a smug grin.

At that, Ludie drew in a sharp breath. "Roxy? Our Roxy?"

"Yep. The one and only. She went hiking with Dennis." She sat back and took a sip of her coffee, giving it a moment for her words to sink in. Ludie's jaw dropped.

"You have to go outdoors to get poison ivy," she protested.

"Well, that's not all. It's *where* she had it."

"Speak."

"Her *ass*," Brynn whispered.

"No way! She's really into this guy." She leaned over and poured a few more Cheerios onto Annie's tray.

"Well. Dennis is a good guy. Ask Ben, he's known him for a long time. In fact," Brynn continued, "remember the time he just happened to drive by when Ben was moving from my house? Saw him in the driveway with boxes."

"And showed back up a few minutes later with his truck and a case of beer. Stuck around till the last box was moved." Ludie smiled.

"Yeah. Great guy." Her eyes narrowed. "But he's so *different* from Roxy. She's a great friend, too, would do anything for you."

"Right. But she's glamorous and sophisticated and successful and…"

"…and gorgeous," Brynn interrupted. "And Dennis is country, laid back. The quintessential gentleman."

"The least pretentious person I've ever met." Ludie set her coffee cup down. "He'll be good to her."

"And she'll be good to him. It's funny, when she first texted me, she joked that she wanted me to send a gorgeous doctor to check on her. When I got down there, Dennis was right by her side, attentive. And a dozen hunky doctors could've walked by and she wouldn't have noticed."

Brynn had always seen Roxy as the epitome of style and sophistication. None of them had ever really known how successful she was, or where she'd gained her success. All they had known was that she had something to do with marketing some type of really expensive lingerie on internet sites.

One day a couple of years before, they'd stumbled on the fact that Roxy had designed her own label, which was sold in the high-end boutiques in LA, New York, and even Paris. Of course, her line was already very popular in Australia, her homeland.

Dennis, however, was as country as could be. He'd been born and raised in Blackwater. He'd spent his younger years riding with the rodeo circuit, bull-riding, if Brynn remembered correctly. Once he'd gotten a little older, he began doing construction work for several different contractors in the area. His truest passion, however, was fighting fires. He devoted much of his time with the Blackwater Volunteer Fire Department.

He'd attended various schools to learn rescue and extrication techniques, gaining his EMT certification. Everyone in the community respected him. He was a favored regular at the Ladybird Café. Birdie had taken him under her wing and never had let him pay for his ticket at the café.

"You serve our community, darlin'," she had told him. "So you're just gonna have to let me serve you," she'd tell him with a wink.

His free time, he spent outdoors. Hunting, fishing, running through mud on all-terrain vehicles were his idea of a day well spent.

Brynn smiled when she thought of the unlikely pair he and Roxy made. Love was a funny thing, though.

Ludie seemed to share her opinion and was glad Roxy and Dennis had found each other. Even if it meant each of them stretching out of their comfort zone's to incorporate the other into their lives. Brynn had a soft heart for romance at the moment, anyway, and Spencer Evans had everything to do with it.

As Brynn and Ludie giggled, Annie began smiling at them and jabbering her little talk until their attention turned to her sweet little face.

"Aunt Brynn loves you," she said, planting a kiss on her tiny little cheek. *And Aunt Brynn is falling in love,* she thought.

* * *

When the weekend rolled around, Spencer was outside in front of Brynn's house loading her bags into the trunk of his car. Piper was standing in the doorway and gave Brynn a quick hug. She was leaning against the doorjamb, but had lost any remaining hint of a limp. The subject of her injury hadn't ever come up again.

"Have fun, Brynn!" She released her and looked her in the eye, "…but not *too* much fun, if you know what I mean." She winked and said, "Go. You don't want to keep your *man* waiting."

Spencer held the car door open for Brynn and closed it once she'd sat down. She just happened to glance up while he was walking around to the driver's side just in time to notice Piper glaring from the window. That was odd, she thought, but then shrugged it off as a misperception and focused on the weekend ahead.

* * *

The road trip was wonderful. She would never have guessed how compatible their musical tastes were until he pushed the buttons on his CD changer and 70's music began blaring. Perfect, she thought. When he had a good mix of 80's as well, she knew she'd struck gold with this one. They turned down the music a bit and had some nice, long talks as well. He spoke of his time with the Houston Police Department. She could easily read from his expression that he had loved his work. After an animated discussion of some of the funnier adventures he'd been on, the conversation turned serious.

"Were you ever afraid?" she asked him, looking over at him for his response.

"I had my moments," he answered curtly. His eyes clouded over and she could no longer read his expression.

"It was time to move on." He forced a smile and glanced over at her. "I love respiratory therapy, though. I feel like I'm making a difference, just in a different way now." Noting that he'd so adeptly changed the subject, she didn't press the issue any further. The last thing she wanted to do was to cast a dark cloud over their first weekend away together.

As they arrived in San Antonio, Spencer saw Brynn's excitement grow. He loved seeing her so happy. She was practically sitting on the edge of her seat, as much as her seat belt would allow, with one hand on the door handle, the other on her chest as she looked out the window. Her eyes sparkled as she took in the sights.

He felt incredible tenderness toward her and took great joy in being able to take her away for a nice weekend. He was determined to make it fun and relaxing for her, as well as romantic. His feelings for her had grown considerably in the past few weeks. Watching her with her son touched his heart and reminded him of his own mother who had raised him alone, as Brynn was doing with Blake.

The way she had taken in Piper out of the blue really said something about her. How many people would open their home to someone they hadn't seen since they were kids? Brynn would, and he loved that about her. He looked over at her and was captivated by her beauty. Her hair was a rich, dark chestnut brown, with almost a little hint of red. The flush on her pale cheeks, and the sprinkling of freckles made him smile. But the depth of her blue-green eyes called to him on some primal level. She looked over at him, the corners of her glossy red lips turned upward, and his heart felt a heat burning through it.

They had gotten checked into the hotel in time to take a stroll on the River Walk. One of San Antonio's most alluring features was the river running through it, the very river that had filled with the blood of Mexicans and the determined Texans who bravely stood their ground until the very end.

Walking just beneath a water wall built into the side of a hotel, they ducked their way under and through from Alamo plaza, down a few steps and then came out the other side to the view of the river before them. Rocks formed a foundation for the landscaping that lined the river and, in some areas, stone paths wound their way along the rambling river. There were archways that stretched over the river to allow visitors to cross to the other side, as well as tunnels where couples could duck beneath archways for a quick embrace. Water fountains trickled from stone rocks built into the planters beneath the bridges.

Festive music poured out over the river from open-air restaurants that lined the river. Most of the cafes and bars had open patios with tables and chairs covered with brightly-colored umbrellas on two levels, up at the street level and down at the river level below. The atmosphere drifted as they walked along, transitioning from fun and festive to soft and romantic.

Spencer held her hand as they walked, occasionally stopping to steal a kiss at just the perfect spots along the pathway. When they were in quieter, more hidden-away areas along the stretch, they talked softly between themselves. In more populated places where there were more people and more businesses, they were content just to hold hands and take in the sights and sounds around them.

"Look," Spencer told her. "Over there, it's the outdoor theater." Directly across the river was a stage.

"Are they having any shows there tonight?" she asked, keeping step with him.

"I'm not seeing anything set up, but what I think you'll be most interested in, is above the theater, on the opposite side." He gave a secretive little grin but didn't offer more information.

"It looks like a bunch of white stone steps leading up to columns..." On the side they were on, there were wide steps made of stone, rising up like bleachers to accommodate a decent-sized audience.

"It is. And when you walk underneath those columns you enter La Villita. There are a lot of shops, and that's the part I think you'll like most."

That was all Brynn needed to hear to continue rapidly up the steps and under the columns. Into the courtyard was a historic shopping village with some of the most beautiful shops with accessories, fashion, jewelry, and home décor. It was all gorgeous, handcrafted by artisans. Brynn took it all in with her eyes, convinced she could spend a month here and never see everything she wanted to see.

In one of the shops, there were baskets full of nuts by the pound. Spencer grabbed a bag and bought a whole pound of roasted sunflower seeds in the shells. Brynn laughed, knowing they probably wouldn't last very long.

There were several shops with handmade jewelry and Brynn found a ring and bracelet that were silver and turquoise. Spencer saw the way she admired it and how she picked it up and then put it back down. He could tell she was undecided about whether or not to buy it. She looked at a few other pieces but nothing seemed to catch her eye as much. They ended up strolling around the river walk for most of the afternoon and enjoyed every minute of it. Conversation came easily for them, and she realized she hadn't laughed so much with any guy for as long as she could remember.

After a long day of strolling about, they returned to the hotel to freshen up for dinner. He had made reservations for a very nice restaurant.

When they got back into the room, she hesitated before taking her shower, stalling by slowly gathering her cosmetics and her clothes. she wasn't quite sure if she was comfortable getting out of the shower and dressing in front of him yet. To her relief, he excused himself and told her he had a couple of things to do and would give her time to shower and get ready.

Things were still new between them, and Brynn had a young, impressionable son to raise; his eyes would be on her every move. She would proceed with caution every step of the way in order to protect his best interests. She had the feeling Spencer would respect her wishes. Regardless of when they would take their relationship to the next level, they would need to keep Blake in mind.

Once he'd left the room, she turned the water on and stepped into a steaming hot shower. She reflected on the events of the day while she let the hot water run down over her. It felt good to be fresh and clean, and the water felt so good on her tired, sore muscles.

* * *

A little while later, she was dressed and her hair was dry. It was shiny and had just enough bounce to please her. This was a special evening, and she wanted to look her best. She was standing in front of the mirror applying the final touches of makeup when Spencer returned.

"You look incredible," he told her. Slowly and seductively his eyes raked over her. She was wearing tightly fitting black jeans with a shimmery silver top. She had finished the look with black, peep-toe pumps. The neckline of her top plunged just low enough to reveal her shapely form. He couldn't seem to pull himself away, until she mentioned she was nearly ready.

He stepped over to the dresser where he'd placed a small bag upon his return.

"This is for you," he whispered. She took the bag from him and looked inside. It was the jewelry she'd seen in one of the shops earlier today. She squealed her delight and put the bracelet and ring on, holding her hand out in front of her to admire it.

"There's more," he told her.

She reached into the bag and removed a box. Inside was a beautiful necklace that matched. The silver and turquoise pendant hung on a sturdy silver chain. She had an appreciation for both delicate, pretty jewelry and chunky, trendy jewelry. This was perfect in every way. She turned her back to him and he fastened it carefully, then placed a soft kiss on her neck.

She turned to face him, slipping her arms around his neck.

"Thank you," she whispered softly. "I love it." She stretched upward as even in her high heels he was slightly taller than her, and rewarded him with a kiss.

"It looks great on you. Now, relax for a few minutes while I get cleaned up. I won't be long."

She smiled up at him, and nodded. She crossed the room to the glass French doors and drew back the curtains, gazing down at the river below. She just happened to glance back at him in time to see him removing his shirt. He stood in front of the mirror shirtless, in his jeans, and gathered a few items from his shaving kit. The muscles in his back rippled with even the slightest movements.

When he stepped into the bathroom, she turned back to the view outside. The sun had already begun setting, casting a romantic glow on the city and the river below. The festive, colorful lights that lined the buildings and bridges had slowly begun to flicker on, and couples were strolling by. She saw a boat float past with a large group of people on it. She opened the doors and stepped out onto the balcony. Music filled the air and mingled with the sounds of laughter and happy chatter. The mood was festive and she already felt its magic touching her.

The outfit she was wearing was fitted closely enough to reveal her shapely curves, and the top flowed, shimmering, drawing the eyes upward. Her rich, brown hair and blue-green eyes were accented by the silver and turquoise. Her pumps were delicate and high, and the whole look made her feel sexy. It was a dramatic change from her usual scrubs, and she was glad he appreciated it so much. But then, she remembered, he commented on her beauty when she was at work, worn, makeup fading, at the end of a shift. Her cheeks felt warm in anticipation. Tonight was shaping up to be very romantic and she felt her eagerness overcome her.

When he stepped from the bathroom, she couldn't help but stare. The curtains blew in the breeze behind her, and she took a few steps forward.

His rugged, denim jeans hugged his hips. The shirt he was wearing was dark gray, a little tight, with a Henley collar open enough to reveal his muscular neck. The sleeves were tight on his arms and she knew he must work out. His short, almost shaved haircut was clean and sexy. He had just enough growth on his face to complete his masculine, rugged look. His dark brown eyes were piercing, staring out from a deeply tanned face and threatening to possess her with their intensity. She took a few steps toward him and gave him another kiss. She caught a hint of the musky scent of his aftershave and it took all the discipline she could muster to step away from him and reach for her purse.

* * *

The restaurant he'd chosen was quiet and intimate, candle-lit. He ordered a very nice wine and she loved the way the name of it rolled off his tongue. This was clearly a man who had a taste for the finer things in life.

When they finished eating, they left the restaurant hand in hand, and explored more of the river walk together.

They found a great club down the river a little way and went in. There was a live band covering some of their favorite artists from the 70's and 80's. They also provided a good mix of more contemporary songs after their first set, and Spencer led Brynn onto the dance floor.

When one of the slower songs came on, he pulled her closer and she leaned into his arms, like it was the most natural feeling in the world.

She laid her head on his shoulder, and inhaled the masculine scent of him. There was a tightening at the pit of her stomach, and she knew she had never desired a man more. She lifted her head from his shoulder and looked up at him. There was a smoldering in his eyes, and she knew instantly he was feeling it, too.

They'd had wine with dinner and each of them had ordered one drink at the club before they danced. It was enough to relax them, but nowhere near enough to cloud their judgment or dull the desire they both felt.

He whispered softly into her ear and asked if she was ready to go. She looked at him and nodded with a smile that told him she was very sure of what she wanted.

He led her to the door and they stepped out into the night air outside. The river walk was still lit up, and they held hands as they made their way back toward the hotel. Anticipation burned inside her and any reservations she may have had about being intimate with him had melted away. She was more sure than ever about her feelings toward him and wanted him to know it.

Suddenly, she was torn inside, though, wondering if it was too soon. Just hours before, her thoughts had been focused on setting the right example for her son. Now all she could think about was being alone with Spencer. *Am I just rationalizing?* she asked herself. They stopped next to a fountain and embraced.

"Spencer, there's something I wanted to talk to you about." She looked up at him, uncertain of how she'd put her concerns into words.

"This, our time together... *this*... has been so amazing. I want nothing more than to be with you." She was looking down at the smooth stones beneath her feet. He put one finger under her chin and tipped it upward, forcing her to look into his eyes.

"Brynn, I'm ready when you are. But I know you have concerns, mostly about your son. I want it to be your decision. I won't pressure you at all, but I feel like as you spend more time away from him, you'll probably find yourself feeling a little more free to act on your own desires. But when we're around Blake, I absolutely think we need to set the right example."

She found his words comforting. He was not merely giving her his approval to proceed at her own pace, he was insisting on it. There would be no pressure from him. His smile was warm, reassuring. She couldn't recall a time when she felt more in control of a relationship.

"You call the shots, but there is something I think you should know." His features softened as he held both her hands in his and leaned forward, gazing into her eyes.

"I don't think there's a better time to tell you this, Brynn Callaway, but I'm in love with you."

She saw a flash of concern in his eyes when she didn't respond right away. She knew without a doubt what she would say, but was caught up in prolonging the moment.

"Then I think it's about time I told you that I'm falling in love with you, too." He took her by the hand as they continued their walk, and it seemed like his movements were lighter, with even a little bounce in his step. She shared his enthusiasm, and had no problem keeping up. Joy bubbled up within her.

When they arrived in the hotel room, he took her in his arms and held her to him. His steady gaze bore into her in expectation. She moved her hands sensuously across his expansive chest and shoulders, then began to pull at his shirt, up, then over his head. His bare chest was hard, his abdomen lined with well-defined muscles.

The light was dim in the room, the bed soft and full with smooth, white linens and luxurious bedding. He took her by the hand and led her to the side of the bed. Gently, he lowered her to the bed. A delightful shiver ran through her, her heart pounding in her chest. In mere seconds, she began to feel his heart beating against her own.

"I love you," she murmured.

"I love you, too."

She gave a sigh, murmuring against his throat, then planted small, warm kisses down his neck.

She threw her head back and gave in fully to the sensations that were devouring her: the passion of his touch, the desire she felt building within her, and the love she felt for this man.

* * *

In the morning the sun snuck in on them in a tiny stripe of light across the bed. The curtains were parted slightly, just enough to allow her eyes to take in her surroundings. She opened her eyes and studied the gorgeous man beside her. He was sleeping on his side, facing her. His right arm was draped across her and she loved the way it made her feel protected and cherished. Her lips spread into a slow, confident smile and she relished the feeling of intimacy, of new love growing between them.

"Good morning," he said groggily as he slowly opened his eyes. "You're still here. I was afraid it was all a dream." He planted a small kiss on her forehead.

"Nope, not a dream," she murmured lazily, content. "I'm here. And I'm not going anywhere."

He smiled again, "I should hope not. I could easily get used to this."

"So could I." Bringing herself to a sitting position, she ran a hand lovingly across his chest. "Are you hungry?" she asked.

"Yeah. I could use some coffee, and a huge breakfast. What about you?" He was on his side still, his head propped up on one hand supported by his elbow. "Wanna order room service?"

"Well that would mean staying in for a while." She drew her mouth into a mischievous grin. "I think it's a great idea." He responded by wiggling his eyebrows up and down.

She got up and went to the bathroom for a shower while he opened the menu and called downstairs to room service. Stepping out, she found it hard to believe she'd been so shy the night before. Her comfort level had changed so much overnight. She straightened out the linens on the bed and folded them back neatly. Spencer was in the bathroom when room service arrived. A young man entered with a huge cart full of silver-domed lids on trays.

Once he'd set them up on the table, he excused himself and Brynn poured coffee from a silver carafe. She stirred a bit of half and half, just enough to soften the color a bit, and a packet of sweetener. She poured his cup as well, adding a packet of sugar. Taking a sip of hers, she moaned her pleasure.

"I like to hear that," he said behind her. "Except not about the coffee."

She giggled, turning around to face him.

"But everything tastes so much better when you're in love," she protested, her lips pouty and full. "Here, drink yours. It's just how you like it, one sugar." He took the cup from her hand and took a drink.

"Why am I not surprised you knew exactly what I wanted and gave it to me," his double meaning not lost on her. He gave her a wink and asked what she'd like to do today. They sat down and began eating while discussing possible activities.

They of course would be visiting the Alamo, as they were both Texans and possessed a great deal of pride in their heritage. It was refreshing, seeing San Antonio through his eyes. She'd always loved the city, but never had she enjoyed it like this. It was clear Spencer had spent a great deal of time there, and he truly had a way of making it come to life for her.

After discussing a full day of activities and weighing their options, they ended up forsaking a portion of them in favor of spending a little more time in bed.

Later, as they stepped from the hotel lobby out onto the river walk, he took her hand, more casual, more comfortable than ever before. Their relationship had grown so much lately, especially on this trip. It was the first time the two of them had any length of time to really ignore the daily business of life as usual in order to devote their time to getting to know each other on a deeper level.

* * *

When they arrived at Mercado del Sol, a market square with the Spanish name for "market of the sun," the air was full with the flavor and festivity of the Mexican culture. It was alive with energy, bursting with color and sound.

Spencer was in a playful mood and Brynn kept up, word for word, measure for measure. She was amazed her heart could still summon this level of intimacy, of playful banter, of such complete love for a man.

As they strolled throughout the market, she reflected on the time they'd spent together at home in Blackwater, at work and then later when he finally met Blake. The instant rapport he'd developed with her son touched her on a deep level. She couldn't see herself in a serious relationship with a man Blake didn't feel comfortable with. When she pictured the two of them laughing together, she could barely suppress a squeal of excitement.

Then, suddenly she remembered the awkward way Piper had taken advantage of his chivalrous ways and imposed upon his kindness to practically carry her back into the house. She felt a flash of concern when she recalled the icy glare she'd seen on Piper's face as they began to pull out of the driveway on the way out of town.

Spencer broke into her thoughts. "What's wrong, Babe?" he asked, his brows knit together in concern.

"Oh, I'm sorry, it's nothing," she quickly responded. "I was just thinking about our last night at my house with Blake and Piper. I'm just hoping everything's okay back home."

He squeezed her hand affectionately.

"Everything's great at home. Blake is with your brother and sister-in-law, two of the most responsible adults on the planet, from what I've heard. And you've got Piper house-sitting."

She gave a nervous chuckle. "That's what I'm worried about," she confessed. "To be honest, I'm glad Sarge is with Blake. I don't know if I trust her home alone with him."

"I admit she's, um, unusual, I guess," he said, choosing his words carefully "But I think she's probably pretty harmless." At the time, neither of them knew the dangers that lay ahead.

"I think you're probably right. Maybe I'm just reading too much into things." She smiled weakly.

"It all comes down to maturity," he offered. "Even though you're only, what... five years older than her, I think she's just maybe got some jealousy issues. Getting used to a new roommate takes some time, especially under these circumstances."

She reminded herself that Piper had just lost her mother and was grieving. Grief affected behavior, she knew. "I know you're right. I think I just over-reacted."

Determined not to let her concerns about Piper interfere with their weekend, she forced the thoughts from her mind and focused on the man she was with.

He stopped, giving her a sweet, reassuring grin and kissed her softly.

Chapter 14

On the return trip home, she found herself wishing she could make their weekend together last forever. Spencer was so easy to be with, that after only a few months, she couldn't imagine her life without him. He had made such an impact on her life already. Glancing over at him, she let out a giggle. He was holding the steering wheel and singing with the music. He was just plain silly, she realized. He sang the main words, and mouthed the backups, so animated that his expressions changed when the music went from part to part.

When they returned home, Piper's car was in the driveway. Brynn was planning to get her things inside and unpack them before going to pick up Blake at Ben and Ludie's. That way she could focus her time and attention solely on her son once she picked him up.

She handed Spencer her keys and he turned the key in the lock. When he pushed the door opened, Brynn was surprised to see Blake standing in the foyer, grinning from ear to ear.

"Hi, honey!" she sang out, pulling him into a tight hug. "What are you doing home? I was going to pick you up at Uncle Ben's house."

"Piper went and picked me up so I could be home when you got here. We have a surprise for you!" His face barely contained his enthusiasm.

"Come on!" he urged his Mom, taking her by the hand and leading her toward the living room.

She could hardly believe what she saw. Piper, grinning from ear to ear, waved her arm in an expansive gesture toward the living room.

"I decorated it for you!" she said proudly.

The walls had been covered with a stark white wallpaper imprinted with tiny black fleur de lis and flourishes. The heavy curtains were white with wide black stripes. On the sofa were black and white throw pillows scattered across. On the coffee table were a few decorative items in busy black and white patterns with a black iron fleur de lis. The floor had a thick, plush rug that was white with black splotches similar to an animal print of some sort. On the wall across from the fireplace was a decal of a huge fleur de lis with very busy smaller, scattered floral print decals, all in black.

Brynn bit her lip hard and choked back a barrage of words. "Um, what have you done?" she asked. Piper stood in front of the fireplace, beaming proudly.

"You deserved it," Piper said pointedly. "You work hard, and I know how badly you wanted to redo your living room." She glanced quickly between Brynn, Spencer and Blake to gauge their reactions. Blake's face held a look of eagerness, since anything that would be a great surprise for his Mom was a great idea as far as he was concerned.

Brynn held her reaction in check. "Piper, um, I had already picked out my colors and themes, and as you know, I had wanted to stay away from black and white."

Piper's expression was passive.

"I'm sorry, Piper. I don't want to hurt your feelings but don't you remember all the soft beach tones I had picked out?"

Piper's mouth flew open, her jaw hanging in faux astonishment. "I thought it was the other way around!" she exclaimed. "I'm so sorry," she dripped in honey sweet words. Brynn saw through her act and could scarcely believe the level of manipulation the woman had gone to.

Piper's lips formed into a pout, her chin nearly resting on her chest. She looked up through heavy lids and lashes and murmured how sorry she was to have ruined everything.

"I only wanted to surprise you. I didn't mean to make you angry. I'll take everything back, and as for the wallpaper, I can try to get it all scraped off." Tears formed on her lower lashes and she let out one small, quiet sob, then burst into tears and ran down the hallway to her room.

A hard reality rushed over Brynn, and it occurred to her to look at Spencer and Blake for their reaction. They were both staring at her, unsure of how to perceive her response.

She dropped her head and looked down. It was a no-win situation. She did not believe for one moment that Piper had merely "forgotten" that she didn't like print, fleur de lis, and black and white. She had specifically vetoed those when they had gone shopping, and had pointed out all the swatches she loved most. She couldn't just pretend it was all okay and chalk it up to a misunderstanding. *Could she?*

But on the other hand, she had always tried to teach Blake to be gracious and that when someone did something nice for him to accept it and express his gratitude. She'd told him not to ever say he didn't like something or to complain about a gift or a favor. She'd taught him to accept it graciously and thank them, then discuss it privately with her later. If she stood her ground on this, he wouldn't understand. She knew she had to apologize, or at the very least explain herself.

Then there was the other matter. She had left Blake with Ben and Ludie thinking he would be there with them when she got back. She was almost certain Piper had gone over there and told them how she had planned a wonderful surprise for Brynn and that she wanted Blake to be home for when she saw her surprise. Ben and Ludie wouldn't have suspected anything was wrong and would have likely been happy to help ensure her surprise would go well.

Brynn tried to shake off her frustration and focus on what to do next. The room was hideous; it might have been perfectly suited to someone else's tastes, but she had made it clear she wasn't big on the black and white theme. Piper had deliberately set her up to make her look bad in front of the others.

She felt eyes on her and looked up yet again to see both Piper and Blake watching her, anxious for her reaction. Spencer was surveying the room, obviously trying to figure out if this was a good thing or a bad thing. Blake was clearly puzzled at his mother's reaction. Piper was still in her room, and Brynn wasn't sure exactly what to say.

Clearly she had lost this round. Anything else she could say at this point would only be in Piper's favor. It would merely lead to further histrionics. Piper had played this well. The only thing she couldn't figure out was *why*.

With what remaining dignity she had, Brynn explained, "I know. I over-reacted. I went to such great lengths to pick out the colors I wanted, and I even showed her all my color samples when we went shopping. She knew I didn't want the blacks and whites or any prints. I just don't get it." She sighed.

"I'm sure she just forgot," Spencer offered, trying his best to ease a difficult situation. Blake looked from Spencer to his Mom and back, obviously trying to form his reaction based on theirs.

"Mom, I don't think she would go to this kind of trouble and spend all that money just to do the opposite of what you wanted," Blake offered, an unspoken question on his lips. "She must have just forgotten, like Spencer said."

Brynn looked at her son, really looked at him and studied his face. He wasn't a little boy anymore. He was growing up. And here he was, trying to use this as a teachable moment with *her*. He wanted her to be gracious. How could she feel so conflicted, and yet so proud of her son, all in one moment?

"I know. You're probably right. I guess it just caught me by surprise." Brynn decided then and there to not bring it up again. She would say no more about the matter, and she would gradually begin to replace things, perhaps one throw pillow at a time until she got the room she wanted. Piper would be finding an apartment before too long, and she would have her living room exactly how she wanted it after that.

Spencer brought her bags in and put them on her bed. They stood in the bedroom and held each other for a few moments. Saying goodbye to this man was getting harder and harder each time for her. She looked up at him and slipped her arms around his neck. She stood back, taking in the sight of him, head to toe. "I'm memorizing how you look," she said.

"I'm not going far. You'll see me tomorrow." He planted a kiss on her cheek. "You're not going to be able to get rid of me very easily."

She bit her bottom lip and her eyes darted about the room as her mind reached to make sense of her emotions. He pulled her close again.

"I miss you already. Thank you for coming with me."

"Thank *you* for taking me. I loved it."

"I should go, I need to get home and do some laundry before I go back to work tomorrow. Will I see you tomorrow?" He eyed her expectantly.

"I'm still off work. I go back in two days. But I'll be here tomorrow if you want to stop by before work tomorrow evening?"

"Yes, I think I will," he laughed. "I can't seem to get enough of you these days."

* * *

After Spencer left, Brynn went to check on Blake and Sarge. They were in the backyard, and Blake was throwing a tennis ball. Each time, the dog quickly retrieved it and brought it immediately back to him.

Piper was still in her room, when Brynn came back inside, and she briefly contemplated going in and speaking to her. She decided against it and instead went and unpacked her overnight bag. She was just putting away her cosmetics when she heard a soft tap-tapping on her door. She looked up to see Piper standing in the doorway.

"Can we talk?" she asked.

Brynn drew in a deep breath and paused before answering. "Um yea, come on in."

"I'm sorry," Piper muttered. "I just wasn't thinking. I wanted so badly to surprise you and I guess I just got mixed up on what you liked and didn't like."

Brynn didn't believe for one minute she had forgotten about the fleur de lis, especially after she'd been so clear about her distaste for it.

"My memory has been so bad, ever since Mom first got sick," Piper continued. "Then when she died, well, it's all I can do sometimes to remember what to do every day." Her faint smile held a touch of remorse.

"I'm so sorry, I can take everything back if you want; I would totally understand." She held an expression of hope that Brynn would forgive her.

Brynn of all people knew exactly how it felt to lose her mother. Everyone grieves differently, she reminded herself. It was probably good that Piper had found something to do, something to help another, in fact. Brynn felt a quick flash of shame over her reaction.

"No, Piper, I'm sorry." She dropped her head, staring at the carpet while she formed her words. "Instead of appreciating what you did for me, I got angry over a stupid misunderstanding." The words rolled off her tongue more easily than she thought they would, but they left a bitter taste in her mouth. She had to play this carefully, or she'd never be able to figure out Piper's game and what exactly she was trying to do to her. She found herself wondering if she'd made a mistake in agreeing to look out for her. She'd definitely gotten more than she had bargained for.

"Maybe we could shop together?" Piper suggested. "Then you could pick out some pillows and a throw for the sofa in the colors you like and I'll get them for you." She brushed her hands free of some imaginary thing and clapped them together, nodding confidently. "That's what we'll do! And we won't stop until you love it!"

"That sounds good," Brynn answered. When Piper moved forward with a hug, Brynn responded with a squeeze.

"So we're good?" Piper's eyes were wide.

"Yeah, we're good." Brynn forced a smile and kept it there until Piper had left the room, closing the door behind her. Righteous indignation washed over Brynn, yet she knew she'd been a little hard on her. When she had lost her own mother, it had taken a while to feel like herself again. She remembered going through the motions every day, almost devoid of emotion.

Blake had been only two years old at the time, and she had forced herself to continue living

135

each day for his sake. She pushed herself to get up every morning and go about the business of living. She had not long since been divorced at the time, so there was no one else there to take care of Blake, so she knew she had to pull up her bootstraps and do it.

Her ex-husband, Mark, was no longer in the picture at that time. Their marriage had been brief. He'd been unkind to her, but things seemed to improve when she got pregnant with Blake. At the time she told herself that now that he knew he was going to be a father, he realized what he was doing. He'd just needed that wake-up call to remind him what was at stake.

The improvement was short-lived, however, and soon after Blake was born, he returned to his angry outbursts. He even became violent on a few occasions, and she knew she couldn't take a chance on him hurting the baby.

As much as it hurt her to see her son grow up without a father, she was not going to risk him being subjected to an abusive one. So by the time she lost her mother, she was alone and knew she had to pull herself together for Blake. She had her younger brother, Ben, in her life and, although he was only three years her junior, she still felt as though she needed to keep it together for his sake, too. Piper, on the other hand, had no one, and Brynn knew she should cut her some slack.

Sighing, she went into the living room. Blake was on the couch watching TV, with Sarge right at his feet, as usual. Blake was completely focused on what he was watching, and Sarge was vigilant as always, looking out for his boy.

Her phone rang, pulling her from her thoughts. She picked it up to see Spencer's smiling face on her screen.

"Hey, how are you?" she breathed into the phone.

"Better now that I'm hearing your voice. How are things going? If you can't talk right now, I'll understand."

"No, I'm glad to hear from you. We're all okay." She took the phone and walked out to the back patio, and Sarge got up and followed her. She pulled a patio chair out from the table and sat down.

"Piper came into my room and apologized. She said she got mixed up and forgot which ones I liked and didn't like."

"Do you believe her?"

"I didn't at first, it seemed all too obvious. I told her that day how much I wanted to stay away from black and white themes and that I preferred solids to prints. I showed her the colors I wanted, they were nothing like what she picked out. I couldn't imagine getting it *that* wrong, but then I started thinking about how she had lost her mother. I know how that feels." She swallowed hard. "I guess it's not worth being upset over, it's an easy enough fix I suppose."

"I know, but you wanted it a certain way," he pointed out. "What are you going to do?"

"Well, I'm just gonna let it go for now. I'm going to just leave it like it is, and Piper suggested we do some shopping and pick up a couple of pillows and other things here and there and put a few colorful accents around. Eventually it'll be exactly what I wanted."

"You're a good sport," he said. "I like it. I like it a lot."

"Oh you do, do you?" she flirted. "What else do you like?" she purred seductively into the phone. He began to elaborate, and Brynn was so enthralled with their conversation that she didn't notice Piper standing just outside the gate listening. Sarge had gone back inside with Blake a few minutes earlier, so there was no alert to the eavesdropper.

Spencer reminded her he had to work the next night but that he was going to try to come by on his way in to work. Brynn was delighted and told him so, then hung up to go back inside and spend a little time with her son. As much fun as her romantic getaway with Spencer was, she missed her little boy.

Chapter 15

As the middle of the week rolled around, Brynn thought it would be nice to have Ben and Ludie over for dinner on the weekend to meet Spencer. She'd missed them lately, as she'd been spending more and more time with Spencer as of late. He had become someone very special to her and it was time for him to meet her family. She called Ludie and Ben to invite them. Ludie answered the phone on the second ring.

"Hey, how's my favorite sister-in-law?"

"Your *only* sister-in-law." Brynn couldn't resist smiling. "Great. Really good. I've missed you."

"I know. We've missed you, too. How are things going with your man?"

"Actually, that's what I wanted to talk to you about." She grabbed a cup of coffee and took her phone outside to chat.

"I've been thinking… I'd like for you to meet Spencer. I was thinking maybe you and Ben would like to come over for dinner Saturday? It would give you a chance to meet him and see how things go. Plus, did I mention I've *missed* you?"

Ludie chuckled. "You might have said something about that. Yea, I think that'll be fine. I need to talk to Ben but I'm pretty sure we don't have anything going. What can I bring?"

"Hmmm… bring a salad."

"Okay," Ludie answered.

"I'm going to make chicken alfredo, or veal parmesan, something Italian, I think."

"Okay, great, then I'll do a green salad, maybe Caesar. How about a dessert? Something chocolate?"

"You know I can't resist that. Of course! And I can't wait for you to meet Spencer." She traced the rim of the cup with her finger. "He's so good to me." She breathed a sigh of pleasure.

"Girl, you've got it *bad.*" Ludie laughed.

"Trust me, I know the feeling because I was just as bad when I got to know your brother. So, is it getting serious?"

"Um, yeah. He told me he's in love with me." She felt a smile tugging at the corners of her mouth, yet again. She couldn't remember ever smiling so much.

"Did you say it back?"

"Of course I did! I'm glad he finally said it because I was afraid I would say it first," she giggled. "Just wait till you meet him, you'll see what I mean." Looking at the clock, she said, "Oh I've got to get ready for work! If I don't see you when I drop Blake off, I'll see you tomorrow.

"Sounds good."

"I think I'm gonna call Roxy and see if she and Dennis wanna come too. Let me know when you talk to Ben, okay?"

* * *

When she got to work Spencer was waiting for her at the time clock.

"I was wondering when you were gonna get here." He gave her a quick hug and took her bag from her, carrying it while they walked. "How was your day?"

"It was good. But better now." She cast a sideways glance at him.

"Oh yeah? I was thinking the exact same thing." When they arrived near the door where the hallway to her unit led in one direction and his department the other, they stopped for a moment.

"I meant to call you, but I was running late. Remember when I told you I wanted you to meet my family?" Without waiting for his answer, she continued.

"Well, I talked to Ludie today, I think she and Ben will be over Saturday for dinner. I told her I'm making something Italian. She's going to bring salad and a dessert. Wanna bring some wine again and join us?"

"Sure. I'll be meeting your brother and sister-in-law for the first time. Maybe I should bring something a little stronger than wine," he joked.

"Oh please, it'll be fine. They'll love you." She eyed him speculatively. "Like I do." She flashed him a persuasive grin. "Oh, and I want to invite my friend, Roxy, and her boyfriend, Dennis, too."

"Stop. You're making me nervous." When she bit her lip and looked away, he responded with a wink.

"I'm kidding… it'll be fine. Now get to work." Looking both ways to ensure no one was watching, he gave her a quick kiss. "Before I get us both in trouble for PDA."

"PDA? What are you, in seventh grade?"

"I'll have you know, you never outgrow public displays of affection." He pretended to look hurt. "Or the need for paychecks. Now walk away so I can get to work. You know I can't leave till you walk away." He handed her bag to her.

She turned and looked back after she had only taken a few steps. He looked back at the same time and blew her a kiss.

When she arrived on the unit, she was thrilled to see Lindsey on the assignment board, but not as happy to see Thea. Every unit had a "Ms. Perfect Nurse," and on this unit it was Thea.

The fact that she was the charge nurse only made it worse. She held everyone to a certain standard and raised hell when it wasn't met. That would have been a good thing, if her ridiculously high standards had anything at all to do with actual patient care. No, for Thea, it meant focusing on details like paperwork and updates to charts and filing things neatly in the charts, she wanted them to put busy work ahead of patients all too often.

Patient care came first in Brynn's book, and Lindsey's, too. Most of the nursing staff had issues with Thea because she got some sort of thrill out of talking down to them in front of anyone who happened to be in the hallways, patients included. Thea was a tiny woman, barely five feet tall with a small frame. Dark, snappy eyes danced about nervously, as if she feared she might miss something. She was of Asian heritage with olive skin and almond-shaped eyes. Her movements were quick, jerky. Brynn was of the impression that Thea felt the need to compensate for her small stature by being loud and authoritative. She was certainly intelligent enough, but seemed to focus on inconsequential things instead of trusting her nurses to manage their patients.

Brynn wasn't too surprised when she arrived to find Thea at the nurses' station barking orders at the staff. Taking her with a grain of salt, she grabbed her report sheet, rolled her eyes and sat down for shift change report. She turned around in her chair to glance at the assignment board once more.

Piper was doing clinical rotations and was supposed to be on her unit. She made a mental note to look for her and let her shadow her for the shift. She had promised Sylvia she would look out for her and help her get herself through the program and settled into a job at the hospital, and that's what she would do.

As it turned out, she didn't have to go out of her way to seek her out. She was in the hall talking to Lindsey, when a small group of nervous young students made their way onto the unit. They wore their freshly starched white uniforms, shiny white shoes, and had their stethoscopes draped over their necks.

"They're so cute when they're little," Brynn muttered to Lindsey.

"You're so bad," Lindsey said, laughing.

"Brynn!" Piper called out as they approached. "I'm assigned to your unit tonight!"

"I know, you wanna shadow me, or did your instructor assign y'all to certain nurses already?"

"Nope, she told us we can choose our own nurses. I want you." She flashed an eager but nervous grin.

The night seemed to go well, with only a few minor situations that required intensive interventions. Brynn told Piper that when a code was called or there was an emergent situation, it was best to jump in and help, or at the very least observe.

"That's the way you learn. Trust me, you'll get way more out of actually going through the situations than you will from a textbook." She started walking and Piper walked with her.

"It's valuable experience, and you'll need that, particularly if you do decide to go further and get your nursing license."

"I definitely want to," she nodded eagerly. "So far I've loved my clinicals, especially ER."

Brynn laughed. The students and new nurses always seemed to love the ER. She had to admit, she did also. She had learned in the emergency room that she thrived under pressure. She had signed on to a medical unit first to get some good, solid experience, but her ultimate goal would be to transfer either to the emergency department or labor and delivery one day.

Brynn was pleasantly surprised that she and Piper seemed to work well together. Certainly their work situation was less awkward than their personal one. Considering the fragile state of their friendship lately, she had been a little concerned, but tonight was helping to shed her uncertainties.

Piper was quick and eager to learn, and didn't attempt to challenge Brynn's authority in any way. She kept a small notebook and jotted down notes when Brynn told her something important to remember.

After passing out medications, Brynn checked in on Piper who was busy giving baths to some of the patients. She had just finished giving a sponge bath to a patient with a new hip replacement when Brynn found her.

"Are you ready to get back to the desk and get caught up on some things?" Brynn motioned for her to follow. "The nursing assistant who's working on this hall with me and Lindsey tonight is Christy and she's excellent. She can show you where to record all your vitals and other notes."

When they got back to the desk, Thea was lecturing some nurses. Brynn was surprised that this time it actually involved patient care rather than hospital politics that made little difference to the patients. Thea had apparently just discovered that someone had cut away some steri-strips that had rolled up from a surgical incision.

"You never remove steri-strips" she said, speaking slowly and patronizing them like she was speaking to small children. "They are put there by the surgeon for a reason, and they stay there until they fall off." She was actually pacing the floor as she spoke and looked more like a drill instructor than a nurse. Brynn cast a glance over at Lindsey, suppressing a chuckle. Not that the patient's issue was laughable, but Thea's behavior certainly was.

"Now I don't know who did it," Thea continued in her whining, tinny voice, "because there were no initials on the dressing change. But if I see it again I *will* get to the bottom of it, and it won't be pretty."

Brynn walked away before she said something she might regret. Many of the nurses on the unit had been practicing far longer than Thea. Brynn and Lindsey were still fairly new but had the common sense to not go ripping off steri-strips from surgical patients.

Piper followed not too far behind. "What was all that about?"

"You probably won't have to worry too much about it, but just for future reference, steri-strips are little tapes that are applied across incisions to reinforce them. They're designed to roll up on the edges and eventually curl up and fall off on their own. Sometimes you can kind of trim the edges a little, especially if leaving them like that will cause any kind of pulling or tearing if they get caught on anything. But you never, ever just pull them off."

"Will they find out who did it?" Piper asked, wide-eyed and clearly concerned.

"Probably not, but it's really not as big of a deal if the patient's not bleeding and the incision is still well intact, as apparently this one was. I think Thea just wanted to make an example of it, and to have something to complain about. To be honest, this was worthy of a complaint because it could easily have jeopardized a patient's healing."

"I see." Piper was jotting notes in her trusty little notebook.

"Most of the time when we do a dressing change or wound care, we take a Sharpie marker and initial and put the date and time on the dressing. That way there's no question as to who did the dressing change last and when it was done."

As it turned out, Thea had no further basis for interrogating the nurses. The patient with the steri-strips ended up telling her nurse what had happened.

"Oh, by the way, these little tapes were coming loose after I took my shower," she told her nurse, "so I peeled them off." Apparently Thea had failed to ask the patient that question and had just assumed it was one of the staff. When the nurse went back to the nurses' station and reported what the patient had said, Thea flushed, mumbled something, and stormed off, busying herself elsewhere. She was certainly above apologizing.

The rest of the shift passed without major incident. Spencer was on the unit briefly a few times, but he was either racing back and forth between his patients or Brynn was tied up with patients anytime he had a few moments to spare. They did manage to make eye contact a few times, and Spencer would give her a wink, or she would blow him a kiss. They had to be careful not to draw too much attention to themselves so they wouldn't jeopardize being able to work on the same units. Although the night didn't leave much time for chatting, there was an upside to the busyness. Thea stayed focused on her chart-checks and appeared to put a lot less time into scrutinizing her nurses so much.

When the students were preparing to leave after their portion of the shift, Brynn spoke some words of encouragement to Piper, focusing on what seemed to be her strong points. She believed in balancing positive comments with any criticism and she would be no different with Piper.

"Thank you so much, Brynn," Piper gushed. "I learned so much with you tonight!"

"It's no problem. You know my schedule, so if you want to sign up to shadow me in the next few weeks, please do." She gave her a quick hug and said goodbye. "I'll see you at home later."

Once again, Brynn chastised herself for having gotten so upset with her over the living room issue.

"What's on your mind?" Lindsey asked, coming up beside her. "You look like you're a thousand miles away."

"Yeah, it's Piper."

"The steri-strip thing?"

"That, and, well… I just can't put a finger on it, but there's something about her." Biting her lip, she looked away.

"I know what you need," Lindsey smiled. "Star Bar, after work."

"You're on."

Chapter 16

A couple of days later, Brynn and Spencer each got a text message from Piper inviting both of them to have lunch with her. They both replied and said they'd be there. Brynn was determined to make the effort. The three of them texted back and forth about the details. Later on, Spencer texted Brynn to let her know he'd just meet her at the restaurant since he'd be in a meeting at work before then.

Brynn was ready in plenty of time and when she arrived at the restaurant she grabbed a booth and told the hostess she'd be expecting two others.

At the same time, Spencer was sitting at a table at the Ladybird Café, craning his neck to watch for Brynn who hadn't yet arrived. Piper arrived shortly after him and sat across the table chattering on about hospital business, the weather, anything that might distract him from watching for Brynn.

Birdie came over and spoke to them. "You ready to order, Sugar?" she asked Spencer.

"Thanks, Birdie," Spencer said. "But we'll wait until Brynn gets here to place our orders." He checked his phone, hoping there would be a text from Brynn. Nothing. He laid it on the table so he'd be sure not to miss a phone call or message.

Piper began regaling him of tales of her life in Houston, hoping to find some common ground with him as he'd once been a police officer in Houston. She went on to speak of her ex-boyfriend, Michael, and his unwillingness to let go.

"I'm not sure what he'll do," she said, "I'm afraid to be alone."

"Then it's a good thing you're not alone," he replied. "He doesn't even know where you live, does he?"

"Well, no," she stammered, "but I wouldn't be surprised if he tracked me down."

Finally, Spencer excused himself to the men's room, barely aware he'd left his phone on the table. As soon as he'd stepped away, Piper grabbed it and went into the settings, adjusting them to ensure it wouldn't ring or vibrate.

Once he'd returned to the table, he commented once again that he was worried about Brynn. Piper attempted to distract him, continuing her annoying chatter.

Eventually, he checked his phone again and was dismayed to find it in silent mode. He was immediately suspicious of Piper, knowing he didn't remember silencing it. He'd missed a phone call and two texts from Brynn, who was sitting alone at another restaurant across town.

Piper appeared shocked and reached into her purse to retrieve her phone. "Oh nooo," she drawled. "Mine was on silent, too! We must have gotten our wires crossed about where to meet somehow!"

Spencer tried to control his irritation at her mistake. Calling Birdie over to the table, he apologized and explained their misunderstanding. She waved him away and assured him it was no problem, she'd see them next time.

"Where are you going?" Piper asked. "Don't you want to just wait for her to get here?"

"She's not coming," Spencer snapped. "She's at another restaurant, but that's okay, we've decided on a completely separate place to meet." The line of his mouth tightened, his jaw clenched in anger.

While Piper gathered up her purse and fished for her keys, he was already near the door.

"But wait!" she called out to him. "You didn't tell me where we're going to meet?" Her words fell on deaf ears, however, as he was already out the door.

* * *

Saturday night came around quickly, and Brynn was almost giddy. Excitement bubbled up in her, and gave her the energy she needed to get everything ready. She had taken some time to clean house with a little help from Piper and Blake. Knowing she would be introducing Spencer to her family and friends made the night all the more exciting. She really wanted Ben and Ludie to love him like she did. Roxy, too, of course. He had made a great impression on Blake, so she felt pretty sure they would like him, too.

Brynn had made chicken fettuccine alfredo for dinner. She'd gotten an early start, making her sauces homemade, giving them time to simmer and the spices to blend. She had purchased two loaves of crusty French bread and would warm it just prior to serving. She had blended softened butter with roasted garlic, parmesan cheese and parsley to put on the bread.

Piper was a big help in the kitchen, helping her prepare things. She made a big picture of iced tea and stayed in the kitchen, chattering pleasantly and keeping Brynn company.

"Are you nervous?" Piper looked up from what she was doing. "About Spencer meeting your family, I mean."

"Not really, I think they'll be able to see in him what I do, that he's a great guy. He's smart, motivated, genuine, and compassionate. He's the total package...what's not to love?" She realized how it sounded, the way she was singing his praises. "A bit much, huh?"

"Ya think?" Piper answered with sarcasm. She popped an olive into her mouth. "Don't worry about it, you're right. I'm sure they'll like him. Especially when they see how happy you are around him."

Brynn was relieved that the tension between her and Piper had diminished. There were a couple of topics that were taboo, including the living room makeover, that they just didn't bring up. And the lunch date mix-up, which was surely just a misunderstanding. Overall their relationship had taken on an easier, more relaxed tone and Brynn was glad.

Spencer arrived early, bottle of wine in hand, gorgeous grin on his tanned face. Brynn wondered how he could bring about this reaction in her every time she saw him. He kissed her on the cheek and told her he'd missed her. The scent of his cologne nearly intoxicated her. Who needs wine, she wondered.

"But I worked with you just last night," she told him, a flirtatious grin spreading on her face.

"I know, but the patients kept taking you away from me, so it doesn't count."

"Ah, I see. Well then I'm glad you're here." She stood on her tiptoes, wrapped her arms around his neck, and gave him a tender kiss.

"Does this count?"

"It most definitely counts. You're on your way to extra credit."

"Ahem..." They both stopped, focusing their attention on Piper, who stood in the entry to the kitchen with a cookie sheet in one hand and a loaf of French bread in the other. "Want me to slice these up and put them in the oven?" she asked.

"Um, yea, thanks," Brynn replied cheerfully. "The seasoned butter is over by the fridge. It's softened enough so it should be easy to spread."

It wasn't long before Ben and Ludie arrived. Ben was carrying Annie on his hip. She wiggled, trying to free herself from his grasp and he finally put her down. She immediately made her way to toward Blake and Sarge. Brynn couldn't wait to get her hands on her niece, but stopped to make introductions.

"Spencer, this is my brother, Ben and his wife, Ludie, who also just happens to be his better half." She winked when Ben pretended to be offended. Spencer stepped forward and shook his hand.

"It's nice to meet you. I've heard a lot about you both." His smile was genuine, and Brynn thought he seemed comfortable meeting them.

"I hope at least some of it was good?" Ben asked, casting a glance at his sister.

"All of it was good, actually. She credits you and your lovely wife with helping Blake turn out to be such a cool young man." Blake was just walking up behind them and beamed at the compliment.

"It's true," Brynn shrugged, throwing up her arms in mock surrender. "I couldn't do a thing with the kid, so I had to call in the troops." Blake shot his Mom a silly look. "Yea, right."

Roxy and Dennis arrived a short time later, which meant another round of introductions for Spencer. He handled it with finesse, as usual.

"It's great to finally meet you," Spencer said, shaking Dennis's hand. Brynn thought they might have a lot in common with Dennis's fire and rescue job and Spencer's previous career in law enforcement.

"Good to meet you too, Buddy." The men ended up in the living room, talking about everything from sports to hunting and fishing. Brynn overheard them from time to time when they'd start laughing and getting loud. Exactly what she'd been hoping for.

Ludie and Piper and Roxy were in the kitchen helping Brynn get things set up, and the mood was light with them as well. Twice, Piper gravitated toward the guys in the living room, and Brynn called her back the first time to help fill the glasses with ice. The next time, it was time to come to the table so she called all of them, Piper

154

and the guys, to come join them in the dining room.

Ludie had made a tossed salad and made a four-layer chocolate dessert with whipped cream, chocolate pudding, cream cheese and powdered sugar all poured onto a baked pecan crust. She had topped it all off with a grated chocolate bar. Blake threatened to eat that first and have all the other stuff for dessert.

"No you most certainly will not," Brynn countered. "See what I deal with?" she asked Spencer. "I'm gonna turn him over to his aunt and uncle if he doesn't straighten up." She locked eyes with Blake and gave him a warm smile. "The truth is, Ludie has become quite an expert on low- sugar desserts. There are limits, but we can afford to indulge every now and then," she finished with a wink in her son's direction.

The main course was Brynn's fabulous chicken fettuccine alfredo along with eggplant parmesan. When she took them out of the oven, everyone's mouths were watering. Sarge came through to the dining room and curled up on the floor just under the edge of the table. He apparently didn't want to take a chance on missing out on anything, especially dropped morsels and crumbs.

They all took their seats as Brynn was putting the last few things on the table. They joined hands to ask a blessing before dinner. Brynn knew that it may not be the norm for most people, but it made her happy and secure, and she was delighted that her family was so willing to participate in giving thanks.

The mood was light, and everyone seemed to be having a good time. Piper was on her best behavior throughout dinner, and Brynn was relieved. She was actually making conversation with Ben and Ludie, and she made a huge fuss over Annie. Ben had set up her booster seat at the table, and Annie was making a mess of the pasta Ludie had put on her little plate.

Roxy and Dennis were really a great match for the other two couples, Brynn thought. With Roxy's uptown sophistication, she could still be one of the most down-to-earth, refreshingly honest people she'd ever met.

Dennis, on the other hand, was Southeast Texas all the way. One of the good old boys that, no matter their lifestyle, were always going to have integrity and treat others well. Dennis was the type to hang out with firefighters, or his hunting and fishing buddies, and then go out to dinner with other couples and fit in, having quite a bit to add to the conversation. Very well-rounded. And he made Roxy smile.

It was also very clear to Brynn that Spencer was going to fit in to the whole family very well if tonight was any indication. Blake was on his best behavior, and Brynn couldn't have been prouder. He doted over his sweet little cousin, Annie, and did his best to make everyone feel at home. If anyone needed a refill of their iced tea or anything else, he was the first to offer to get it.

The subject came around to moral dilemmas, somehow, and it became a game. "Okay," she said, setting up a scenario. "You're at a bus station, and you see someone, an old lady, heading for her bus," Roxy drawled for effect. "The lady had been sitting next to you and she's left her travel bag on the bench next to you." She rubbed her hands together and cast her eyes upward, letting her imagination help her create the scenario. "Let's say the little old lady is boarding her bus, and you see her."

Brynn said, "You chase after her and give her the bag, no question."

"That's what I'd do," Ludie echoed.

"I'm not finished yet." Roxy looked as if she were grabbing the words from the air. "You suddenly realize the time, and your own bus is leaving very, very soon, and you have to run to catch it. What do you do?"

"Good one," Spencer said. "Wait, how long do you have until there's another bus to your destination?"

"Yeah," Ben said. "That makes a huge difference."

"It's 24 hours until the next bus to your destination." Roxy turned a little in her chair, a self-satisfied smile on her face. They were clearly stumped.

"What's in the bag?" Blake asked her, sincerity evident on his face. "Cause if it's money, I'd have to think really hard."

"You don't have time to think, Son," Brynn told him. "What's the right thing to do?"

They didn't completely decide on the one right way to handle it, but instead compromised by saying they'd grab a security guard or railway employee and hand them the bag, pointing them to the bus the lady's boarding.

"I have one!" Piper blurted. "Say you have a great friend, and she's seeing someone you're interested in." She took a sip from her wine glass, licking her lips, pausing for drama.

"You know he's into you just by the way he looks at you." She cast her eyes downward, demurely. "What do you do? Give in to your feelings or back away. And what's the best way to get him to become yours?" She grinned, obviously quiet proud of herself for having come up with such a dilemma.

"I think you just leave them alone and let them work out their relationship." Ludie said, a look of incredulity on her expression.

"Nooo," Piper added, waving her off with a gesture. "I mean for him to notice you and leave her, what's the best way to go about it?"

Just then, all eyes were on Roxy. Roxy, the only one who would say what she meant, when she meant it. She didn't fail to disappoint.

"I'd think, but of course this is just me, that you should bugger off and stay the hell away from both of them until you get your own issues worked out."

Piper's mouth flew open, and she pointed to her chest. "Me? You thought I was talking about me?" She threw her head back and laughed. "No, it's hypothetical. I thought that's what we were doing. Roxy, did you actually find a bag some old lady left at the bus terminal?"

"No, actually, I didn't. But if I did, I'd hand it off to you and load you on the next bus out of town." Roxy gave a sarcastic wink and took a sip of her wine.

Brynn froze, not saying a word. *Where was this going?* she wondered.

"There's no stupid travel bag, anyway," Piper said with a laugh.

"And there are no available men here," Roxy's voice dripped with honey. "So I guess we don't have a dilemma after all."

Piper pushed her chair back and came to her feet. Her eyes burned into Roxy, who continued drinking her wine, not in the least bothered by Piper's display of emotion.

Piper tossed her head and burned into Roxy with her gaze. She stiffened with the sting of being put in her place. She grabbed up her dinner plate and took it to the kitchen before making her way down the hall to her bedroom, sullen.

"Whoa," Spencer said, hoping to lighten the mood. "So when *is* the next bus out of town?"

Brynn suppressed a tiny wave of guilt for letting the situation escalate. "I'm sorry, Rox, I don't know what's going on with her."

"Don't worry yourself, Luv," Roxy told her. "She just sees that I've worked her out and know what she's about. She'll be all right." Dennis held up his glass and clinked it to Roxy's glass.

The conversation took on a lighter tone. After dessert, Brynn surveyed the dining room and, as her eyes moved across everyone present, she was thankful for the people closest to her. She missed her parents terribly, but having Ben and Ludie and Annie in hers and Blake's lives made their sense of family complete. She tried not to think much about Piper and the old connection that extended the family in a small way, through memories of past connections.

Things were different now, Brynn reminded herself.

The conversation turned to Brynn and Spencer's recent trip to San Antonio. She hadn't been sure how everyone was feeling about her romantic weekend alone with Spencer. When she began talking about some of her favorite things they saw there, everyone seemed interested. When she spoke of the fun and excitement, then alternately the time they spent relaxing on their last morning, Ludie's interest was piqued.

"I'd love to get away for a weekend," Ludie said, looking at Ben. Her bottom lip poked out, just in case he wasn't certain that she was pouting. "We should all go camping on the beach one weekend," she said, using her eyes to enlist Brynn to join her in talking him into it.

"Count me in," Roxy added, casting a glance at Dennis.

"Spencer, how about it?" Brynn asked. "What do you think of us all going together? We could make it kind of a family trip. Even the kids."

"I'm good with that. It sounds like fun," he answered, looking back at her.

Piper had slowly wandered back out of her room and was walking toward the kitchen. She cocked her head to listen, as if she were pointedly making an effort to be included in the conversation and the trip they were planning, but looking down at her wine glass, lost in deep thought. No one seemed to notice.

"Another weekend away sounds great to me," Brynn said.

"I can stay here and keep an eye on the house for you," Piper said slowly, drawing herself into the conversation.

Ludie and Brynn exchanged a look, each of them trying to gauge the idea of including her in the trip. So she wasn't particularly socially gifted. It would be cruel to make plans in front of her and not include her. Brynn gave a slight, brief nod to Ludie, and she knew what to do.

"Piper," Ludie said. "You're coming, too, right?" Ludie eyed her expectantly.

"I'm sorry, Piper," Brynn said. "I didn't think to mention it, I know you're busy with your classes and clinical rotations, but if you can be off on the days we decide to go, I hope you'll join us." Piper looked from Ludie to Brynn as if to question whether her invitation was legitimate or just an effort to soothe her hurt feelings.

"Really," Brynn added. "We'd love for you to join us. Even if you've got your own place by then, it would be great! That way we'll still be in touch and making plans together." Brynn felt awful for not immediately including Piper from the very beginning of the conversation, but she would make up for it now. She brought out a calendar and they tried in vain to find a weekend coming up. When Brynn and Spencer both had a weekend off, Ludie and Ben wouldn't be able to get away from the shop.

Ludie leaned over to peer at Brynn's calendar. "Wait a minute," she said. "We have someone helping out at the shop not next weekend, but the one after. We had planned on going to a friend's going away party but her plans changed."

"She met a guy and suddenly she's not going anywhere," Ben teased.

"Hey," Ludie said, "I'm happy for her! She found her one and only, just like I did. And I, for one, am glad her plans changed." At that, he smiled, nudging his wife playfully.

"Well, maybe this will be your chance, if we can ever get a weekend scheduled." Ludie said it in such a final way that everyone accepted it as settled. But then Ludie's face suddenly lit up, and she sat up straight in her chair. She leaned over to whisper something in Ben's ear. He listened, then smiled before speaking up.

"I know everyone was thinking San Antonio," he offered, "but Ludie and I love to take the camper down near Galveston and camp out on the beach."

"That would be great!" Ludie agreed. "We get a big enough campsite when we go, and it would be so much fun!"

"It's October," Roxy said. "Won't it be too cool to be out on the beach?" Dennis flashed her a grin, knowing she wouldn't dare resist another outdoor challenge, even if she thought it impractical.

"No way," Ludie replied. "We go all the time in the fall. It's perfect weather for camping on the beach. You know how it is with Texas weather, if it's warm, we'll be wearing shorts. If it's cool, we can always build a campfire, you'll love it."

Roxy brought her wine glass to her lips and took a sip. "Are you sure it won't be too windy?"

"I have a tent y'all can use," Ben told Spencer. "It's seriously a big tent, and it's one of the nicer ones; we got it before we got the RV.

162

We even have an air mattress that fits in it. Ludie's idea of roughing it, well, it's not the same as mine." She cut her eyes at him and clicked her tongue, pretending to be exasperated with him.

"Sounds good to me," Spencer said. He cast a look at Brynn, gauging her response. She was smiling. "As far as the tent, it would be more than comfortable, with the weather the way it is." Brynn's expression encouraged him further.

They were quick to consider Roxy's level of commitment to the trip, and all their gazes fell on her expectantly. Before anyone could speak, she held up a hand. "I'm always good for a trip to the beach, but I'll be hiring a car to sleep in. I don't *camp*." Everyone laughed, knowing she'd make the weekend fun in spite of her reluctance.

Ludie had quickly warmed to the idea. "It's not like you'd even really *be* roughing it. We've got a full kitchen in the RV, and a shower. We always build a campfire and cook outside. We love to camp at Crystal Beach. We can put the tent right next to the camper, that way you'd be sleeping right next to us and could come in to use the bathroom and shower." She was rambling now, and Brynn found herself caught up in the excitement.

"I can bring some marshmallows and hot dogs and we can make a fire. Blake loves a campfire." She looked around. "Where is Blake?" she asked.

"He went to his room to play his games, I think." Piper offered, "I'll go get him." She got up and marched down the hall toward his room.

"Blake," she called out.

Brynn leaned over to Ludie and whispered, "Are you sure it's okay if Piper does decide to come?"

Ludie softened. "Of course, the more the merrier. It may actually help make things easier between the two of you. You're gonna bring Sarge, too, right? Dogs love the beach. And he's used to being around us anyway, when we have Blake."

When Piper and Blake came back into the room, they told Blake what the plans were. Before they could reassure Piper that she was welcome to join them, Blake asked, "Can we make a campfire and roast hot dogs?" Just as Brynn had predicted.

Piper had already begun to walk away, silently, heading for her room, when Brynn called out, "Get back here, Piper! We gotta get this planned."

Piper put a hand up to her chest. "Me?" she asked. "You really want me to come with you?"

"Why the hell not?" Roxy said, laughing.

"Of course," Ludie answered, cutting her eyes at Roxy, silently scolding her. "Piper, you're not getting off so easily, what are you going to bring?"

Roxy seemed to mellow a bit after that, much to Brynn's relief. A couple of times, however, she caught Roxy studying Piper as if she were trying to solve a puzzle.

A little later, the men were in the living room once again talking sports and cars. Blake, of course, was right there with them, soaking it all in. Brynn loved to see it. The male role models were good for him, and it was nice to see her son scrambling to keep up with their conversations. They were all three admirable men, in her opinion, and she was thrilled to have them in Blake's life.

After the women had gotten the dishes all put away, everyone sat down and played cards for a while. Sarge remained on the floor in the dining room corner, only now he was further behind the table. He slept intermittently with his chin on his paws. His eyes opened from time to time, with his ear perked up, when they would laugh a little too loudly. Once he realized they were just laughing or teasing he would again lay his head down and relax.

The mood from Piper's outburst eased a bit after a particularly aggressive hand of cards where the girls beat the guys. The teamwork brought on by a "boys-against-the-girls" game seemed to ease the awkward tension between Brynn and Piper. And Roxy and Piper. Ludie, as always, was a neutral party. Brynn loved that about her sister-in-law. Always the peacemaker.

The night had gone well, Brynn thought. She was amazed at how quickly Ben and Spencer had found common interests and subjects for conversation. Dennis was one of the most easy-going men Brynn knew and she was pleased at how well he seemed to fit into their conversations. Both Ben and Ludie seemed to get along well enough with Piper, and she was as relieved about that as anything else. The tension between Roxy and Piper had eased up, but hadn't gone away.

Alone in the kitchen for a moment, Roxy confided in Brynn that she just didn't get a good vibe from her. "It's a good idea to keep an eye on that one."

Brynn tried to dismiss the uneasy feeling that crept over her, hoping her issues with Piper were just a series of misunderstandings. Little did she know, these days were just the calm before the storm.

Chapter 17

A couple of nights later, Brynn was scheduled to work. Unfortunately, it was one of Spencer's days off. Piper would be doing the evening shift with her class and leaving at 11:00 pm. Brynn checked the assignment board when she arrived at 7:00 pm and asked if she could take one of the students to help her with her patients for the evening. Piper was delighted, of course, and very enthusiastic.

She still appeared to be catching on rather quickly, which came as a great relief to Brynn since she'd already prematurely recommended her for a job. On several occasions she had noticed Piper answering call lights that weren't even her own patients, which was a sign of great teamwork. She spoke very kindly to the patients, which was a huge attribute for anyone involved in healthcare.

At one point about halfway into the shift, Brynn had entered a patient's room to discover Piper changing the patient's gown and linens with the patient in bed. She was very careful to log roll her with care and seemed more than proficient at changing the sheets with the patient still in the bed. Brynn's eyes took in the scene before her and realized something was terribly wrong. She had just happened to glance at the feeding pump and realized that the formula was flowing through the patient's feeding tube with the patient lying flat on her back.

Brynn crossed the room quickly and flicked the machine off. Piper's eyes were wide with fear, taking in Brynn's actions. Brynn began elevating the head of the patient's bed. Removing the stethoscope from around her neck, she placed it on the patient's chest and began listening carefully.

Removing a large, needleless syringe, she pushed the tip into a port on the side of the tube nearest the patient and aspirated. The syringe quickly filled with a backflow of cream-colored formula. Piper continued watching, clearly unnerved. Brynn unplugged the machine and leaned over the patient.

"I just needed to check your feeding tube setup for a moment. We're going to leave it off for a little while and give your stomach a break, okay? You just relax here and I'll be back in to check on you in a little while."

Piper was still taking everything in when Brynn excused herself from the room. She followed her and caught up with her in the hallway.

"Brynn? Can I talk to you?" Piper's voice trembled. Brynn stopped in her tracks and paused there a moment before turning around.

"Do you realize what could have happened in there?" Brynn asked, trying to control her tone. She spun around to face her.

"No," Piper replied, almost in tears.

"Never, *ever* is it okay to run tube-feeding with the patient lying flat. The head of her bed should've been up at least to a 30 degree angle, I'd recommend 45 until you've gotten a little experience and know what to look for." She placed her hand over her face and looked down, still trying to control her anger.

"But Brynn," she whined, "I'm not even allowed to give tube feedings, nurses' aides can't do that, so I don't see how I did anything wrong. Weren't you the one who hooked up her feeding and started it?"

Brynn inhaled sharply, attempting to manage slow, deep breaths in and out a few times before speaking.

"That's right. You don't do tube feedings. I do, and I started hers. But you *are* qualified to bath and clean the patient in the bed, and when you do so, the tube-feeding has to be stopped. Then after you're finished, you come and get me. I'll listen to her lungs, check for placement, then restart it."

Piper stared at her, her mouth gaping open. "I'm sorry, I didn't realize."

Brynn snapped her head up and, asked, nearly shouting, "What? How could you not realize?" She took in a deep breath, trying to control her frustration.

"Um, they didn't tell us that part yet." She looked down, tears forming in her eyes. "I'm sorry. I didn't know." Piper's eyes darted nervously about, checking to make sure no one was witnessing the confrontation. Relieved to see that no one was around, she met Brynn's stare and continued to listen, blinking to force the tears back.

"If the patient is lying flat, the fluid that's going in through the tube can flow upward into the lungs. If they aspirate, they can get pneumonia, quickly. And I'm not talking about the kind that slowly develops and they get antibiotics until they're all better." Again, she took a deep breath and swallowed, determined to control her tone and volume.

"I'm sorry," Piper said, tears pooling on her lashes, threatening to spill over.

"Aspiration pneumonia happens fast, and sometimes there's nothing we can do. Older patients have weakened GI and respiratory tracts and can't always control what happens. That's why a lot of them have feeding tubes in the first place."

Piper's eyes were full of tears now, big heavy teardrops rolling down her cheeks. She choked back a sob, desperate to control her humiliation. "I said I was sorry. Now that I know, I promise it won't happen again."

Brynn softened a bit at that moment. Perhaps she really *hadn't* been told yet. Maybe Brynn had sent her to do a task that Piper wasn't completely ready to perform alone. She considered the possibility that the students really *hadn't* yet been instructed on this.

"I'm sorry. I'm not mad at you." Brynn stepped toward her, closing the distance between them. "I didn't realize they hadn't gone over that yet. It just really scared me." Sighing, she looked around.

"I'm sorry." Piper's tears had left several large, wet splatters on her scrub top.

Brynn nodded. "I know. I've just seen several times what can happen when a patient aspirates, and it's not pretty. I may have overreacted. Just please, never let that happen again, okay?"

Piper nodded quickly. "I won't. I promise." When Brynn forced a half-smile and turned to walk away, Piper stepped forward. "Wait." When Brynn turned to face her, she continued. "When I said I didn't know, I meant it. I promise, you can even ask my instructor. They haven't taught us that yet."

Brynn thought for a moment before answering. "No, that won't be necessary. I believe you. And now that we've talked about it, there's no chance of it being repeated. And again, I'm sorry, too."

Piper nodded her head and swallowed hard. "I won't let you down, Brynn. I told you I would do a good job here and that you wouldn't regret recommending me, and I meant it."

"Thank you."

* * *

Later in the night, the nursing assistant students were leaving for their post-conference session before going home. Brynn made a mental note to become more informed about what level of skills the students actually had before delegating patient assignments. That would apply, she decided, to student aides and student nurses as well.

Around midnight, when things had calmed down a bit, she noticed a text message on her phone. Checking it, she found a message from Spencer. He was just letting her know he was still awake and that he would love to hear from her, if she had time.

She slipped into the doctor's dictation room after quickly checking to make sure it wasn't in use, and sat down, dialing his number.

"Hey," he answered. She loved hearing his rich, deep voice. Oh, how she missed him on nights he wasn't scheduled to work.

"Hey, what's up?" she asked.

"Not much, Babe. Just watching a movie."

"Let me guess. Star Wars?"

He gasped. "How did you know? You know me too well." He sighed, pretending defeat.

"Yes I do, I'm a fast learner and don't you forget it."

"So how are things at work?"

"Oh, fine," she said, but her voice revealed more tension than she was able to hide.

"Talk to me. What's going on?" He was always so genuine with his concern, and she knew he wasn't going to give up until she talked.

She told him what had happened with Piper. And how awful she felt about it.

"You didn't know they hadn't taught that yet. How could you?" It occurred to her that it was just like him to always have her back.

"To be honest," he assured her, "as a respiratory therapist, if I had entered a patient room and found that, I would've gone off on whoever was doing it. Trust me, when patients aspirate, you know RTs are the ones who end up coming to help y'all deal with that. It's hard to see a patient like that. I would've been very upset with her."

"I guess, but I really should have asked before I sent her to the patient's room. The patient was okay, but I know what could easily have happened."

"Yea, so do I. Every pneumonia, every aspiration, and who do you call? Superman? No. Spencer. Respiratory to the rescue." He mocked a very superior hero voice, and she couldn't help but laugh. He seemed to always know how to calm her down.

By the time they hung up, she was in a much better mood. Amazing how he always seemed to make her feel better. Unfortunately, the mood didn't last. Thea was at the desk just before 1:00 am, asking for Brynn, who was coming up the hallway when she heard her name.

"Right here," she answered, walking behind the desk. Thea was furious, her short little body trembling and her tiny jaw working itself into a frenzy as she clenched and unclenched it.

The little woman inhaled, sucking in a sharp breath before beginning. "What have I told you about taking off steri-strips?"

Brynn began to defend herself, but was interrupted. Apparently Thea wasn't finished.

"After what happened not too long ago, I didn't think it could *possibly* happen again."

"The patient took those off herself, remember?" Brynn countered.

"Yes, I remember perfectly well. And we went and reinforced educating the patient on not removing them again. We had a staff meeting and memos were issued." She was pacing now, becoming more and more animated as she went on. "Which is why I never thought a nurse would go in and remove them from another patient." She stopped then, focusing her dark little eyes on Brynn. Her expression held an edge of contempt. "Especially you of all people."

Brynn's mouth flew open in protest, but when she spoke it came out as a suffocated whisper. "Agh! How dare you accuse me of that! You know that's not something I would ever do," she choked out. Intense shock registered on her face.

"I wouldn't have thought so, no," breathed Thea, her eyes shining with aggressive hostility. Brynn knew she was difficult, but never expected such a cold and unlikely accusation.

"Follow me," snapped Thea. "When I show you the dressing change, you will stand quietly, and observe. I do not want the patient to know there is a problem. There is no point frightening her."

Brynn could hardly believe what she was hearing. "What patient? I have a couple of them with steri-strips."

"221. Mrs. Darnell. Total knee replacement. Unfortunately, Mrs. Darnell has been unable to speak since her postop stroke, so she can't speak for herself."

Brynn's mouth flew open in exasperation. "I would *never* pull strips off a TKR! You know that!" She felt rage growing within her. *What on earth is happening*, she wondered.

Moments later, she stood at the bedside while Thea pulled back the sheet to reveal a dry gauze pad, taped into place. On the tape, in black permanent ink, were her initials: BC.

I didn't sign my initials there, Brynn thought. *What is going on?*

Thea loosened the tape and pulled back the gauze, revealing an incision with only two tiny steri-strips remaining at the middle of the incision. Brynn was speechless. Her mind was spinning with confusion. She glanced up to see Thea staring at her with accusation. Against her wishes, a soft gasp escaped from her lips. She turned on her heel and walked stiffly from the room, biting back tears, leaving Thea to speak softly to the patient as she re-secured her dressing with more strips.

Brynn raced for the bathroom, careful not to make eye contact with anyone. Once inside, she turned on the water to conceal the noise, and burst into tears. What on earth was happening? Those were her initials, exactly. Right down to the hook on the top of the B and the way the C overlapped the B. But why? And who would do this? Was Thea that determined to make her look bad? She was petty and confrontational, but never before had she sunk *this* low.

Brynn was looking into the mirror, carefully wiping smudged mascara from underneath her eyes when, suddenly, she was hit with a jolt of recollection. Piper had been humiliated by her mistake earlier about the feeding tube. Brynn had apologized to her and she had given the impression all was forgiven. Apparently it hadn't been.

But this, Brynn thought, *this was uncalled for*. A patient's safety had been jeopardized. This was getting out of hand and it needed to be settled.

Brynn asked to speak to Thea privately. Once they were out of earshot of the other staff, Brynn reiterated her innocence.

"Thea, you know I didn't do that." When her charge nurse's eyebrows raised in question, she continued, more emphatically. "When have I ever done something, intentionally, that would harm a patient or put them at risk? Name a time, just one."

Thea looked down at her shoes, her brow furrowed with concern. She was clearly giving it some thought. When her eyes returned to Brynn, she had a look of resignation about her. "Okay, I'll give you that. You've never given me reason to believe you'd ever put a patient at risk like that. But what explanation could there be? Those were *your* initials. Who else would do such a thing to make you look bad, and why?"

She hesitated, wondering just how wise it would be to share her suspicions about Piper with someone who was so intent on catching people's faults. If she didn't believe her, Brynn knew, she could make things very difficult for her in the future.

Brynn sighed deeply. If she didn't speak up now, though, no one knew how far this might go. So she met Thea's gaze with the intensity of her own and began. She told her of several things that Piper had done in recent weeks, careful to only include the small, albeit unverifiable, situations that involved work. There was no way she would reveal all that was happening at home. This needed to remain professional, and she wasn't about to mix personal issues with business.

Thea seemed to soften a bit, and responded by assuring Brynn that this conversation would be kept confidential. She encouraged her to keep her eyes open and to monitor Piper's work carefully. She finished with specific instructions for Brynn to watch her back, especially where her patients were concerned.

When the conversation was over, Brynn had no real way to know if Thea had believed what she'd said or thought she was out of her mind. She would either be trustworthy, or not. But Brynn couldn't regret speaking to her. *What else could I do?* she wondered.

Chapter 18

The next few nights, Brynn was scheduled to work. Her shifts rotated, and she often worked several twelve-hour shifts in a row in order to have four or five days off at a time. It was a fair payoff, she had decided, as it gave her more time to plan things with Blake. *And now Spencer*, she thought with a warm glow spreading inside her at the thought of him. He had brought so much to her life so soon. The fact that he often found ways to include her son in their plans was a bonus, and it gave her a great deal of confidence when she thought about a future with him.

He had begun staying overnight from time to time. They didn't make a habit of it, but when he did stay, it was nice. Blake went to bed early on school nights, and he often stopped and gave both his mother and Spencer good night hugs on his way to bed. To Brynn, that was to be cherished because at her son's age she knew it wouldn't last. Spencer was at the house with her most of his nights off, and after dinner, if he didn't spend the night, he at least stayed late to have more time with her.

* * *

She was glad to discover that Spencer would be working most of the same shifts as she would on the upcoming schedule. Lindsey, too. Piper's class had a couple of more rotations that week as well. Brynn didn't confront Piper right away about the issues, and instead had her accompany her on rounds. While doing some dressing changes, she was careful to observe Piper's expressions, and reinforced the standard instructions that nursing assistants weren't to remove dressings from wounds or surgical incisions.

"If a dressing is saturated with drainage or is no longer intact, you come and get me or whoever the nurse is for that patient. Don't remove it on your own."

Piper nodded her understanding, and assured her she would comply. Brynn never let on that anything was wrong, and even began to question her own suspicions. *But who else could have done it?* she wondered. *And why?* Finally, she realized it would do no good to torture herself with her suspicions. It was unlikely to solve anything and would likely only serve to drive herself crazy.

On the second shift Piper worked after that, Thea called Brynn aside, craning her neck to ensure no one saw or heard her. They ducked into the physician's dictation room, certain that no one had seen them. It was the wee hours of the morning so they were unlikely to be disturbed at this time, as most doctors made evening rounds and it would be several more hours before morning rounds would begin. Brynn braced herself for another accusation and instantly regretted not pushing the previous issues in her own defense.

Thea leaned in with a whisper. "I saw something," she said, "and I thought you needed to know about it." She had a conspiratorial look on her face and nervously, she kept her eyes on the door.

"What do you mean?" Brynn asked, unsure of where this was going. She gripped the back of a chair and waited.

"I was walking past a patient's room earlier, and it was pretty dark inside. I wouldn't have even stopped and noticed anything, except the curtain was pulled and I saw legs in scrubs. I stopped outside the door and listened, and it was Piper. I could almost swear I heard her tell the patient that her name was Brynn and that she was just going to help her get repositioned in the bed."

"What?" Brynn asked. "Why would she do that?"

"I have no idea. I was hoping you'd know." Thea studied her face, waiting for a response.

A quick and disturbing thought came to mind. "What are we going to do about it?" Brynn asked her.

"Nothing. What *can* we do?" Thea's eyes were cast downward. Brynn knew she must be feeling bad for having accused her on that other night.

"Why not? She claimed to be me! We have to do *something*." Panic rioted within her.

"That's just it. I can't be 100% sure, and I never confronted her about it. I just stood at the door and listened, and she was speaking softly.

They won't take my complaint seriously since I didn't act on it right there on the spot. Now I wish I would have, but at the time I didn't want to confront her in front of the patient. I can't prove anything, and she doesn't even know I was out there."

"Then why are you telling me this? If there's nothing we can do?" Her face clouded with resignation.

"Because," Thea answered, the first glance of compassion she'd ever shown, "I owe it to you to give you the benefit of the doubt. I couldn't imagine that girl having any good reason to set you up." She shrugged. "I just thought you should know. So you can watch your back. And," her gaze softened, "I'll be watching, too."

Brynn never mentioned any of the previous events to Piper, but she was watching her closely. There were no more questionable events over the next few days, and Brynn even wondered a few times if she'd imagined most of it. Thea wasn't even sure she'd heard correctly, she reminded herself. And she might have only been suspicious after Brynn had put the thoughts in her mind.

Brynn didn't mention her concerns to anyone else. Up until then, it seemed she was constantly talking about some strange thing Piper had done, and it seemed no one else ever really witnessed anything suspicious. Even the living room redesign, she remembered, looked to Spencer and Blake like a generous favor, a pleasant surprise that had gone wrong. And very unappreciated. No, she was going to keep this to herself. But she'd be watching.

The weekend of the camping trip near Galveston was getting close, and Brynn's anticipation was dampened by the prospect of Piper coming along. As she began discussing final details on the phone with Ludie one day, she hung up to see Piper standing in the kitchen a few feet away.

"Oh hey," Piper said. "I didn't mean to be eavesdropping, but I thought you should know. I won't be able to go to Crystal Beach with y'all Friday."

Brynn looked up from the mail she'd been sifting through and tried to disguise the relief she felt, until Piper continued.

"I've got a late shift on Friday, so I'll have to drive down there by myself on Saturday."
Brynn hid her disappointment.

"All right, no problem." Brynn exhaled. "And hey," she continued, "if it's too much for you, I don't want you to feel like you have to come."

"I *want* to come," Piper said. "I wouldn't miss this for the world." She flashed a sweet grin, marched out to the living room and plopped on the couch. Sarge was resting beneath the coffee table and gave a low short growl when she sat down. Brynn tossed the mail onto the table and sat down. There was no understanding this girl.

* * *

Friday afternoon when Blake got out of school, Spencer and Brynn were waiting for him. Brynn's SUV was packed to the brim, leaving plenty of room for Blake to slide in next to Sarge.

He was delighted to find his Gameboy on the seat next to him and immediately began playing.

Glancing up briefly from the backseat, he asked where Uncle Ben and Aunt Ludie were.

"They're already at the beach," Brynn told him. "They're setting up camp."

"Cool," he said, returning to his game. He barely spoke the rest of the way. Brynn and Spencer listened to music, chatting occasionally. She turned to look in the backseat a couple of times, glad to see Blake smiling contentedly. She was glad he was involved with his game, or else he'd be asking every five minutes if they're almost there. At moments like these, it was hard to believe he was already twelve. He could easily have been in that exact same pose, doing the exact same thing, when he was only six or seven.

* * *

They arrived at the beach to find very few others camping. There were far fewer beach houses along Crystal Beach than in previous years before the last big hurricane. The few remaining homes stood proudly on their stilts, daring the tides to surge and challenge them again. Boards on homes ranged from brand new wood and siding to varying degrees of older, weathered timber, making all the frequent repairs obvious.

The forecast for the Galveston area predicted no temperatures higher than 72 for the coming weekend. It was perfect weather, Spencer knew, to stay in a tent. If it even began to get too warm, the breeze from the beach would cool them. Besides, he remembered, Ben had offered an oscillating fan that could be connected from the camper with an extension cord. Considering the forecast, it was doubtful they'd even need it.

When they pulled up to the campsite, Ben and Ludie had most everything set up nicely. The awning was stretched across the side of their camper, giving shade to the blanket and toys set up for Annie. Ben had already set up the patio table and lawn chairs he'd unloaded from the truck.

Spencer and Ben began setting up the tent, and Blake was proud to assist. He moved about confidently, and Brynn smiled to herself. He was turning into a young man. Once again, she was hit with a surge of relief that he had such wonderful male role models. His father had chosen not to be in the picture, and it had taken Brynn a long time to accept that as a good thing. Now she knew. When she watched Blake, she knew he was turning into a smart, kind gentleman. She had done okay, she realized. And again, she eyed Ben and Spencer and silently thanked God for their presence in his life.

A loud, deep sound jolted her from her thoughts. It was more like a foghorn than a car horn. *Or perhaps a semi*, Brynn thought. There it went again, deep and low, repeatedly, four, then five times. Squinting to make out a shape in the distance, all she could see was what appeared to be a very large truck surrounded by a cloud of dust. She wasn't the only one who noticed.

Spencer, Ben and Blake had stopped what they were doing and stepped from the other side of the tent to watch the road.

Whatever it was seemed to be getting closer. It slowed to a crawl, then made a very wide, precarious turn toward their campsite. It was an RV. A very large, monstrous, very fancy RV.

As it drew closer, the passenger side was the side nearest their campsite. A bright, floral scarf with vivid reds, pinks and oranges waved wildly out the window. It was Roxy, and Dennis was apparently behind the wheel.

"Hello, darlings!" Roxy shouted. "We've arrived! They party can start now!"

Ben and Spencer crossed the small road, which was merely ruts in the sand that had been delineated by the weight of vehicles pulling in and out over time. The two men took positions opposite each other and directed Dennis into parking the monstrosity he was commanding.

Stepping down from her perch high on the seat, Roxy shouted.

"What do you think? I've hired us a little camper to help us get through the weekend." Flagging her scarf at Brynn she sneered, "And you thought I couldn't handle a weekend in the outdoors? Ha!"

"I've seen your bare ass covered in poison ivy, Roxanne. And I had the professional integrity to not ask you how you managed to have *that* part exposed to the great outdoors." Brynn's eyes held a touch of mischief, and Roxy paused for a moment, speechless. Suddenly, she threw her head back and released a loud, throaty laugh.

"Wouldn't you like to know?" she responded in a sing-song voice, playfully swatting at her.

Once Roxy and Dennis were in the capable hands of Ben and Spencer, Brynn joined Ludie in the camper.

"What the hell was *that?*" Ludie asked. "I had my hands full in here and couldn't check it out. "I heard Roxy's voice, but only *after* it sounded like the circus had just arrived in town."

Ludie was changing Annie's diaper, and as soon as she had refastened her and pulled up her pants, she handed her over to Brynn.

"She's 'hired herself a camper' for the weekend," she laughed. "More like the Taj Mahal on wheels."

"Hi sweet girl!" Brynn said, holding her niece up high, and kissing her tummy before bringing her back to eye level. Annie burst into giggles. There was no sound sweeter, Brynn knew, and found herself briefly wondering if she and Spencer might ever have children. She felt certain they had a future together, judging by some of the things he'd said, but they hadn't discussed children. The level of comfort he showed around Blake and little Annie told her he was a natural, and her mouth grew into a wide grin. When the guys joined them in the camper, her face colored. It was hard to believe her expression hadn't broadcast her every private thought to the others.

"What were you thinking just now?" Spencer whispered, sliding next to her on the bench cushions. "You had a huge smile on your face. It was beautiful."

"Oh, um, I was just enjoying Annie. I don't get to spend nearly as much time with her as I'd like. She's growing up too fast." She looked back at Annie who was giggling. Spencer took her from Brynn and put her on his lap. Annie smiled at him, then gave huge belly laughs. They couldn't help but laugh in response. Ludie had gone outside with Ben and Blake, so it was just the two of them inside with the toddler.

"I look at Blake sometimes," she confessed, "and I can't believe he's already twelve. It seems like he was just this age last week!" She cast her eyes downward. "I just don't want Annie to grow up too fast. Maybe Ben and Ludie will give me another niece or nephew in a couple of years. I'm just not ready for the little ones to be all grown up."

"Sooo...." Spencer began, testing the waters, "you've decided you don't ever want anymore kids?" He gave her a questioning look, his face showing he was hanging on her answer.

"No," she said, "I've always thought Blake would make an excellent big brother. You've seen him with Annie, right?" She flushed slightly. "I just didn't want to bring another child into a situation of being raised by a single parent. I had kinda given up on ever finding someone, so I never gave much more thought to the possibility." She slowly looked up at him from only the corner of her eye, wondering what his reaction would be.

"No, don't give up!" He seemed shocked by the sudden volume of his own voice, so this time he spoke more softly. "I mean, you're too young to just give up on having more children. You're a great Mom, and I'd hate to see you deprive another child of the wonderful life you've given Blake. Any baby would be lucky to have you as a Mom." At that precise moment, Annie began babbling, laughing so hard it was impossible to interpret what she was saying in her baby-talk jibberish. It was almost as if she were echoing Spencer's assessment of the situation. Spencer looked as though he wanted to say something else, but instead closed his mouth and got up to see if Ben needed help outside.

When Spencer closed the door behind him, Brynn pulled Annie to her chest and held her close. *Did he just say what I thought he said?*

Spencer had seemed adamant that she should eventually give Blake a little brother or sister. He had also made it apparent in recent weeks that he wanted their futures to include each other. She couldn't put a finger on any one thing he'd said in particular, but she knew he had made it clear.

For the first time in a long time, she allowed herself to dream of having a family. For all Blake's life it had just been the two of them.

Suddenly, a thought occurred to her, unbidden and unexpected. He *had* seemed encouraging about having more children, but he hadn't once brought up their being together during that conversation.

He had told her "don't give up," and suggested she was still young enough to start over with a family. But he hadn't at all mentioned himself in that scenario. *What if I've ruined it all?* she thought. Their relationship had been progressing at a steady rate, and then she had to go and bring up having children. *He must think I'm desperate, trying to lasso him and pull him into a ready-made family.* The pangs of regret wracked her and she wished she hadn't spoken.

Annie was pulling on Brynn's hand and asking if they could go outside when Ludie and Roxy walked into the camper.

"What was *that* all about?" Ludie asked, pointing over her shoulder to the outside.

"What do you mean?" Brynn eyed her expectantly.

"Spencer just came outside and it's almost like he was talking to himself, and he didn't even know we were there.

"What did he say?" Brynn had scooted to the edge of her seat, handing Annie up to her mommy who was reaching for her.

"The bloke's completely smitten," Roxy said, the thrill of a juicy story carried on her words.

"Something about kids, I don't know." Ludie's eyes narrowed. "Have you two talked about that?"

"Kinda." She had a baffled look on her face. "Just now, actually."

"Grownups are so silly, aren't they?" Ludie said to Annie.

Chapter 19

Once they'd returned outside, Brynn noticed Spencer alone, leaning against the side of the picnic table. He had a bottle of cold beer in his hand and he was silent, staring out at the beach. The expression on his face wasn't exactly a look of unhappiness, but it was clearly a serious one. He looked down, kicking his foot around in the sand. He was absent-mindedly peeling the label from the bottle, occasionally looking up at the waves, squinting against the wind that picked up occasionally.

"Getting your eyes full?" Roxy whispered behind her. "He *is* quite handsome. What's he spitting into the fire?" she asked.

"Sunflower seeds. It's a nasty habit."

"At least it's not tobacco, like Dennis."

"True enough. And you're right, Spencer *is* handsome, and I never get tired of looking at him. That's not it…" Unsettled, she crossed her arms and looked away.

"No, you don't," Roxy said. "You've got a gorgeous man who's crazy about you. Why are you acting like you've lost your best friend?" She grabbed a lawn chair from near the camper, far enough away from Spencer to allow them to talk freely. The others were busy moving about the campsite, not paying any attention to their conversation.

Pulling another chair closer, she gestured to Brynn to sit down. "All right," she demanded. "Spill it."

Brynn took the seat and began. "We were talking about children," she breathed, and I think I've said too much."

"He doesn't want to have children?" Roxy asked. "Give him time, of course he will."

"No, it's not that. He never said he didn't. But I just realized, he was encouraging *me*. Telling me I shouldn't give up, that I'd make a great Mom to another one, that I have what it takes." Her voice broke slightly.

"You're worrying too much, Luv. I'm sure if he didn't see children in his future he would've said so. And he certainly wouldn't have been telling you what a great Mum you'd be."

"It's not what he said," Brynn mumbled. "It's what he didn't say." She looked up, taking note that he was still in the same spot, still deep in thought.

"I really think you've got yourself worked up for nothing, Luv. Why don't you give it a while and maybe see if the subject comes up again." She pursed her lips, then gave a sympathetic cluck.

"Right now I think you could use a drink."

"You're right. I definitely need a drink."

* * *

As the afternoon progressed to evening they were planning a campfire, much to Blake's delight. He and his Uncle Ben spent part of the evening walking on the side of camp farthest from the beach, picking up sticks in the areas closest to bushes and trees.

Everyone had been busily unloading and setting things up, but Brynn couldn't help but notice Spencer had been quieter over the past few hours since their talk. He didn't appear angry or upset, just quiet. And pensive. After they'd done their part to help the others, Brynn looked to Spencer.

"Hey."

"Hey," he echoed.

"You okay?" she asked.

"Yeah, why?"

"I don't know, you just seemed quiet, like you have something on your mind."

He merely nodded, a small but clearly perceptible nod, but didn't answer. A flicker of apprehension ran through her.

"Wanna go for a walk?" she asked him.

"Sure." Without another word, he joined her, falling into step.

Wordlessly, they walked. Any other time, she would've found it pleasant, a welcome refuge from the constant chatter around the campsite. She'd always found a great deal of solace and comfort from her time with Spencer, even when neither of them spoke. But after their earlier conversation, and then his wall of silence, not so much.

The two of them were walking silently, when Sarge came up to them. Up until that point, he'd been with Blake and Ben. He was staying close in spite of not being on a leash, first with

Blake, and now with Brynn. He enjoyed walking along the very edge of the sand where it met the water, but would quickly step away from the waves when they would surge forward. He didn't mind his paws getting wet but he didn't like to be splashed.

The waves crashed in, then subsided and with each surge the fine mist of salt tickled her nose.

The fact that their easy companionship had become tenuous wasn't lost on her. Their comfortable rapport had given way to tension and she felt powerless to reverse it. Her conscience nudged her. *Why do you always assume the worst?* She tugged at her bottom lip with her teeth.

Finally, Spencer stopped in his tracks and broke the silence. "What are you so worried about? You look like you're about to bite your lip off." Facing her, he lifted a hand and gently smoothed the wrinkle in her brow. "Relax, babe. It's a great evening. I don't want you so uptight you're unable to enjoy it."

"I'm sorry," she breathed. "I've just had a lot on my mind. Especially since we talked earlier."

"That's what I thought." He let out a deep rush of breath. "I've been thinking about it, too. I'm afraid I pushed the issue."

She looked up suddenly, meeting his anxious gaze. "What do you mean?" She was nearly breathless waiting for his response.

"I didn't even stop to think about whether you were comfortable with such serious talk," he said in a rush. "I assumed that just because I felt ready to consider the next steps that you would be as well." They stood facing each other and he was shuffling his foot back and forth, nervously. "I'm sorry."

A nervous laugh escaped from her. "No, no," she said quickly. "I thought my comments pressured you. You kept saying you thought I shouldn't give up, that I'd make a great mom to another child. Then I realized you were talking about me, and only me. You didn't mention yourself in the plans."

An expression of huge relief swept across his face and he embraced her, lifting her slightly and swinging her around. "I *want* to be in the picture. I *am* in the picture. Heck, I'll even hire the photographer because there's nothing I want more than to be in a picture with you!"

She felt her heart slow to a more normal beat and her breaths grew more even, less labored. She couldn't help but draw a comparison to their professions. Always considering heart rhythms, respiratory status. She almost mentioned it, knowing he would find it humorous, too, but she didn't. She would just focus on their discovery that they were of the same mindset.

"I'm glad we talked," she breathed. "I've always dreamed of having more children. That instead of it being just me and Blake, that there would be another child. But it would have to mean having someone special in my life."

"Of course," Spencer said slowly, nodding. "I think being a single mom would be one of the hardest jobs in the world, and you've done a fantastic job with Blake." He was trudging along next to her, looking at his feet in the sand. "But I wouldn't ask you to do that again." He stopped walking again and looked her in the eyes. She stopped alongside him and looked up at him as he continued to speak.

"It's no secret that I want you in my life, but maybe I haven't said it enough. I love you, Brynn, and whatever you decide to do with your life, getting Blake through sports and high school and into college, having more children…" He looked down again, shuffling his foot in the sand.

She nodded, tears in her eyes, but she was speechless.

"…whatever your future holds," he continued, "I want to be part of it."

Wordless, she stepped up on her tiptoes and kissed him square on the mouth, firmly. Her arms tightened around his neck and she wasn't letting go.

"Um, does that mean you're okay with it?" he asked, shyly.

"Um, yeah!" she told him, laughing. "Apparently you haven't noticed, but I'm crazy about you. I just didn't ever want you to feel pressured."

"I've never felt pressured," he protested, reaching down to brush a wayward strand of hair from her eyes. "I want to be with you, and since I've gotten to know Blake, I can just, I dunno, I just sort of see us all together as a family."

The wind was starting to pick up along the beach, and they started walking again, this time arm in arm. She huddled herself closer to him, partly for the warmth, and partly to test the waters of them closer together, as a couple. If she could find a way to make this moment last forever, she would. Except that would hold them back, from exploring the life they would map out together.

The family traditions they would have, the vacations, the simple, relaxed days at home doing silly little family things together. And if there were another baby in the family? Another little person that would complete the picture? She would love it if that little tiny person just happened to have Spencer's eyes, and his smile. She continued to walk, enjoying the steady rhythm of their pace and the warmth of Spencer's body against hers.

Sarge was walking back toward them, a stick in his mouth. He stopped just short of them and dropped it at Spencer's feet.

"Looks like I'm not the only one who has plans for you," Brynn said with a laugh. They turned around and headed back toward the campsite. Spencer threw the stick and Sarge lunged forward to get it and run back with it. They repeated it again and again. Sarge never seemed to tire, even though he was running circles around them, almost literally.

In the distance she saw Ben and Blake walking back toward the campsite from another direction, loaded down with sticks and branches. Sarge raced off to meet them. They arrived at the campsite pretty much at the same time, and Blake made it known that he was ready for his campfire.

The men began arranging the sticks into the campfire area, breaking branches as needed to make them fit. They showed Blake and he caught on quickly and began helping them. The look on his face was serious, he was learning "guy stuff," and Brynn's heart swelled at the site of him.

"You've got a crazy, happy glow." Ludie interrupted Brynn's thoughts. "What's going on? You look all mushy and lovesick."

"Um, you mean like you were when you kept hanging around my candle shop even on days when I didn't need you?" Brynn's lips pursed. Ludie blushed, looking down at her shoes.

"What? I don't know what you're talking about." She feigned innocence. "I just liked making candles." She looked down, working at a loose cuticle on her finger. "So what if I made better candles when Ben was working than when I was working with you?" They giggled, knowing that the joy Brynn was experiencing wasn't new to Ludie. She had fallen for Brynn's brother, hard, while working with him in the shop. Brynn couldn't ask for a better sister-in-law and friend.

"So what's going on with you two?" Ludie asked, looking her in the eyes to convey her seriousness.

"When you walked in earlier," she swallowed hard, "and I was holding Annie? Well, right before that, we were just talking about babies, and the subject came to whether or not I had ever thought of having another one." Her features became more animated as she spoke.

"Oh? He asked if you wanted to have kids with him?" Ludie pressed.

"Not exactly. He just told me I'd make a great mother, that I *am* a great mother, to Blake."

"What did you tell him?"

"I said I would love another child, but that I didn't feel it was fair to raise another child without a father." Her voice was quiet, laced with awe.

197

"He just," she trailed off and shrugged, her voice broken, her eyes filled with tears.

"Say no more," Ludie nodded. "I know how this goes."

Brynn laughed, loving how Ludie was the voice of experience. "I was thinking how much I would love to have a family with Spencer, but then I wasn't really sure if I was jumping to conclusions. About the future, I mean."

"And?" Ludie searched her face for more.

"And... when we went for a walk," she looked up and smiled as she continued, "he made it clear that I wasn't."

Once they'd all filed back out to the campsite, the sun had nearly disappeared from the horizon. Ludie cleared her throat and looked behind her at the campfire. The guys had gotten quiet, standing back and admiring their roaring fire.

"Guess we better get the marshmallows," Blake announced.

"*After* the hot dogs," Brynn corrected him.

"Aw, man," Blake stormed off into the camper. "I'll get them."

Ludie got up and followed after him. "Let me help you."

Brynn took a few steps toward Spencer, who was leaning against the SUV and facing the fire. Looking up as she approached, he openly admired her. Her hair was loose, blowing in the breeze. Her eyes sparkled in the moonlight, reflecting the flames from the fire. He opened his arms, pulling her into them, with her back to his chest. He circled his arms around her waist in front of her and she relaxed into his grip. They stood there for a while, both of them staring at the fire, neither of them feeling the need to speak.

Ludie walked up, a glass of white wine in each hand. "Here you go," she said, handing them each one.

"Thanks," Spencer said, taking one.

"Mm," Brynn nodded, taking a sip.It was crisp and tart, cool in the back of her throat. Ben helped Blake and together they piled the table up with hot dog buns, mustard and relish. Brynn stepped forward to help, adding napkins, chips and paper plates to the table. Spencer turned around and opened the car door, bringing out some wire hangers he had straightened for roasting hot dogs and marshmallows.

"Can you handle getting these ready?" he asked Blake. Blake took them eagerly and began putting hot dogs on them. Brynn glanced up from the table and met Spencer's gaze. *Thank you,* she mouthed, looking over at the campfire.

He knew she was referring to teaching her son to build a campfire and showing him how to do things boys should learn. Spencer wanted to correct her, and tell her it was *she* that deserved the thanks. She had given him the opportunity to be a part of her son's life. He was learning all the things he'd been missing by not having a child of his own. Now he knew the joy a man could have just from having a child look up to him. The joy of being part of a family. If she only knew what she had done for him just by letting him in.

Chapter 20

It was a cool, crisp evening and the October wind carried a chill. This first night on the beach was ideal, and Brynn looked forward to the rest of the weekend. She gathered a small fleece throw around her shoulders and arms and took a seat near the fire. Just then she heard tires on gravel coming up one of the side roads that led down toward the beach. A small, sporty blue car made its way toward them, then came to a stop. A door opened and Piper stepped out. As she walked toward them, Brynn nearly spit out her wine.

Piper was dressed for the middle of summer. She had a short, half-shirt type halter, and shorts. Short cut-off shorts that left little to the imagination. True, the Texas Gulf coast was warmer than most places even through the early fall sometimes, but this was over the top. Her platinum blonde hair was pulled back from her face with sunglasses perched atop her head. *It was evening,* Brynn thought. The sun had long since gone down. Piper's tanned skin was far from natural, as she often mentioned her time in the tanning beds. Silver and gold bracelets dangled on her arms, multiple rings glittered on her hands. Her lips were brothel red, and her breasts threatened to spill over atop the lacy black bra that rose above the halter top. She strode toward them on long, bronzed legs in high heels. In the sand.

Ludie and Brynn exchanged a look, rolling their eyes. They both cut their eyes over to Roxy, who was biting her lip. "Don't make eye contact," Ludie whispered. Ben, Spencer, and Blake had six eyes focused firmly on Piper. What else could they do? She clearly screamed for attention.

Brynn tried to disguise her annoyance in front of the others. There was no reason for Piper to show up a day earlier than she had planned, and dressed more appropriately for a men's magazine photo shoot than a family weekend. Her shorts were ridiculously short, and her top shockingly low cut. Blake didn't need to be exposed to that, not at his age. He was just reaching puberty and was very impressionable.

She tried to convince herself that Blake was her only reason for being upset at Piper's exhibitionism, but she knew it was more than that. She didn't want Spencer looking at her. *Since when was I the jealous type?* she pondered. She decided to avert her eyes from the walking advertisement before she reached the group. It was ridiculous, watching her high heels sink into the sand as she struggled to reach them.

"Well, hello, everyone!" she sang out. "Guess who got away from clinicals early?"

Roxy looked her up and down, then answered. "The stripper who got away from her pole?" Brynn literally had to bite her lip. Hard.

Piper gave her a sarcastic glare and then made her best attempt at ignoring her. She took a seat near the center of the campsite, stretching her legs and crossing them. "The fire is lovely," she purred, reaching over and picking up Spencer's wine glass that sat on the table in front of him.

"You don't mind, do you?" She took a sip, and the corners of her lips turned up in a seductive smile.

A little while later, everyone was busily occupied roasting hot dogs and eating dinner. Annie was growing sleepier by the minute. She was toddling around, fighting sleep. Ludie didn't want her near the campfire and had to redirect her several times. Brynn reached down and picked her up. She looked over at Ludie.

"Want me to try to get her to sleep?"

"Sure, that'd be great, thanks!"

Brynn held her close, getting up to pace around a bit in hopes of soothing her. She felt eyes on her and glanced up to see Spencer watching her. He had a gentle smile on his face, a serene expression of deep thought. He stepped closer to her.

"You have a way with her," he whispered. "I told you you're great with kids. You're a great mom to Blake, and Annie is lucky to have you as an aunt." He leaned over and planted a small kiss on Annie's forehead. The child was growing sleepier, her lids getting heavier by the moment.

"Awww, let me hold her!" squealed Piper, reaching for the tired toddler. Annie opened her eyes, her face twisting into a grimace. She immediately began wailing. "Aw, see? She wants her Auntie Piper to hold her." She put her hands on each side of her underneath her arms and took her from Brynn.

Spencer, Ludie and Ben looked on, astonished at Piper's behavior. Brynn jumped to her feet and stormed off into the camper. Spencer followed her inside.

"That was ridiculous," he told her, taking a seat next to her on the sofa-bench.

"Why does she do that?" she snapped. "She's offensive!"

"Have you spoken to her about her behavior?" he asked, genuinely.

"Yeah. In some ways, I suppose. It's just, she honestly doesn't get it. I think she truly believes it's acceptable." She shook her head, trying to make sense of it all.

"I do think you're going to have to draw the line when it comes to her inappropriateness around Blake," he said. She was happy to hear him side with her. Especially about that.

"I know when I was that age, the sight of a half-dressed girl left me a bumbling mess, no matter how old she was."

Okay, she thought. *You can stop there.*

"Look," he continued. "I know she's your friend and you two have a long history, but there have to be some boundaries and I think she's crossed more than a few."

"She has, but it seems like when I try to bring them up to her, she either swears she's totally innocent or acts like what she's done is perfectly acceptable. Then when I push the issue, she starts crying."

"When is she supposed to get an apartment?" His concern was genuine.

"She was supposed to have an apartment ready before she moved to Blackwater. But we couldn't find anything within her budget, so I told her she could stay until she finished the certified nurse's aide program."

"When is that?"

"She'll finish in a couple of weeks. Then she can start working. The hospital has already agreed to take her on. I think they're only hiring four from her class. As soon as she gets her first paycheck, I really want her to go." She looked up at him.

"Does that make me an awful person?"

"Nope." He slapped the palm of his hand down on her thigh playfully. "It makes you a person who wants to keep her sanity. Want some coffee?"

"No thanks, but you can go ahead and make some if you want it."

"Okay. Back to Piper's plans. Her first paycheck...that shouldn't take more than a month, all things considered, right?"

"Right." She put her head on his shoulder and nuzzled his neck. "Let's talk about something else, okay?"

"You don't have to tell me again." He tipped her chin up with one finger and kissed her softly on the lips. They shared a moment of togetherness and she knew without a doubt that they stood together; no matter what else anyone on the outside did, they were solid.

* * *

The next day, there was debate about what to do. The sun had come up and other beachgoers had started to move around. It was October and even in the Texas climate it was a little cool for swimming, but there were still enough people who just seemed content to camp out on the beach and enjoy the serene view.

It was Saturday, and the day stretched out before them. The sun was high in the sky, and Brynn enjoyed its warmth on her skin. She stepped out in front of the camper and around the other side of the tent. What she saw next sent her into a fit of rage.

Blake was seated on a lawn chair holding his handheld gaming system, distractedly. And the reason for his distraction lay a few feet away on a blanket. Piper was stretched out in a bikini, face down, with the straps to her top untied.

Brynn sucked in a sharp breath, looking twice to ensure she hadn't dreamed it.

"Blake, I need you to go in the camper," she ordered.

"But Mom, Aunt Ludie said I could sit here and play my game if I didn't run off," he protested.

"Go. Now. We'll talk later." At his crestfallen expression, she quickly added, "You're not in trouble." She forced a reassuring smile on her face, realizing he must have thought he had done something bad. At this point, Piper had realized something was wrong and lifted her head up to look at Brynn. In doing so, she raised up from the blanket, barely able to contain her breasts in the scant pieces of fabric that made up her bikini top.

"Hey. What's going on?" she asked, as casually as if she were asking about the weather.

"What's going on is that you're half-naked in front of my twelve-year-old son."

"I'm dressed!" she argued. I have a swimsuit on, since when is that illegal?" She attempted a laugh but it came out awkward.

"You're the only one in a string bikini in October, Piper. And your top isn't even tied."

She sat up defensively, struggling to keep her top intact while she fought with the strings. She was literally bubbling over, bursting at the seams. Their voices had grown louder, and they suddenly realized they had drawn attention to themselves. Ludie and Ben were standing just on the other side of the tent and had seen the whole thing. Spencer came up behind them and just shook his head at what he saw. Blake had obeyed his mother by going into the camper, but couldn't resist eavesdropping from the doorway.

"Piper, you've got to think about what you're doing," Brynn said, fighting to control her voice. "He's at an impressionable age. And besides that, none of the rest of us are dressed that way. Do you ever look at anyone else and try to pick up on social cues? Or do you just do what you want, everyone else be damned?" She shook her head in disgust, and started pacing furiously, trying to control her anger.

Piper's eyes were filling with tears and she cried out, "I'm sorry, I didn't know I was *offending* anyone. It seems like everything I do upsets someone." She stood up and grabbed the blanket, wrapping it up around her. "I better cover up with this so I don't offend anyone or scar them for life!" She began grabbing things, her bag, her purse and keys, and stormed off toward her car. She opened the trunk and folded her blanket, placing it in the trunk. She pulled a t-shirt over her head and fumbled around in the bottom of her purse for a comb. She began pulling the comb through her blonde hair feverishly. She stepped into her shoes and took off walking down the beach alone, leaving six adults and one very perplexed young boy staring after her.

Spencer put a hand on Brynn's back, soothingly talking to her. "Listen, no one will blame you if you have to tell her to go ahead and move out," he told her.

Brynn sighed heavily. "I know. I mean, I thought about that, but, I made a promise. She has nowhere to go and I told her mother I would help her." She looked down, her forehead in her hand, and let out a frustrated moan.

"I don't know, Spencer."

"Then don't make a decision yet. Give it some time, okay? Let's see how things go after the weekend and we'll go from there, all right?" He took both her hands in his own and held them up to his mouth, kissing the backs of her hands.

"Whatever you decide, I'm behind you."
When they turned back around to the others, Ludie shrugged her shoulders at Brynn and said,

"Want me to take her out? I will." She spoke with such a degree of seriousness that everyone paused for a good few seconds, then burst out laughing.

"What?" she asked, furious. "Y'all don't think I would?"

Ben threw his arms around her and laughed. "That's my girl!" he shouted, then craned his neck to look at Blake, who was still in the doorway of the camper, his mouth agape, watching every move and listening to every word.

"And as for you, go play with your Gameboy for a while." Blake nodded and went back inside, happy to do just that.

Ludie looked at Brynn and Spencer. "Hey, why don't you two make a run into Galveston. Take Blake if you want, or he can stay here with us. If you go in the afternoons like this, the Bolivar ferry is a blast."

Brynn looked at Spencer to gauge his reaction.

Ben added, "Yeah, it takes like, twenty minutes, and you can get out of your car and climb to the top deck."

"And you can see the dolphins!" Ludie added, barely able to contain her excitement. "We do it all the time! Blake would love it!"

"Sold," Spencer said, looking at Brynn. "Wanna go?"

"Yeah, I actually think that's a great idea. Want me to ask Blake?"

"Of course! Better yet, let me." His eagerness got the best of him and it was moments like this that made her fall more in love with him. He went into the camper and within seconds he came charging out, with Blake close behind.

Ludie and Ben told them to take their time, they'd keep an eye on the campsite. It was unspoken but certainly understood what that entailed. Roxy and Dennis were still in the luxury beast they'd brought and had missed Piper's show. Brynn couldn't help but laugh as she imagined what Roxy's reaction might have been.

As they piled into her SUV, Brynn stared out the window, taking in the views around them. There was no sign of Piper on the beach, which was fine with her. She was grateful to Ludie for suggesting a day trip to Galveston, as she really needed a break.

Before they even made it onto the ferry, Spencer had music blaring and he and Blake were singing along. *Who knew they could rap?* Brynn smiled secretly.

They got out of the car and climbed the narrow stairs to the top level of the ferry. They were able to see a few dolphins, as she'd hoped. As they crossed, they were able to get a good view of about five of them that were following right along with the ferry. They seemed so playful, and Brynn wondered how many trips they made back and forth each day.

Once they'd made it across the ferry onto Galveston Island, they made their way to Moody Gardens. It was a resort area that included a luxury hotel, aquarium, rain forest, a 3D Imax, and more. They had a paddleboat that gave tours and there was also a huge man-made beach within its parameters that included palm trees, waterfalls and lagoons. The beach area was closed this time of year but Brynn could see how it would be lots of fun in the summer. She promised Blake they would return during the right season.

They took in a nature show in the huge theater, then strolled through the aquarium. There was an incredible penguin display and Spencer bought them tickets for a "penguin experience" where they were taken to the back of the penguin habitat and actually got to pet one of the penguins.

By the time they were ready to leave Moody Gardens, Blake was telling them he was hungry. They made their way to the car and headed out, driving through town to look for a good place to eat. They parked near The Strand. It was the historic downtown district and a very popular tourist attraction. There were a few dining establishments and even though Brynn and Spencer were always in the mood for seafood, they told Blake he could choose. He picked out a little restaurant with outdoor dining that was enclosed on one side with a huge waterfall on the side of a building. Blake loved it, far more interested in sitting practically underneath a waterfall as he was in the food. Once they'd eaten and strolled in and out of a few shops, they were all getting tired and ready to head back to camp.

The sun hung low in the sky, and the evening atmosphere was kicking into gear. Even in the off seasons, Galveston attracted many visitors. The historic homes alone were enough to draw the interest of visitors, and that was before most of them even reached the beach from the causeway, the huge bridge that most people crossed to get onto the island.

Blake was quiet in the backseat on the way back. Spencer looked over at Brynn and gave her a smile that melted her heart even more. This was a man who could've complained that he wasn't getting enough alone time with her, and yet he was perfectly content to bring her son along for family-type fun. She'd caught him several times watching Blake, a look of pure pride on his face.

Chapter 21

By the time they arrived back at camp, there was no sign of Piper. Her car was gone and Ben explained that after her walk, she had returned and apologized for any problems she might have caused. She had decided to go ahead and pack up and go home, not wanting to cause any more tension.

"I really think she was sincere," Ludie added. "She looked like she had been crying."

Brynn felt her heart sink, conflicted by her torn emotions. She knew she had to take a stand when it came to her son, but she began to question her rush to judgment about some of the smaller, more insignificant things. Regret overcame her, and she wished she had chosen her battles more wisely.

The guys began building another campfire, not only at Blake's request but also because the night air had a chill to it. Ben was mixing margaritas, and Ludie was slicing the limes and salting the glass rims.

Spencer cranked up some music and he and Blake stoked the fire. When the others came back outside with a tray of drinks, Spencer handed one each to Brynn and Roxy, then took one for himself.

"Here, you both deserve this," he said with a wink. Brynn accepted hers gratefully and drank up, smiling over the rim at him.

"You're a peach, Love," Roxy said to him. She cast a glance at Brynn. "You've got yourself a good one. Nicely done."

As bad as Brynn felt about the situation with Piper, she was determined not to let it spoil the fun for everyone else. She absolutely wasn't going to waste a single moment of family time stressing over something she could do nothing to fix. Vague uneasiness about Piper being in the house alone threatened to surface; after all, she'd already completely changed her entire living room, for the worst, without her there. *Surely she wouldn't dare try anything else.* She decided once again not to let it ruin her time with the family, and forced it out of her consciousness.

"Let's play charades!" Blake suggested, and they all agreed. Within moments, everyone was laughing hysterically, and the mood was festive once again. Roxy's performances, in particular, were stellar. Her personality was always fun and vibrant, and Brynn was glad they'd invited her and Dennis to join them. Dennis was one of the most laid-back men she'd ever known, and seemed to be crazy about Roxy.

Brynn couldn't help but be in a good mood around the two of them. They couldn't be more polar opposite from each other: Roxy was glamorous and sophisticated, while Dennis was more of a *what you see is what you get* kind of man.

For some reason, it played off well. Dennis was a tall, lanky country boy. He had never struck Brynn as the type to participate in any kind of silly games such as these, but to impress Roxy, there he was, in the middle of the gang, performing his heart out at charades, glancing over at Roxy every few seconds to gauge her reaction. And she never disappointed. The woman couldn't take her eyes off him, and he never failed to impress her.

The breeze off the beach was nice, and the fire was more than cozy. Sarge was stretched out between Blake and the campfire. He was drowsy and relaxed but as always he kept one ear up and alert for the sound of any intruders.

The beauty of the night was not lost on Spencer. Brynn followed his movements with her eyes, captivated by his bold sense of humor. He was now acting out a movie that had action heroes in it and, because he was competing with a preteen boy, he was pulling out all the stops. Brynn knew that this night, this trip, meant a lot to him. He didn't have much family of his own; his mother lived in Houston but traveled a great deal.

Only recently had Brynn realized what the idea of marriage and family meant to him and, watching him now, she wanted nothing more than to give him that dream. She wanted it as much for Blake as well. As wonderful as her brother, Ben had been as a role model for him, she knew he longed for a father. He asked about his own father from time to time, mostly surrounding life events like starting junior high, Annie's birth, the time he tried out for little league baseball. Those were the milestones, the times when a boy needed his dad.

And there were times when she needed a husband.

Brynn caught some motion out of her periphery and realized Spencer was finished with his skit and moving toward her. She felt her cheeks color, as if her thoughts were transparent and he had seen them. *And if he had?* she demanded of herself. He would be thrilled; he loved the idea of being part of her family.

They played late into the night. Once they'd finished several lively rounds of charades, Blake found a deck of cards in the camper. Brynn couldn't remember laughing so hard in a long time. Little Annie wasn't even phased. She lay sleeping across her daddy's shoulder, her cherubic little cheeks rosy by the light of the fire. Ben and Ludie exchanged looks a time or two, and Brynn knew exactly how to read them. Ludie was the love of her brother's life and that feeling was completely mutual. Brynn silently thanked God for bringing Ludie into their lives and for blessing them all with Annie.

* * *

Sunday evening they had cleaned up the campsite and gotten everything packed for the trip home. It had been a fun, relaxing weekend for all of them in spite of Piper's chaos but it was time to get back to their routines. Roxy and Dennis were the first to pull out of the campsite. Roxy had gone on about the RV she had rented. She had been quite a trooper over the weekend and Dennis had declared her a happy camper. As they prepared to leave camp, she had announced that she and Dennis were going to the dealership the following morning so she could handle the paperwork to purchase it, or at least one like it. She affectionately named it the "silver beast," and deemed it quite worthy of her comfort the next time they decided to "rough it."

Brynn was pleased with Blake's glucose levels over the weekend. He'd seemed to be learning moderation in recent weeks, and had only eaten two of the roasted marshmallows, heeding his mother's warnings.

Brynn would need to have Blake back in plenty of time to be ready for school on Monday morning. Ben and Ludie needed to get back because they would need to open the shop on Monday. They had staff members keeping the shop open on the weekend but it was time to go back and manage orders for wholesale accounts and to build up inventory. As it was growing cooler outside, sales had picked up, and they would need more candles than ever. Brynn always helped out in the fall and, when she mentioned it to Spencer, he expressed an interest in helping out as well. Since they were both working the minimum of three- 12 hour shifts per week, meeting the basic requirement of thirty-six hours, they had more free time for each other.

They had both decided to put in for day shifts at the hospital and were hoping to be able to switch over soon. His department had another respiratory therapist who wanted to work the night shift so Spencer wouldn't have a hard time making a trade. Brynn simply needed to speak to her supervisor about finding out if any of the nurses on her unit were interested in switching to night shifts. Brynn and Spencer knew that day shifts would not only be more conducive to their growing relationship, but that it would also be a wonderful change for Blake.

He loved his time with his Uncle Ben and Aunt Ludie, but it would be best for him to have a solid routine of being at home every night. Brynn found herself dreaming of being home every night and having dinner as a family. She stared out the window as Spencer drove back home from the beach, her daydreams keeping her silent and wistful.

Blake was in the backseat, nearly asleep. It had been a fun weekend for him, but a long one, and he would need to get back into his routine quickly. When they pulled into the driveway, Piper's car was there. Brynn sucked in a deep breath, bracing for whatever was ahead.

Spencer squeezed her hand reassuringly. As they trudged toward the front door, bags on their shoulders, Sarge followed them obediently across the yard toward the door. He immediately began sniffing around, securing the parameters as always. Piper met them at the door, anxiously stammering on about Michael.

"I know it was him!" she cried. "I wanted to call you, but I knew you'd be home soon." Piper was wringing her hands, and pacing frantically.

Brynn placed her hands on each of Piper's shoulders. "Slow down. Take a deep breath and tell me what you're talking about."

"The door. I think Michael has found me. He broke the glass at the back door, but when I shouted out that I'm calling the police, I guess it scared him away." She anxiously looked back and forth between Brynn and Spencer, gauging them for their reactions. They followed her towards the back door, and found shattered glass swept into a pile. "Where is your dustpan?" Piper asked Brynn.

"Did you call the police?" Spencer asked, looking at the broken glass and inspecting the lock.

"No, I just now discovered it broken." Piper said. "I was trying to get it swept up, and…"

"You *discovered* it?" he demanded. "I thought you heard him when he broke the glass." He eyed her suspiciously.

"I mean, well, I heard something outside, I was in my room and I came out to the living room to look around." She was reaching for words, clearly caught in her own web. "That's when I called out that I was calling the police."

Brynn stood facing her, shaking her head slowly.

"What?" Piper's eyes filled with tears. "You act like you don't believe me!"

Spencer shook his head, a look of disbelief on his face. "Piper, I just don't know, I don't understand why you didn't call the police. And did you hear him break the glass or discover it broken?"

"I don't know, I guess, well, I think he must have broken it when I was still in my bedroom. I didn't exactly hear the glass breaking." She looked nervously between the two of them. "I'm sorry! I'll pay for the window," she said, then stormed off to her room.

Just then, Blake came through the front door, Sarge at his side. "What happened?"

"Just a little accident with the back door," Spencer said, exchanging glances with Brynn.

"Don't go near it for now, I don't want you getting cut," Brynn said. Blake shrugged, heading for his room to put his things away.

"What do you make of this?" Brynn asked, looking up at Spencer for his take on the situation.

"Honestly? I think she's full of crap."

"I thought the same thing. I just have to be so careful accusing her." She brought her hands up, cupping her face and shaking her head. "It's so precarious right now. Why did I ever offer to let her move in?"

"Don't blame yourself, you had no way of knowing." He reached up and pulled her hands away from her face and planted a gentle kiss on her forehead. "And as far as falsely accusing her, I'm pretty sure you're not. She changed her story, and then offered to pay for the broken window. That, and her body language, told me more than I need to know. She's lying."

Brynn sighed heavily. "You know, when we were on the way home, I was actually feeling guilty, wishing I had handled the situation at the beach differently. I was gonna apologize. Now I think I am the one who's due an apology."

She got the opportunity to express that thought when Piper asked her for a few minutes alone. They went into Piper's room and closed the door. Piper took a deep breath, forcing herself to stand straight and look Brynn in the eye.

"I just wanted to thank you for letting me be a part of your beach trip, and to tell you I'm really sorry about what happened." She looked down at the floor. "I mean, about the glass in the door, *and* about the beach. You were right about Blake being impressionable, and if I had given it a minute's thought I would have realized it. Anyway," she continued, "I'm really sorry, and it won't happen again." She was searching Brynn's face for a reaction.

"Thank you, Piper. For realizing it and for apologizing." She forced a reassuring smile. "I probably shouldn't have reacted so strongly."

"Oh, no, you had every right," Piper said, shaking her head. "I just need to think before I do things." She reached out and gave her a quick hug.

"About the door..." Brynn started.

"I know, and I'll pay for it. And I'll have a talk with Michael. He can't continue this."

Brynn looked down at the floor and took in a breath. "Piper, what really happened here?"

For a minute, it looked like Piper was ready to confess making it up, but then she said, "I don't know. I'm really confused about the whole thing. I was really scared, and that's why I couldn't get my story straight, that's all. I know I heard something, but I'm not sure when he broke the glass."

"Is that the story you're going to give the police?" Spencer asked from the doorway. Brynn wondered how much of their conversation he had heard.

Piper looked up at him, and a look of realization came over her face. She knew she was defeated.

"I'm sorry," she said, looking at them both. Her eyes quickly filled with tears. "All right. Please don't call the police. I locked myself out, and had to break the window to unlock the back door."

Spencer shook his head, clearly not trusting her story. *Stories,* he corrected himself. Wordlessly, he turned and left the room, leaving Brynn to confront her with her admission of guilt.

"Piper, we can't continue like this..." she began.

"I know," she interrupted. "I've been meaning to tell you, I've been looking at some apartments. Hoping to find the right one soon. I'm considering one on the street behind the candle shop, it's cozy, perfect for me, but not quite vacant yet."

"Are you sure you'll like it," Brynn asked, "since you obviously haven't been able to even see it yet, if it's not vacant."

"Oh, they let me look at one just like it. It's a small complex, there's one on the other side that's already been rented but they let me look at it before the people moved in."

"How soon will it be ready?" she asked.

"In a couple of weeks?" Her answer was uncertain.

Brynn thought carefully before she spoke. "I'm glad. I think it's for the best."

Chapter 22

The next morning when they'd gotten Blake off to school, Brynn and Spencer reported for duty at Blackwater Candle Company. Brynn, having founded the company, needed no instructions but Spencer was a different story. She showed him how to wick jars and he stayed busy for quite some time. He was curious about the whole process and appeared impressed that they had built such a devoted clientele. When he caught sight of the orders he realized most of them were for mail orders and wholesale.

They all settled into a routine, music playing in the background. Brynn couldn't help but love it, knowing it was a family business and taking pride in starting something that would be lucrative not only for herself and her son, but also for her brother and his wife.

When lunchtime came, Ludie gave them the rest of the day off. "You've both been amazing help! Now, go play!" she ordered them.

Brynn protested, and Spencer agreed, but Ludie wouldn't hear it. "We're just about caught up. Blake's already planning to ride the bus here after school and he can hang out with us."

"Oh, no," Brynn said, "We're not just gonna leave you high and dry." She looked at Spencer, who turned out to be no help at all.

"You're not," Ludie said. "I told you. We're caught up."

Brynn caught Ludie and Ben exchanging a look and Spencer nodding as if he was in on it. She didn't know what to think, but she shrugged it off, happy that he was hitting it off so well with her family.

"You don't have to tell us twice," Spencer said. "My hands are tired from all that wicking." Turning to Brynn he asked, "What do you want to do today?"

"Hmmm…. Let me think about that."

They headed down the sidewalk to the Ladybird Café for lunch. Brynn loved the owners and their staff, and it was one of her favorite spots. They slid into a booth and ordered two iced teas.

Perusing the menu, Spencer decided on a chicken fried steak sandwich with fries and Brynn ordered the chicken salad sandwich. He asked her about her plans for the next day and she told him she wasn't doing anything that she knew of.

"You are now," he smiled.

"Oh really?"

"Really. Come have a picnic with me."

"I'm intrigued." Brynn raised an eyebrow in question. "Where are we going?"

"I know the perfect spot." His eyes sparkled as the ideas came forth.

"I'm in good hands, then."

"More than you know." His eyes held a faint glimpse of mischief.

"All right then. Tomorrow. I'm all yours."

"Hey!" he said suddenly. "Let's go to Houston today and get some things. There's a market in Rice Village that has all kinds of good things for picnics. Besides, I like to stock up on other things while I'm there. They've got all kinds of cheeses, my favorite kind of olives, you'll love it."

"Well look at you, my secret culinary hero! I had no idea," she giggled.

"Oh I wouldn't go that far," he laughed.

"You have a favorite olive."

He laughed. "Seriously, I don't really cook much, I just know all the stuff I like to eat and how to find it there. They make it easy for guys like me."

After lunch they got onto I-10 and headed west toward Houston. Driving through the Rice Village area, Brynn was captivated as always by the shops and houses in the area. Spencer seemed to share her enthusiasm, finding something he liked in just about anything.

When they arrived at the market, she fussed at him for not telling her about it sooner. "I *love* this place!" she told him. "Why have you been holding out on me?"

"I'm sharing it now. My Mom was a chef, and we didn't just snack. We *experienced*. You'll have to come with me to her house for dinner one night. Prepare to be amazed."

"I'm already amazed."

"When you taste her cooking, you'll redefine the emotion of amazement."

"I can't wait to meet her."

"She feels the same way. I wish she was in town, we'd go by there now."

"Where is she?"

"In Connecticut, with her sister. She goes every year."

They ended up buying several different types of cheese, some sourdough bread, summer sausage, and Spencer's favorite olives, giant ones stuffed with garlic and pimentos. Brynn found some very thin, crisp ginger cookies, some biscotti, and a few spices for the kitchen. Once they'd loaded up on a few other things, they headed to the wine department. Spencer selected a few different bottles of wine and even some really nice champagne.

"Champagne?" she quizzed him.

"Yeah. Looks like a really good one."

"Expensive," she observed. Shouldn't that be something for a special occasion?"

"Who knows when we'll make it back here," he reasoned. "And besides, you never know when people are going to drop in unexpectedly. I just think it's always good to have a few things on hand."

"You had me at champagne," she breathed dramatically. "Vee must have zee bubbly for zee visitors, no?" she said, in her finest French accent. "Oiu, oiu!"

"Now you're talking." He winked at her.

That evening when they got home, he sorted out his purchases for their picnic to take home with him. They left a few of the things she'd bought in her kitchen, and she planned on saving some of the meats and cheeses and even the cookies for their next family movie night. She had the perfect trays, she decided, and the ingredients would make the perfect spread. She was confident that if he could make the quintessential picnic preparations, she could make a perfect party hors d'oeuvre tray for their next night together around the house.

Ben came over a little later to bring Blake home. As soon as Blake saw a package of ginger cookies on the counter he was ready to dig in.

"Ohhhh, no you don't!" Brynn stopped him. "I've got that planned for something."

He dropped his head, disappointment flooding his eyes. "Mom! I never get to eat *any*thing," he whined.

"Oh, noooo," cried Ben. "That's child neglect! The horror of it all!" Blake couldn't suppress the grin that broke across his face.

"You know what I mean, Uncle Ben."

"No, why don't you tell us what you mean," ordered his mother.

"Sometimes I just want to eat something sweet and I don't know what I want and then I finally *see* something I want and I can't have it." He tried to pout but couldn't keep a straight face. His mother and uncle both burst into laughter and fed his drama. Everyone knew his mother made sure he had things he liked to eat while still managing to keep his diabetes under control.

Ben escorted him to the table as if he were unable to walk. Brynn began grabbing items from the pantry and refrigerator, calling them out as if she were announcing items pulled from a crash cart at work.

"Cookies."

"Cookies, check." Ben replied.

"Yogurt."

"Yogurt." .

"Cheese," she said, slapping it into Ben's hand with a whack.

"Cheese," he replied, slapping it into Spencer's hand.

"Very funny," Blake said. "Laugh all you want, but I'm getting weaker by the minute. I'm fading, hurry." He clutched his chest with a fist and squeezed out every word.

"I.... must.... have... all of it!" He announced, grabbing a string cheese and a yogurt cup and racing around the bar, escaping the clutches of his evil Uncle Ben."

"You're abusing this poor kid," Spencer said. "Don't worry, Blake, I've got your back."

"What's so funny?" they heard from the direction of the living room. They turned to see Piper, in her pajamas, padding down the hallway from her room.

"Oh, we're having to hurry and feed this poor growing boy who never gets anything good to eat," Brynn said, laughing.

"Hmm, that's horrible! At his age, even," she hissed, going along with the game.

He flashed a grin at her. "Very funny."

She rounded the corner into the kitchen and opened the fridge. "I don't know what you're so worried about," she told him, rummaging.

"There's lots of good stuff here to eat."

Ben stood in the entryway of the dining room, relaying the events of the afternoon, including homework assignments, to Brynn.

"He already did his spelling words and the math problems. And, more importantly, he used a death ray laser to annihilate his enemies and reached another level."

"Oh, of course!" said Brynn. "As long as he achieved that, right?"

"C'mon, see?" Piper joined in. "He's a good kid. "You should really feed him more often." She held a paper plate with cracked wheat rounds, honey mustard, and gourmet deli cheese. Some of the food for tomorrow's picnic.

"This is good," Piper mumbled, her mouth full of the gourmet spoils. Brynn sucked in her breath and began counting to ten. Slowly.

* * *

Later in the evening, while Blake was getting ready for bed and Piper was in the shower, the phone rang. Brynn picked up on the second ring.

A male voice spoke. "May I speak with Piper?"

"She's not available at the moment, may I tell her who called?"

"Michael. So I did reach the right number, then. It took me quite a while to find her."

"I'll bet it did, *Michael.* I'll tell you what, don't ever call here again." She hung up before he could speak. Her heart hammered in her chest. *Michael is real,* she thought. *He's real and he's looking for Piper.* Suddenly, she felt horrible for having doubted her. It was clearly time for her to cut Piper some slack.

* * *

The next morning, Brynn relaxed around the house in her t-shirt and shorts. It was a lazy kind of day, and she took full advantage of it. Spencer wouldn't be here to pick her up until around noon, so she had the morning to herself. She poured a cup of coffee and took it into the living room, sinking into the cushions of the couch. Picking up the remote, she surfed until she found a design show.

The designers on the show were transforming a bedroom into a nursery, and she found herself completely drawn in to the process. She even made a few conscious mental notes for possible future reference.

Picking up her coffee cup, she held it in both hands, warming her hands on the ceramic sides. Leaning back into the cushion she daydreamed, imagining the possibilities that lay before her. She allowed herself to wonder if Spencer knew how strong her feelings for him were. He had told her he wanted a future with her, but she wondered if they were anywhere close to being on the same page about the timing. She couldn't help but question whether he was thinking long-term or short-term about taking their relationship to a more serious level.

Sarge walked over to the couch and laid his chin on her thigh. He looked up at her with his sad puppy dog eyes, eyes that could melt her heart with just a glance. She patted him on the head and scratched behind his ears and he rewarded her with a cold, wet lick on her leg that she wasn't expecting.

Suddenly, he pulled away from her, growling and showing his teeth. Right on cue, Piper came walking down the hallway. She could've guessed immediately when Sarge started growling. He never had gotten used to her.

"Good morning," Piper said. "Want some coffee?"

Brynn hushed Sarge, calming him down.

"I'm way ahead of you," she said, holding her cup in the air.

"Okay, I'll join you." She walked past her, heading into the kitchen.

Brynn debated briefly on whether to tell Piper about the phone call from Michael last night., then decided against telling her just yet. She didn't need any upsets or setbacks at the time.

"I don't know why that dog hates me so much," Piper said from the kitchen. Maybe he knows I like cats more than dogs."

"Um, I think it just takes him a while to get to know people," she offered. "You'll be in your own place before you know it and then you can get a cat." She drank the last bit of coffee in her mug.

"Speaking of which, any word on when you'll be hired on as an employee?" Not wanting to make her feel pressured, she added, "I know it'll be better for you, getting paid to be there instead of as a student."

"Yeah, about that. I can start fairly soon, I think. She said I could start orienting next week with another patient care tech, but I won't be released to work the floor on my own until I take the state test." She returned to the living room with a cup of coffee and sat on the easy chair, her legs draped over one arm of it.

"When *is* the state test?" Brynn asked, careful not to sound too eager.

"I take it next Friday. And we'll have the results that day."

"That's great!" She gave her a warm smile. "I'm happy for you, Piper. You've worked hard."

"Thanks."

"Maybe we can go one day this week and you can show me that apartment you're considering." In spite of Piper's questionable actions, Brynn couldn't help but feel sympathy for her. It was clear that she had some emotional struggles. *She's alone in this world,* Brynn reminder herself. I'm all she has.

"Yeah, okay."

"When you get your things out of storage to move into your place, I want to see what all you've got. I need to get some ideas for housewarming gifts."

"Oh, there's no rush," Piper said with a dismissive wave. "It's gonna take a bit to get settled into the job and then get a few paychecks under my belt." She picked up the remote and clicked on the guide. "There's plenty of time."

For the umpteenth time in just a few short weeks, Brynn practiced the highest level of self-restraint she knew was possible.

Chapter 23

Spencer arrived right about noon and she was ready when he got there. She was more than ready, in fact, to get out of the house and away from Piper. Knowing she would have the pleasure of Piper's company even longer than she had anticipated was not a pleasant thought. But she was determined not to let thoughts of Piper's drama interfere with her date.

She and Spencer were growing closer by the day and it was reaching the point where she dreaded saying goodbye each time. She had been in a couple of relationships since Mark, Blake's father and her ex-husband. The relationships, for the most part, had been casual and she didn't see them going anywhere. She hadn't brought them into Blake's life for that very reason. There was no point in getting him attached to someone only to have them out of the picture later on.

With Spencer, however, it was different. She wouldn't have dreamed of not introducing him to Blake because she knew that he would benefit just from knowing Spencer. He already had been a positive influence in his life and for that she was grateful.

She dressed casually, a cute teal-colored silky top with jeans and boots. Spencer came to the door in jeans and a black shirt that hugged his masculine body and reminded her of what was underneath. His close-cropped hair and moustache were just icing on the cake. This man was handsome and sexy. And he was *hers*. She felt the color rush to her cheeks, worried that her eyes raking over him would reveal her secret thoughts.

"Penny for your thoughts?" he said, waving a hand in front of her face to get her attention.

"Oh, they'll cost you a lot more than a penny, trust me," she winked, brushing past him at the front door.

"Fair enough!" he replied with a light slap on her behind. She rewarded him with a suggestive smile on her way to the car.

"We can go by the bank if you'd like!"

He laughed, opening the car door for her. They drove a few miles, not too far away, to an area down at Blackwater Creek that had picnic tables, park benches, a gazebo and a foot bridge. It was one of the more scenic parts of the creek, one that Brynn loved. There were other areas that were located in thick patches of brush, in swampy areas. Water moccasins slithered in and out of the water, alligators sunned themselves, sometimes slipping beneath the murky water to reveal only their black eyes. In some of those areas the cypress knees were so thick and mangled it looked like a horror movie might come to life at any time.

The part of the creek that Spencer had brought her to, however, was lovely. It was kept clear and the park area was well maintained. In the spring and summer it was fairly crowded, especially along the bike and jogging trails. But since today was a weekday in the fall, they had the place to themselves. The leaves were all turning and displayed broad strokes of nature's paintbrushes in shades of orange, red, brown and green.

When they drove up and Spencer parked the car, he opened the door for her and led her toward the water. She protested briefly, reminding him they needed to get the picnic things out of the car.

"You did remember to pack them in the back of your car, right?" she asked him.

He merely shrugged and kept walking, holding her hand firmly.

When they stepped past a winding curve in the path just around a cluster of trees, she took in a sharp breath.

There, beneath the gazebo, was a table set up for a romantic lunch for two. A red-checkered tablecloth had an array of items laid out carefully on top. A big wicker basket sat at one side, and a silver ice bucket held a bottle of champagne, the one he'd bought in Houston. A small arrangement of flowers sat in the middle of the table and coordinated beautifully with the rich fall colors that surrounded them.

Her heart fluttered in her chest. She felt completely and blissfully alive at this moment and her love for Spencer grew leaps and bounds at the thought that he would go to such lengths for her. She was seeing more and more every day that this was just like him, and he never ceased to amaze her.

As they approached the gazebo, she could barely contain herself.

"Spencer, you did all this, for me..." She looked up at him, into his steel-blue eyes.

"You deserve it."

"But this is too much..."

"This doesn't even scratch the surface of the things I want to do for you. Besides," he continued. "I did it just as much for me. Think of it this way: I've got you to myself, I'm in a beautiful location with a beautiful woman, and some of my favorite foods are in that basket. See?" He gestured grandly. "It's for me, too."

"Oh, yes," she laughed. "It just goes to show how very selfish you are!" she said with a laugh. He squeezed her hand and led her up the steps of the gazebo. When he began pulling items out of the basket, she was impressed with the variety. He'd gone to a lot of trouble. Not only were there items from the epicurean market they'd gone to, but other items as well. There were red grapes in a ceramic bowl, and a small tray with petit fours arranged on it. In the middle of the table was a big, square box, in elegant wrapping paper and a huge bow. When she asked about it, he shrugged it off and told her he'd get back to her on that.

As they ate their lunch they enjoyed the beauty of nature around them. It was a beautiful day, slightly cool, but the sun was shining. The air held the distant aroma of burning leaves. Herons dipped in and out of the water in the creek and the birds made up a cheerful chorus in the trees above.

Time flew quickly, and their conversation flowed more smoothly than the creek nearby. Her time with him was precious, and on days like this she stood in amazement at the level of the connection between them. They talked about their careers and how being involved in healthcare made them feel as though they really were making a difference in the lives of others. For both of them, that was important. They also both believed in using their time away from the hospital to laugh and play because, as caregivers, they had to take care of themselves before they could care for others.

Spencer grew silent as they finished their meal. She raised her eyes to find him watching her, a look of bold appraisal and deep satisfaction on his face. He stood and extended his hand to her.

"Let's take a walk," he said. "We can come back to this."

"That sounds great," she told him, taking his offered hand and rising to her feet. Just as they began to step away from the gazebo he turned back and reached for the present. He still hadn't said what it was for and though she was curious, she didn't ask.

They walked toward the creek with the sound of leaves crunching beneath their boots. The air was cool, but not uncomfortably so. A light breeze picked up a few leaves and scattered them about in tiny whirlpools swirling above the ground. As they reached the creek he led her to the footbridge and they stepped to the top of it where it arched to allow small boats and kayaks to pass underneath. There was a park bench at the top, and they both took a seat. He handed her the box and told her to open it.

"It's not my birthday," she said.

"It doesn't have to be."

She carefully removed the bow and began pulling the paper away cautiously to avoiding tearing it.

"Just rip it open!"

"Okay, okay," she said. "Although I'm not even sure why you're giving me a gift, Christmas is weeks away."

"I don't need an occasion to give you something. It's an occasion every time I get to see you." The glow of his smile warmed her.

She finally had dispensed with the paper and removed the lid to find layers of tissue paper. Removing them, she revealed a beautiful throw pillow, accented with tiny beads and intricate embroidery. It was in a soft shade of ocean blue and she loved it. It was exactly what she'd had in mind for her living room.

"Thank you!" she told him, giving him a kiss. "I love it! You know me so well!"

"It's my pleasure. I'm glad you like it."

"I do!"

He snatched it from her hand.

"Okay," she told him, puzzled. She had planned on placing it carefully back in the box to avoid it getting damaged. He took the pillow and tossed it on the bridge in front of the bench.

"What...?"

"This." He flashed a devilish smile.

Her eyes held a look of confusion but before she could ask him why, he got up from the bench and went down to the ground, one knee on the pillow.

"Brynn Callaway, you mean the world to me. I never knew I was missing half my heart until I heard it beating in your chest."

"Spencer!" she gasped.

"I love you, and can't imagine my life without you in it. You're an incredible woman in so many ways, you're kind, generous, lovable, an amazing lover and friend. You're a wonderful mother, and when I see you with children I fall in love with you all over again. Will you do me the honor of becoming my wife?" Tears shimmered in his eyes.

She drew in air, wondering how she was even able to breath. He opened a tiny box in front of her and revealed a gorgeous princess cut diamond set in platinum.. Her hands shook so much she was afraid he wouldn't be able to get it on her finger, but he held her hand steady within his own.

The ring went on beautifully and she realized it wasn't just her hands but her whole body that was shaking. She couldn't speak, all she could do was nod. Tears pooled in her eyes before spilling over to her cheeks. He got to his feet and, holding her hands, drew her up next to him. He pulled her into a warm embrace and held her, trembling against him.

For what seemed like a long time, they stood there together, in each other's arms, while the whole world spun about them. Life as usual was going on all over the world but at this moment, for the two of them, time had stopped.

When they made it back to the gazebo, he popped the cork on the champagne and they drank a toast to their engagement. She was glad she'd taken a moment to take a few pictures of the results of all his efforts when they'd first arrived: the beautiful flowers, the tablecloth and all the wonderful foods he'd prepared. Now she stopped to take a photo of the champagne glasses and they leaned in close to snap a picture of the two of them together. This day would stand in her memory forever.

That afternoon they picked Blake up from school so they could tell him their good news. He slid into the backseat, tossing his backpack onto the floorboard next to him.

"What's for dinner?" he asked.

"That will be your choice," Spencer said.

"But pick somewhere nice since we're celebrating," Brynn smiled mischievously.

"Cool. Can it be in Houston?" he asked, apparently not even noticing the comment about celebrating. "I like the Aquarium! They have one at the Kemah Boardwalk and one in Houston. I don't have any homework, I did it all in study hall last period."

"I think the Aquarium would be perfect for a celebration," Brynn added. "Especially one like this. Maybe we should see if Ben and Ludie want to come."

"Wait," Blake added, speaking slowly. "Um, what are we celebrating?"

"Maybe you should ask your future stepdad."

Blake's jaw dropped and he stared, blinking. "What did you say?"

Brynn was beaming, and looked back at Blake, her eyes filling with tears yet again. Spencer continued driving, looking straight ahead, with a huge grin plastered across his face.

"I've asked your mother to marry me," Spencer told him. "and she said 'yes.'" Blake was so ecstatic he could hardly sit still in the seat. He was full of questions, blurting them out before they could even answer any of them. When would the wedding be, was he going to be in it, would he have to wear a tux, and were they going to have babies. They laughed, enjoying his enthusiasm. They stopped at home so he could get changed, and to put their things from the picnic away.

While he cleaned up a bit and changed clothes, Brynn called Ludie and asked if they wanted to meet them for dinner in Kemah. She didn't let on the reason, only that she and Spencer really would love it if they joined them, and that it was Spencer's treat.

"Um, yeah," Ludie told Brynn over the phone. "Roxy and Dennis are over here right now..." she hesitated, unsure.

"Bring 'em!" Brynn nearly shouted.

"Let me ask," Ludie said, then held her hand over the mouthpiece of the phone for a moment. Brynn could hear her mumbling before she spoke into the phone again.

"Yep. They're hungry, too."

Blake's excited chatter continued, and he rattled on all the way to Kemah to the Boardwalk. His Mom made him promise not to breathe a word of the good news until they could announce it together. Brynn gave Spencer her ring, hating to take it off but knowing it would spoil the surprise if anyone saw the ring before they could announce it.

Since it was a weekday evening, the Aquarium was able to seat them without a reservation or a lengthy wait. They asked to be seated next to the aquariums, since Blake liked to watch the fish. Annie would love it, too. The largest tank was a huge cylinder that rose vertically from the ground floor to the very top, positioned centrally for optimum views. It was hugged by the spiral staircase that extended to every floor.

They were waiting for Ben and Ludie and the others to arrive, and Blake could hardly contain himself. He asked Spencer if he could call him Dad, and Brynn teared up instantly, fighting to regain control of her emotions. She dabbed at her eyes with a tissue, determined to keep it together. Spencer told Blake he'd be honored to have him call him "Dad." Before they saw Ben and Ludie reaching the top of the staircase to join them, they heard Annie's excited squeals. She was so excited about the "little fishies" she could barely contain herself. Roxy and Dennis were right behind them, reaching the top of the stairs while Ben took Annie from Ludie. She was kicking her little legs with excitement, both at seeing her Aunt Brynn as well as all the bright, tropical fish.

When they had given hugs to everyone, Ben began helping Annie into a booster seat, securing the safety belt around her. Once they had all taken their seats, Spencer got everyone's attention.

"I have something I'd like to tell you," he began. "I hope you'll be as happy as I am when I tell you that Brynn has agreed to do me the honor of becoming my wife."

He opened the tiny ring box and removed the ring from the box. She held out her hand and he took it in his, sliding it onto her finger. Ludie cried out, tears forming in her eyes. She and Ben were both thrilled. Roxy jumped to her feet, nearly knocking Brynn off her chair with an enthusiastic hug.

"That's fabulous!" she shouted. Brynn just happened to glance over at Dennis just in time to barely notice an almost imperceptible look between him and Roxy. She decided to ask more about that later.

Little Annie was happy simply because everyone else was happy, and because she saw the little "fishies," as she called them.

Brynn and Spencer spoke of their plans over dinner, and made it clear they wanted each member of the family that was present today to be a part of the wedding. As they discussed wedding plans, Roxy and Ludie said they would need at least until spring to plan a nice wedding. Brynn gloried in the shared moment, knowing these two women were more like sisters than friends.

The women spent every moment they could huddled together talking about wedding plans. The guys had to remind them they would have plenty of time to work out the details. Ludie looked up and reminded the guys that they didn't have a clue what all goes into planning a wedding. Ludie admired the beautiful ring, and told Spencer he'd chosen well. Even Roxy, with her sophisticated, high-end taste voiced her admiration.

"Nicely done, mate," she eyed Spencer admiringly.

"I had to," he answered her, "it's for the most beautiful woman in the world, and she deserves beautiful things."

"Then I've said "nicely done" to the wrong person!" She winked at Brynn. "Good job!"

Spencer leaned over and cupped his fiancé's chin in his hand, planting a soft kiss on her lips.

"Now that I've found my other half, I hope I'll always be able to do nice things for her."

"Just being here is the nicest thing you could ever do for me," she told him, her eyes misting once again.

Blake clanged his knife on his ice tea glass, just as he'd seen in the movies. "Ahem!" Everyone turned, surprised at his outburst. "Am I gonna have to wear a tux?" he demanded. They all burst into laughter, and his mother told him that most assuredly he would be wearing a tux that day.

Once they'd all pretty much finished with their entrees, their waiter brought out two beautiful flaming deserts with candles putting off sparkles in the air. They were the same style dessert usually delivered for birthdays, but they served the purpose well for an occasion such as an engagement. Everyone in their party was in a festive, happy mood.

After they'd shared their desserts, they somehow managed to pull a fascinated Annie away from the giant aquarium next to their table.

She had been pressing her little hands to the glass and was talking to the "fishies," and squealed with delight each time one would swim near her.

After dinner they made their way down the huge spiral staircase encased in tropical, coral-textured walls and strolled through the gift shop toward the stingray aquarium. They purchased tiny trays of feeder fish to feed the stingrays, who were docile and extremely grateful. There was an aquarium worker who instructed them to grasp the fish outward from the outside of their hands between their fingers. To feed the fish, they would need to hold their hands with closed fists against the inside of the tank below. The wall surrounding it was low enough that Blake was able to easily reach in and feed them. Immediately upon placing their hands against the walls, giant stingrays made their way close and covered their hands with giant, gaping mouths. Blake loved every minute of it, but Annie wanted no part of the icky fish, so Ben and Spencer did it for her. At first she was afraid from all the splashing, but when Ludie picked her up and she was able to actually see the stingrays, she bgan squealing with excitement as they neared the sides of the tank.

With a tender heart, Brynn watched Spencer and his stop-at-nothing tactics to entertain both Blake and Annie, and fell in love all over again. She knew that a man who would go to such lengths at the risk of his own personal dignity just to please a child was a man worth holding on to, and that was exactly what she was going to do.

He glanced up at her from his position bent over the tank and suspended precariously above the giant stingrays and she blew him a kiss. More and more she found herself silently thanking God for bringing such a man into her life. She had already seen him with patients many times and knew he was a man of great compassion, but these past few weeks seeing him around her family and with the children in particular, she knew there would be no doubts about her relationship with him. She couldn't wait to be married to this man.

Roxy, being from the Gold Coast of Australia, knew a thing or two about sting-rays and other tropical fish, and surprised them with a few interesting facts. She was quite a good sport about getting her hands dirty to feed the creatures.

Once they'd finished washing up from the stingray experience, they strolled across the boardwalk, taking in the sights and sounds. Music drifted through the air, and laughter echoed. Amusement park rides nearby emitted the sounds of screams and all the bells and whistles of roller coasters and ferris wheels. There would be no time for amusement rides for them this time as the kids were both tired and it was a weeknight.

They began loading up in vehicles to head home. Annie was asleep in her daddy's arms before they had even made it to the car and Ludie wondered aloud if she'd stay asleep the whole way.

Blake was tired, but happy. Brynn glanced back a few times in the backseat to find her son staring out the window through heavy eyelids, with a soft smile of satisfaction on his lips.

As much as she wanted Spencer to stay the night at her house with her, he had brought up a valid point. It was a school night and had been an eventful day. Blake was overwhelmed with the excitement of their new lives together, but even though the changes were positive ones, they were changes nonetheless. Brynn and Spencer had decided together to keep things as close to the routine for Blake as possible, especially during the school weeks. On the weekends, it was a different story, but for now, it was important to both of them to keep Blake's routine consistent during the school week.

Chapter 24

When they arrived home Sarge was waiting for them at the front door. He sidled up to Blake and brushed against his legs. Blake reached down to pet him and apologized for being gone so long. Clouded by drowsiness, he promised Sarge he could sleep in his room with him, then ambled toward the bathroom to brush his teeth. When he was finished he went straight for his room and Sarge followed, not about to let him back out of his promise.

Spencer helped Brynn unload and then kissed her goodnight and left for home. Brynn locked the door behind him and headed down the hall towards her bedroom. She just happened to be outside Blake's door when he knelt down to pet him and whispered to him. "Mom's getting married, Sarge, and we're gonna be a family."

She didn't let on that she had heard, but stopped, leaning against the wall outside his room for a moment. With her hand on her chest, she sighed. Life couldn't be any sweeter than it was at that very moment. Knowing that their decision impacted Blake by providing an additional layer of security in his life, her heart nearly burst with love.

Just as she was stepping away from the wall to walk away, Piper came out of her room and stormed past her, not saying a word. *More drama,* Brynn thought. *Exactly what we don't need tonight.* Against her better judgment, however, she followed her to the kitchen to investigate, hoping to learn the source of her attitude.

"What's going on?" she asked, honestly not knowing what she could've possibly done to upset her *this* time. Piper set down the glass she was holding and stared down at the granite countertop for a moment before speaking. Finally, she looked up, an expression of bitter disappointment on her face.

"It's just hard to see pictures posted on social media about what a lovely time you're all having at a family celebration. Dinner out, to celebrate wonderful news that no one bothered to tell me."   She shook her head in disgust and headed for the fridge to fill her glass with ice and water. Brynn leaned back against the bar and closed her eyes for a moment.

"What on earth are you talking about?" she asked through clenched teeth. "We literally *just* got engaged this afternoon and only told the family a little while ago at dinner. We were coming home and were going to tell you, but when I saw you were so furious, well, let's just say that's not conducive to sharing such wonderful news."

Piper turned back to her and hissed, "What ever happened to you considering *me* a part of the family?" Her eyes shone with tears that threatened to spill over.

Brynn let out a slow breath. "Piper, I'm sorry. When we picked up Blake from school we came home to get freshened up a bit and let him change from his school clothes. You weren't here, and we assumed you must be working. I never really know when you will and won't be home so it's hard to know. If you had been here, we would have asked you to come."

"Don't worry about it." Piper hung her head low, pitifully, then glanced up slowly. "It was for family only." Taking a few steps down the hallway, she stopped and turned around. "I shouldn't have made assumptions. For what it's worth," she continued, "congratulations."

Brynn stood at the bar, wiping the countertop and was still going over the conversation in her head. Sometimes she was literally infuriated with the things Piper said and did, and others, like tonight, she felt truly awful for not including her. When she really took the time to think about it, Piper had no one. Not a single relative, not a sibling, no one. And Brynn and Blake, although not true blood family, were all Piper had in this world.

Sighing, she threw down the dishtowel she was using, and headed down the hallway to her bedroom. She quickly put things away, then stepped into the shower. She stayed for a long time, loving the feel of the hot water pouring over her. She'd always felt the shower was perfect not only for washing the day's dirt and grime away, but for thinking about the day's events, and unwinding from them.

Tonight, she stood in the shower thinking about how much had changed just since this

248

morning. Engaged! Even now, in this moment, all alone, she could feel her face stretched into a wide smile that wouldn't go away. It was amazing how well Spencer rounded out their family. What she wouldn't have given to have met him sooner. *If only he could have been Blake's father,* she wished. Quickly, she shook the thought away and thanked God for bringing them together, here and now. She had been through her share of heartache, years of parenting on her own, and Spencer had survived broken hearts as well, but they were both a product of what they'd endured. The scars, the baggage, every single obstacle they'd each endured had made them what they were today: perfect for each other.

Rinsing the suds off her body, she felt a deep sense of satisfaction and contentment within. Not only was she content, she was excited. There was an unbelievable sense of exhilaration that came with falling in love, and she was feeling every bit of it. The way things looked and smelled were heightened, as were her senses in appreciating each one of them. Even the mundane daily things seemed less like chores now. At work, performing the same tasks every night were not a problem. Nursing presented its own set of challenges with each new day and each new patient, so she never found it boring, but now every shift held a tinge of renewed excitement. There was the chance of running into Spencer at any given moment when they worked the same shifts and her heart skipped a beat every time.

They worked well together, each respecting the other for their distinct body of knowledge regarding patient care. As a nurse, she held her own knowledge in overall care, but when a patient was in any form of respiratory distress, she quickly deferred to his knowledge.

He was amazing, she had to admit, and not just from her bias. She had watched him in code situations and he was impressive. Not that she watched the way his smooth muscles rippled beneath his scrub top while he performed chest compressions. Or the bold confidence she heard in his voice when he took on an authoritative note in a crisis. There was no doubt about it, she was in love with this man and everything she knew about him.

Oh and she'd seen him watching her as well. He'd see her in certain situations and would tell her he was impressed with the way she could multitask and handle any combination of problems with ease, and he told her so, often. She would sometimes glance up from something she was doing and see him at a distance. He would give her an intimate smile, one only meant for her, and it made her feel wonderful. It let her know she was his girl and there was no greater feeling in the world.

She stepped out of the shower and wrapped herself in a thick, plush towel. How was it that Spencer could invade her thoughts no matter what she was doing? She quickly dried off and crossed the room, throwing on a t-shirt and panties before climbing into bed. She shivered at the feel of being fresh and clean and climbing into crisp, clean sheets. Her muscles relaxed as she stretched out in her bed. She had barely pulled the soft, light comforter over her when sleep overcame her and her last thoughts were of Spencer.

* * *

It was the earliest hours of morning when Piper suddenly woke up. Her first conscious thoughts were of this family, a family who had taken her in when she'd felt the most alone, then tossed her aside just as quickly once she had gotten in the way. They'd embraced her, only to throw her away like she'd meant nothing. If only they knew, she thought, the first pleasant thought she'd had in a while. But they didn't. And wouldn't, not until she was ready for them to know.

She threw back her covers and sat on the edge of her bed for a moment, listening. The house was quiet, still. The air conditioner kicked on, a soft, welcome, white noise. She hesitated, then decided she must be the only one awake. But the dog, the dog was a different story. He always slept with one ear open. Damn mutt growled at her every time she got near it. Hopefully he was in the kid's room, asleep.

She stepped into the hallway and padded softly, quietly, into Brynn's room. She stood over her and watched her sleep, seeing that her breath was slow, deep and even. Her dark auburn hair fanned out beautifully on the pillow, her delicate features softly framed. Her thick, dark lashes made shadows on her cheeks in the soft light from a streetlight that shone in through the window. She was beautiful, Piper realized. Not that she hadn't noticed before. She practically watched her every move. Followed in her every footstep. She wanted to look like Brynn, dress like Brynn. She looked to her like a big sister. *Sister.*

She laughed quietly at the bitter irony of such a thought and turned away quickly before she might take a chance of waking Brynn. Padding softly to the dresser, she slowly and silently slid the top drawer open. No chance of opening the wrong one, because she had them memorized. Every drawer and its contents. Every piece of clothing.

Reaching in, she pulled out a black, lacy nightie, holding it up to herself, feeling its soft, silky fabric across her skin. Balling it up and clutching it to her chest, she stepped quietly from the room and into the living room. Up on a shelf she found a photo album and removed it from its spot. Just like Brynn's clothes, she knew exactly which photo albums represented which time periods from Brynn's life. Clutching it tightly, she made her way quietly into her own room, setting down her treasures and covering them with her comforter.

She went back out and peered into the kid's room, opening the door so quietly he wouldn't know. Just as she had suspected, that dog was lying on the floor alongside his bed. As usual, there would be no approaching him without getting past Sarge. That was a problem she'd need to deal with. Sooner rather than later, she decided, and felt a thrill up her spine as she remembered her plan.

Back in her own room, Piper closed the door and turned the lock. Stripping down to nothing, she slipped Brynn's nightie over her head, feeling its softness caressing her skin as it fell over her body. It fit her almost exactly like it did Brynn, only her own curves were a bit more generous than Brynn's. Piper had seen Brynn in it. Once, on a night when Spencer had been there, she had snuck down the hallway and opened the door, quietly, carefully, and only a fraction, enough to see inside. Usually they kept it locked, so she was lucky that night.

She knew they were up to something, she could hear the sounds from the pipes stop when the shower was turned off, so she knew exactly when they'd gone to bed. She waited the appropriate amount of time before opening the door. She'd watched them, then. Spencer, she watched because he was so sexy, and she could hardly wait. One day he would be hers. Once he'd finally realized she was a better match for him than Brynn was. But her mission right then was to watch Brynn. She observed every movement, every sound, down to the soft gasps she released and when. She studied her, knowing she'd have to one day mimic her every move. She remained in the doorway to Brynn's bedroom, caught up in the moment, almost too long.

She was so fascinated, enthralled even, that she almost didn't hear the dog get up from where he was sleeping in Blake's room. It was a close call. When the dog stood up, he shook a bit before he came out of the kid's room. If it weren't for his collar jingling, she'd have never known he was on the move and would've been caught. As it was, she had just enough time to back up in the hallway, closing the door to Brynn's bedroom quietly behind her. She pressed her back against the wall, stepping sideways toward the door to her own room. When the beast had approached her, she heard a low, deep growl that began in his throat. She tried to shush him, then realized the more she did the louder he would get. He might even become more aggressive. She'd barely made it back into her room and shut the door when she heard him finally walk away, back into the kid's room. That night, much like this one, she'd felt a secret thrill at watching them when they didn't know she was there.

Later on, in her own room again, Piper shivered at the memory of the close call. This time it had gone much smoother, but the risk was still there. Glad to be safely back in her room, unobserved, she decided to simply enjoy the feel of Brynn's silky lingerie on her body. Sitting on her bed, she flipped open the photo album and eyed the photos with a singular focus on a three part goal. Find, study, and replace. She'd found her, was studying her now, and soon it would be time for phase three. Replace.

Piper found photos of herself and her mother in this album. She compared herself to Brynn in every pose. Brynn was taller, thinner, darker. More beautiful in every way. But time had progressed, and with it there were changes. Her skin was a near match to Brynn's flawless skin.

Once, after she'd visited the tanning beds a few times, Brynn had noticed and complimented her on her tan. After that, she'd taken it a bit too far, tanning too often. She'd finally slacked off and her tan had evened out a bit, a better match to Brynn's. Now her hair was finally grown to the length of Brynn's, so close that it would now only take one cut and color at the salon to match her.

She'd even begun to follow in Brynn's career footsteps. Now she had scrubs like Brynn's, and a stethoscope around her neck. Even her nametag was just like Brynn's unless you happened to be close enough to read the name and see that the initials for her title were CNA instead of RN. But that was only going to be a matter of time.

She retrieved a bottle of perfume she'd once taken from Brynn's dresser and hidden in her own drawer. Spraying it lightly on her wrists, she rubbed them together and felt a tingle of excitement rush through her. She quickly put it back and laid down on her side, with one wrist close enough to her face to smell it as she drifted off to sleep.

Chapter 25

The next morning Brynn awoke, completely oblivious to having been watched, even emulated during the night. She also had not even the slightest of inkling that in the past she and Spencer had ever been violated during one of their most intimate moments.

Instead, Brynn Callaway woke up to the renewed joy of instantly remembering the events of the day before. Sitting up, she held her left hand up and admired her beautiful engagement ring. The light streaming through her bedroom window reflected off it, casting iridescent rainbows around it.

Glancing at the clock, she knew time was limited, so she pulled herself away from her dreamy state and hit the floor running. Stepping into a pair of yoga pants, she got moving quickly. Blake was easy to awaken because Sarge had begun licking his fingers as soon as he had heard Brynn moving around.

"Wake up, Sweetie," she said, standing in his doorway. "School's in half an hour." Satisfied to see him stirring, she sauntered down the hallway to the kitchen. She made some coffee, knowing she'd need it to get the day started. It wasn't but a few minutes later that Blake headed up the hallway, dressed but without his backpack.

"What do you want for breakfast?" she asked him. "We don't have much time."

Before he could answer, there was a knock at the door. Answering it, she saw Spencer on the doorstep, a box from the bakery in his hands.

Smiling, she opened the door wide to let him come in.

He marched past her into the house, announcing his breakfast delivery. He eyed Brynn up and down, and she was suddenly aware of her t-shirt and yoga pants.

"Sexy," he whispered. "I'm looking forward to waking up to that picture every morning."

With a kiss on her cheek, he disappeared into the kitchen, dispensing a few donuts onto a plate, telling Blake he could have one, but only after he ate a ham and cheese kolache.

"Protein before empty carbs," he explained, and Brynn could've hugged him at that moment. She wasn't about to say anything about the donuts in front of Blake, but hearing Spencer insist on something more nourishing first saved her son a cautionary lecture. Spencer was turning out to be a really good influence on her son.

She smiled at the sound of Blake and Spencer talking and laughing in the kitchen and joined them. "Want some coffee?" she asked Spencer.

"No thanks, I'm trying to cut back," Blake answered, cracking them all up.

"I'll take some," Spencer answered. "Get your backpack, Buddy, and brush your teeth. This bus departs in five minutes."

"You're taking him to school for me?" she asked, sweetly, slipping her arms around his neck.

"Well it looks like I have to," he winked. "Look at you, you're a mess." Once again, laughter bubbled up in her.

"Actually, I want you to enjoy your morning. Kick back and sip your coffee, catch up on some reading." He gave her a devilish grin.

"Because I have absolutely nothing else to do when I get finished taking Blake to school." He wiggled his eyebrows at her and departed, giving one last shout out to Blake.

"C'mon, Buddy, let's roll!"

He returned to the house shortly thereafter, and cuddled up with her on the couch. He was wearing a t-shirt and sweatpants, and she couldn't help but love his shape, obvious beneath them. But his comfortable clothes meant ease in snuggling together under a blanket. He pulled her into his arms and she settled eventually with her back against his chest, and he picked up the remote.

To her surprise, he landed on HGTV for a show about couples remodeling homes.

"You watch this stuff?" she asked, turning to look up at him, surprised.

"Not usually, but I need to know some things about your tastes, and if you have any specific plans for this house or wanting to move."

She thought for a moment, then answered.

"You know, since I've raised Blake here, it's the only home he's ever known."

"Okay, then we stay here." He nodded, satisfied with her answer. "Have you ever envisioned any changes?" he asked her sincerely.

"I've always wanted a sunroom," she told him. "But I wasn't sure if I'd ever be able to pull it off."

He gently shifted her from his lap and stood up, looking out the sliding glass door to the backyard. He walked over and stepped out the doors, in his socks, and studied the patio. Coming back in, he shined with boyish enthusiasm.

"You know, it wouldn't be hard to do! You've got a concrete slab already." He slid across the floor in his socks, making her laugh yet again as he eyed every window, every space, verbalizing his plans so seriously, all in his sock feet.

Before long, he returned to the couch to the spot he'd previously occupied and pulled her back into his arms. They stayed like that for quite a while, watching the home renovation shows and talking about their plans. His dream was a man-cave, he told her. She told him about the shed out back and how the only things in there were things that could go in the attic. The lawnmower was in the garage, and could stay there. His eyes widened with excitement and he ran for his shoes, putting them on and heading out to the shed. She couldn't help but chuckle at his boyish excitement.

When he returned, he was wound up tight. She pushed her bottom lip out slightly, pouting.

"What's wrong?" he asked her, suddenly concerned.

"When you build a man-cave it'll be back to me and Blake, all alone again."

"Oh, noooo," he answered emphatically. "Blake will be out in the man-cave with me! He's a man in training!" He gave her a wink and hugged her to him.

"Oh well then I'm relieved," she said. "The queen of the castle gets much needed time to herself, finally."

"Oh yeah?"

"Yeah. If you're gonna spit your nasty sunflower seeds everywhere, you can do it out in your man-cave."

He pulled her to him and tickled her slightly on the ribs. "Oh no, you don't," he scolded her. "I'll only be out there when it's a very special game or something you don't want to watch. Either that or when you get tired of me and throw me out. The rest of the time, I'll be crunching on my sunflower seeds in here, right next to you."

She laughed at him, and told him he'd be lucky to be the only husband with a fancy enough dog house to have a big TV in it.

"Husband." He breathed. "I like the sound of that." He turned her around with her back to his chest and held her to him. He bent down and whispered into her ear, "I love you."

Just about then, Piper surfaced for the morning. Coming out of her room, she came down the hall. She had put on pajama pants and a t-shirt, no bra. She was headed into the kitchen for coffee. When her eyes fell on Spencer and Brynn, she stopped dead in her tracks.

"Oh. I didn't realize you were here," she said. A smile played at the corners of her mouth. Brynn wasn't surprised to hear the lie roll off of Piper's tongue so easily.

"Morning," he murmured, still focused on the DIY project on TV.

"He took Blake to school," Brynn told her. "He brought kolaches and donuts, if you want some."

Piper eyed the two of them carefully, as if not sure how to respond for some reason, then said, "Okay."

She disappeared into the kitchen. When she returned, Sarge was coming down the hallway to inspect the parameter and make sure everything was kosher in the Callaway home. Ambling up to Spencer, he sniffed and rubbed against him, waiting for his hand to stroke him. Spencer obliged, as always, and so did Brynn. Satisfied, he continued on through to the kitchen, letting out a short, low growl at the sight of Piper as he walked past.

A while later, the phone rang. It was Brynn's boss, calling to tell her she would have a day shift for her, starting the following week, if she still wanted it. Brynn was thrilled, and asked her if she could have a moment to discuss it with her family and call right back.

Hanging up, she asked Spencer how things were coming along in his pursuit of a day shift.

"I almost forgot to tell you!" he said. "Scott's going back to school and needs a night shift."

"That's great!" Brynn smiled up at him.

"Thing is, Scott won't be able to make the trade until a few weeks from now."

"I understand." She quickly added, "but if I don't take this shift now, Monday, they'll give it to someone else." She searched his face for a reaction.

"Take it. Call her back right now and take it," he told her, "and in just a few weeks we'll be right where we need to be."

Realizing that it would mean a few weeks working opposite shifts, she looked down, a little sad.

"It's only for a short while," he assured her cheerfully, in hopes of making her feel better about it. While Brynn called her boss back and was talking to her, Piper went over to Spencer and informed him that she was starting out next week on night shift.

"I'll be orienting on nights for a while," she told him. "So you won't feel lonely when Brynn goes to days. I'll be there to keep you company."

It gave him a strange feeling, the intimacy with which she spoke, as if she were insinuating something on a different level altogether. He shrugged it off, deciding to bring it up to Brynn later. For now, he was just happy that both he and his bride-to-be would be working together on the day shift soon, freeing them up for evenings together and keeping them home at night for Blake.

Friday night rolled around and since Brynn and Spencer were both scheduled off, they decided to plan an evening at home watching movies with Blake. At Brynn's insistence, they included Piper. Since she seemed to have her heart set on making Piper feel more included, Spencer made a decision regarding their movie night. He decided to hold off and not mention anything to Brynn yet about the way Piper had been making him feel uncomfortable. Maybe he was just reading more into it than was really there. He would wait and see how she behaved while they were watching the movie.

Spencer left to pick up Blake at school and they went to the store for popcorn and some other movie snacks. They laughed and had a good time together, choosing some chips, dips and, to placate Brynn, they picked up a raw veggie plate with dip. They headed home, with plans to order pizza around six o'clock.

When they arrived home, Brynn was inviting Piper to join them for family movie night. She looked for a second to be planning a sarcastic retort, but then inexplicably she forced a smile and then said she would love to. Brynn wondered what her response was all about, but then shrugged it off, deciding to just make the most of it and make her feel welcome and loved. It was the right thing to do, for not only the memory of Aunt Sylvia, but also the memory of her own dear mother. They'd been practically sisters growing up, and she wanted to be there for her now.

They let Blake choose the movie, and when the pizza arrived, they all piled into the living room, sprawled out on the furniture with paper plates and big fluffy pillows. It was a nice night, Brynn reflected, and she was glad she included Piper, who seemed to be enjoying it immensely. Brynn smiled, knowing she'd done the right thing. That was all Piper had needed, just to feel included.

By the time the second movie ended, Blake was sound asleep, the upper half of his body on the loveseat, his legs propped over the side of Sarge's large body. Sarge had slept for the last part of the movie, seemingly perfectly content to have Blake's legs across him. As long as he could keep his boy close and safe, he was happy. Brynn woke her son gently, telling him it was time to go to bed. He was groggy, but alert enough to give both her and Spencer good night hugs, thanking them for family night.

* * *

Later that night, when Brynn and Spencer were getting ready for bed, Blake had already been asleep for quite a while. The house was quiet and Brynn figured Piper must already be in bed. Once Brynn and Spencer had both showered, they got into bed.

They were both sound asleep a little while later when her phone rang. She grabbed it quickly so as not to wake Spencer, and whispered, "Hello."

"Brynn? Hi, it's Thea. I really hate to bother you, but I had to send a nurse home sick."

Brynn moaned, groggy.

"I thought we could make it," Thea continued, "but ER just hit us with a bunch of admissions. Just when we thought things were settling down."

Brynn started to pretend she hadn't heard her, then hang up, but Thea's insistent voice made her more alert.

"Listen, I really hate to ask this…"

Then don't, Brynn wanted to say, but held her tongue.

"… but could you come in just for a little while? Long enough to help with some admissions, then you can go home, I promise!" Brynn was just about ready to tell her she couldn't, but then Thea continued.

"We can handle the patient load, once they're admitted and into the system. It's just the admission process. You know how it is, until their orders are entered they can't receive any medications, or pretty much anything else. I hate to see them so uncomfortable while they wait."

Dammit, Brynn thought. *She's got me.* "Fine," she muttered. "I'll be there in a few."

Looking over at Spencer, she realized he was sound asleep. Not wanting to bother him, she slipped into her scrubs quietly, and jotted him a quick note.

Spencer, I got called in to help with admissions. I'll be home in a little while. Love, Brynn

She grabbed her stethoscope and her purse and keys and headed out.

Arriving on her unit, she immediately saw the chaos of admissions and jumped right in to help. "Give me the list," she told Thea, trying not to snap at her. She forced a smile and took the clipboard.

"Where do you want me to start?"

Thea was unusually kind, obviously grateful to Brynn for agreeing to come in and help.

"If you could do this one first," she said, pointing to a name on the clipboard, "we could get him in the system. He's here with end-stage pancreatic cancer, and we'll be consulting hospice over the weekend. If you could get him in the system first, we can get him some pain meds ordered." She rifled through a stack of papers, pulled one loose and handed it to Brynn. "Here is a list of the pain meds they gave him in ER, along with the dosages and the times."

Brynn took the paper from her, quickly scanning it and heading for the patient's room. She found him being transferred to the bed by two of the ER staff that had brought him. His wife was next to him, wringing her hands, evidently worried.

What spoke to Brynn the most was their age. Neither the man nor his wife could've been older than in their forties. Glancing at his admission data she saw his date of birth. She was right, he was only 47.

Sighing, she smiled warmly and introduced herself. "Mr. Collins, I'm Brynn." She shook his hand once he was settled into his bed and then shook his wife's hand. "I'm one of the nurses here and I'm going to get you all settled in and comfortable."

The two nurses from ER were finished and, handing Brynn some paperwork, they disappeared into the hallway with their stretcher. Mr. Collins and his wife answered her questions, and Brynn was touched at the closeness between them. They were able to finish each other's sentences, something that would sound cliché to hear it said that way, but it was very true in their case.

The way they looked at each other was so sweet, so loving. Brynn saw in the woman's eyes compassion for her husband, for the pain he was experiencing. In his eyes, she saw compassion for his wife, worried about leaving her alone. *Such an amazing connection,* she thought.

She was delighted to help this sweet couple get settled in. She not only got his medications started so he would be more comfortable, she also gave Mrs. Collins a quick tour of the floor to show her where to find things like extra linens, the coffee pot, vending machines and even the chapel. Out in the hallway, she was able to speak with Mrs. Collins more candidly and asked if she had any questions about his condition or about hospice care. She felt satisfied that she had answered the woman's questions, and Mrs. Collins expressed her gratitude.

Once Mr. Collins was comfortable and Mrs. Collins was settled into a bedside cot, she gave report to one of the night shift nurses and went on to the next patient. Once she'd admitted three patients, a little over three hours had passed. Thea looked at the clock and clucked her tongue.

"Go home!" she ordered. "You've been here for hours, and I didn't mean for that to happen."

Staring at her for a moment, Thea cocked her head to the side and said, "You know, you're a real team player. You didn't have to even come, and you've been here all this time. You really made it an easier night for these patients. Thank you." Thea at first acted as though she would choke on her words, then softened at the realization that Brynn really was the type of nurse to step up and help.

Exhausted, Brynn got in her car and headed home. As she drove up in the driveway, she thought she noticed a small, dim light on in Piper's room. She was surprised, considering this late hour, but parked in the garage and headed inside. Heading down the hallway, she noticed what looked like spots of water as the light from the entryway shone in and reflected off it. Shining the small flashlight on her keychain, she saw wet footprints on the tiles. They led from her own bedroom door to Piper's room. The shock of what she was seeing hit her full force. *What was this?* she wondered.

Her thoughts ran amok as she considered the possibilities. Spencer, she knew, had already taken a shower before bed. Piper had disappeared into her room long before they had gone to bed. The guest bathroom didn't have a shower, only a deep tub, she remembered. Perhaps Piper had wanted a shower and used hers? But to go in there, in the middle of the night, without asking? She shook it off. No, no way.

Stopping just short of Piper's door, she hesitated, about to tap on it, then stopped herself. No, she would go into her own bedroom and assess the situation. Maybe Spencer had given her permission. But that seemed odd, too.

She quietly entered her bedroom to find it dark, the only light a faint glow of moonlight from the window. Spencer was sound asleep, his breaths deep and slow. Curious, she stepped through the doorway to the master bath, only a few steps away from the bed where Spencer slept. She could see a little better in there due to the window above the garden tub. She noticed a candle wick that had clearly *just* been extinguished as the wick was glowing slightly orange at the tip, a faint trail of smoke lingering in the air. She had *just* been in there, Brynn realized with a start.

Her body stiffened, unable to process the scene before her. Stepping back over to the bedside, she saw Spencer, sleeping so sweetly, his face relaxed and free of stress, almost smiling in his sleep.

For a brief moment, she almost wondered if something more was going on than met her eyes. Her breath caught in her lungs. *There was no way.* She felt a deep twinge of guilt for even allowing herself to wonder. Her faith in Spencer wouldn't be shaken by a strange set of events, no doubt brought on by Piper's actions. She and Spencer were solid and nothing anyone could do would shake that.

She quickly undressed, climbing into bed. Shaking off a vague sense of unease, she settled into sleep. Spencer lay next to her, still lost in a deep sleep, undisturbed.

Chapter 26

The next morning, everyone slept in. Sarge was the first one awake, and he nudged Blake's hand, hoping to wake him. Unsuccessful, he scratched at Brynn's door, whining. She heard him and got up, moaning.

"I'm coming, Sarge, hang on." She padded down the hall, groggy, Sarge running ahead of her, pacing at the door. As soon as she opened the door, he bounded outside, racing to find the right spot. As soon as he finished his business, she let him back in. Looking at the clock, she decided she may as well stay up.

She put on some coffee, knowing Spencer wouldn't be far behind her. Memories of the odd events from last night crept into her mind. She pushed them aside, watching and waiting for the coffee to finish brewing. After a few moments she poured herself a cup of coffee.

Wrapping her hands around the mug for warmth, she took a seat on the couch, sinking into the fluffy cushions. She stared straight ahead, giving herself time to wake up gradually. Sarge came up to her, waiting for a quick nuzzle, then settled himself beneath her feet. The two of them remained in that same position, the only sound in the house was the quiet, gentle ticking of the clock over the mantle.

Soon after, Brynn heard the door to Piper's room open. She stiffened, unsure of what to expect and careful not to show any kind of reaction. Piper moved down the hallway, hips moving seductively back and forth, a satisfied grin on her face, almost a smirk. She was in a sexy little pajama set, baby pink, comprised of a tiny tank top that bared her midriff and matching short shorts. Brynn wanted to say something so bad, considering that she had a 12 year old boy in the house, but didn't dare say a word right now, not willing to show a reaction.

"Good morning," Piper sang, her lips pursed as though to hold back words. Brynn restrained herself, careful not to react. "How was your night?" Piper continued, nearly as self-assured as before.

"It was good, thanks," Brynn replied. "I had to go in to work and help out with some admissions." She eyed Piper out of the corner of her eye, careful not to be obvious that she was gauging her reaction.

"Yeah, I know. How did it go?" Piper asked. Brynn wanted so badly to ask her how she knew, considering Spencer was still asleep and the note was left on his nightstand. She bit her lip to keep from asking.

"It was great," Brynn said with a smile. "But even better afterward," she finished.

Piper stopped in her tracks, briefly, resuming her steps quickly in an effort to not show a reaction. As soon as Piper disappeared into the kitchen, Brynn smiled, glad she had the final word and that Piper was the one left wondering and not herself. Just by Piper's reaction she knew the girl was trying to get a rise out of her and that nothing was going on other than a silly attempt to create friction in her relationship.

Just then, Spencer appeared in the hallway, stretching. Damn, he was sexy. He walked straight to Brynn and curled up on the couch next to her, his head in her lap. She ran her fingers over his head, feeling the soft buzz of hair on his head, so close he looked almost bald. His shoulders were broad, his arms and neck muscled as well. A warm glow settled in her belly, and she caught her breath.

Piper came back into the living room with a cup of coffee in her hand just in time to see Spencer reaching Brynn and lying down with his head in her lap. *Dammit.* This was not what she had hoped for.

When she had made it back to her room last night, she had listened quietly as Brynn walked up the hallway. She almost thought she could hear a slight tapping, but she waited a minute and didn't hear anything else. Listening carefully, she pressed her ear against the door and heard Brynn go into her own room and close the door.

She had remained at the door for a while, listening for an argument. Silence. She opened her own door and looked, but the master bedroom was dark. She waited, listening, for raised voices. Nothing. Infuriated, she lay awake for a long time, unable to sleep.

And now, this morning, here they were, the two lovebirds, happier than ever. Neither of them held even a trace of doubt or concern. Piper was furious, but not in any way giving up. *This time next week,* she thought, *it will be a different story. Everything will have changed by then.*

Not to be outdone in this challenge, she pranced into the living room, right in front of them, and stretched her long, tan legs out on the loveseat in front of them. She then draped one leg over the arm of the loveseat, and the other one down in front of her. That left an easy view of her open legs exactly across from Spencer and would be the first thing he would see when he opened his eyes.

Piper waited there for a while and, not getting any kind of reaction from either of them, stood up and stretched, yawning loudly, and disappeared into her room. Brynn couldn't help but smile, knowing she'd won this round, then suddenly wondering when it had become a battle. And why?

By the time Blake woke up and came dragging into the living room, Piper had already gone to her room and reappeared a few moments later, dressed for the day.

"I'm still sleepy," Blake mumbled. He bent down to pet Sarge. "Why didn't you wake me, buddy?" he asked.

"I'm sure he tried," Brynn told him. "He was scratching and whining at my door a little while ago and I let him out."

"I can't believe I slept that hard!" Blake said. "I guess from staying up so late watching movies," he reasoned.

273

"In that case we better start sticking to an earlier bedtime for you," Spencer said, winking.

"No!" Blake protested loudly. "Not on the weekends! I love movie night!"

* * *

Later that afternoon, Brynn was in the kitchen, putting ingredients together for chili. It was getting colder and chili was the perfect food for cold winter weekends. Spencer had gone to run a couple of errands, including returning some books to the library for her.

Brynn was assembling the ingredients and organizing the spices she would need for the chili when she happened to glance out the front window to see Piper at the mailbox. She had the mail in her hand when she came in and was about to set it down on the tray in the entryway.

Piper clearly didn't expect Brynn to stop what she was doing and ask for the mail. She quickly slipped one envelope from the stack and handed her the rest, careful not to let her see.

Brynn *had* seen, though, and asked her pointedly,

"What's in the other one?"

"Oh," Piper stammered. "Um, that one was for me. I mean junk mail." She attempted to hold her composure but Brynn saw through the act.

"Here, want me to throw it away for you?" Brynn asked, extending her hand.

Sidestepping her, Piper said, "No, I got it." She stepped into the kitchen and opened the pantry door. Brynn noticed she seemed to bend over the trash can and took a little longer than necessary to throw something away.

Once Piper had gone off to her room, Brynn went into the kitchen to finish making her chili. Peering down the hall to make sure Piper was still in her room, she looked into the trashcan.

The piece of mail had been pushed down underneath the tray from the raw beef Brynn had used for the chili. *Piper didn't think I would look under all this bloody wrapping,* she thought. She dug beneath the packaging and retrieved a bill from the kitchen, bed and bath store. Stunned, she found a bill with her name on it for over $800.00.

Piper had opened an account in Brynn's name when she decorated her living room so out of keeping with the styles she had wanted most. Carefully wiping it off, she tucked the bill into a clear plastic sandwich bag, saving it to show Spencer. He might be able to make some sense of it. She didn't even know what steps to take next? *Was this considered identity theft?* she wondered.

What reason could she have possibly had to think she could get away with doing all this as a "wonderful surprise gift," and then sending her the bill for it? Maybe she didn't have the credit to do it herself and was going to do it and have it paid off before Brynn could notice. Perhaps that was her intention for being so willing to check the mail all the time, in hopes of intercepting the bill. She sighed deeply. These confusing emotions were exhausting. It was a roller coaster, and she was rapidly tiring of it.

Just then, Sarge rushed out to the hallway, barking, before hurrying back into Blake's room. He was evidently upset about something, and

Brynn felt a surge of panic overtaking her. Glancing quickly at the clock, she realized Blake had been in his room for quite a while, and it had been several hours since he had last eaten.

Snatching up a tube of glucose gel, she raced into her son's room to find him sprawled on the bed, his head jerking back and forth rapidly, as he attempted to push Sarge away from him. He was confused and agitated, and his mother knew exactly what to do. She crawled onto his bed behind him and cradled his head against her. Speaking softly, she gently reassured him while squeezing some of the gel under his tongue.

Blake was biting down on the tube, so she had to work to pry it from beneath. That's why gel or paste were always safer for moments like these. They worked as quickly as juice, maybe even faster, but were less likely to cause him to choke or aspirate than thin liquids.

His agitation slowly began to subside, with no further combative movements. Sarge, dutifully, stood poised at the end of the bed, never taking his eyes off Blake. His concern was clearly evident in his eyes, no one would be able to argue otherwise after witnessing what had just occurred.

Once Blake seemed to calm further, Brynn managed to slide out from behind and beneath him to retrieve a glucose monitor from the desk beside his bed. Grabbing a hand towel from the linen closet in the hallway, she dabbed at the sweat that glistened all over his face. He was able to take the towel from his mother and wipe around his neck and hairline. Brynn quickly pricked his finger to get a glucose reading.

"It was pretty bad this time, huh Mom?" he asked. Her heart nearly broke at his troubled expression.

"A little," she answered softly. "We just need to start being a little more careful with food choices."

"I'm sorry, Mom." He tilted his brow and looked up at her uncertainly.

"Nooo, honey, it's not your fault. We've all gotten a bit careless lately, what with all the celebrating we've been doing." She cast him a playful glance in hopes of cheering him up.

Blake's mouth dropped open as he suddenly became aware of Sarge, still poised and ready for action, at the foot of his bed. "He let you know, Mom?" He bent down to pet him.

"He sure did! He went out to the hallway and barked, then came back in here to be with you. He never left your side after that."

"Good boy," Blake said in baby talk, repeating it several times. "You're such a good boy, thank you, thank you, thank you!" He had gotten down from the bed and was on the floor, his arms around Sarge's neck. He buried his face in the dog's fur, and was rewarded with a few grateful licks.

Brynn broke through the celebration with careful instructions. "It's still reading pretty low, and that was a lot of sugar we just got down you. Come to the kitchen and let's get some protein in your system." She crossed the room to the door, pausing for a moment, her hand on the doorknob. Blake still hadn't moved from his spot.

"Now, Son." She spoke firmly. "The chili's not ready yet, but you can have some cheese and deli meat. We'll recheck it again before dinner."

Chapter 27

By the time the excitement had died down, Brynn realized she hadn't heard a sound from Piper in a while. Her door was closed, and it was quiet. Glancing out the window, she noticed that Piper's car was no longer in the driveway. Sighing, she reminded herself she would need to discuss the incident regarding today's mail with Spencer.

Later, when Spencer arrived, they served up the steaming hot chili in bowls and sat down to eat. After what had happened with Blake earlier, Brynn decided to save the conversation for later. It would be best to have the conversation alone with Spencer. She didn't want to do anything to upset Blake right now. His sudden hypoglycemic episode had really left her rattled this afternoon. Stress wouldn't help matters.

After a while, it occurred to Brynn that Piper had never come back. Walking past her door, she decided to take a quick peek. She didn't know whether she expected to find any glaring answers to her roommate's recent behaviors or not, but she just felt the need to look.

Turning the knob, she opened the door and peeked inside. The bed was neatly made with fresh linens, but Piper's vibrant-colored bedspread and pillows were gone. Her jewelry box and cosmetics caddy, also gone. There were none of the decorative items she had previously kept on her dresser. No bottles of nail polish, magazines. Nothing.

Brynn crossed the room and opened the closet. Aside from a couple of mostly empty boxes, there wasn't much there. She was both surprised and aggravated. She had opened her home to Piper and then managed to overlook her very bizarre behavior. Aside from a few of the most upsetting incidents, she had refrained from addressing the outbursts and mood swings.

And now she was just gone, without a word of gratitude or apology. *When had she done this?* Brynn wondered. There hadn't been any furniture or large objects to move, so she figured Piper must have taken her things to her car in boxes gradually when no one was home. But *why?* she wondered.

Going back into the living room she found Spencer and Blake watching sports. "Spencer, can I talk to you for a moment? I need to show you something."

Breaking away from the TV, Spencer muttered, "Keep watching, buddy, I'll be back in a few."

In Piper's empty room, Spencer stood with his mouth open, clearly as shocked as Brynn at her sudden exit.

"What do you think is going on?" he asked. She went over the events from earlier, and he was barely able to contain his anger.

"That is completely unacceptable," he told her. "And criminal." His jaw was clenching, one hand on the corner of the empty dresser and the other in his pocket, to keep his temper in check, Brynn figured. "We need to report this," he finally said.

"I know," Brynn whispered. "I just wish we didn't have to. She's gone, so maybe there won't be any more problems. Maybe we should offer her a chance to explain her actions.

"She stole your identity, she racked up a huge bill. In *your* name," he hissed. "The only thing we need to *offer* her is a warrant."

"Shhh," whispered Brynn, placing a hand on his chest. "I don't want Blake to know about all this yet."

He hadn't even realized he'd gotten louder. "I'm sorry. I didn't mean to get carried away. It's just that I've seen what all you've done for her, and how you've overlooked her bad behavior. She's gone too far this time."

"Look, I know you're right." She looked up into his eyes and for the first time he noticed there were tears on her lower lashes.

"Promise me you'll take some time," she pleaded. "Think it through, so you're not acting out of anger."

"I will, I promise." He put one hand on each of her shoulders. "But this time we can't ignore it."

"I know," she said softly. "But at least maybe we should talk to someone before we do anything. What if we went over to Ben and Ludie's. Kinda see what they have to say about it."

"Good idea," he said. "I'd rather not discuss it here, because I don't want her walking in on us in the middle of everything." A look of realization flickered across his face. "Does she still have her key?"

"Yeah, I mean, I guess so. She certainly didn't leave it with me."

"I guess not," he murmured. "Well, we need to change the locks pretty soon. I don't want her having access here. She's unstable, clearly, and we don't know what she might do."

Taking Spencer by the hand, Brynn led him to her bedroom where they could sit down with the door closed and talk. She told him about the events at work, and about the night she'd been called in to work and came home to discover Piper had showered in her master bath, where he'd been sleeping only a few feet away. He was furious.

"Why didn't you ever tell me any of this?"

She looked down at her hands, twisting her ring on her finger absent-mindedly while she considered her answer.

"I wasn't sure about some of the things. I kept hoping it was just my imagination. I wanted it to be," she said, looking up at him. "I wanted it to be me over-reacting and not her really being so hateful and manipulative."

He pulled her close to him and simply held her for a little while.

* * *

Together, Brynn, Spencer and Blake crossed the street and down one house toward

Ben and Ludie's house. Spotting Roxy's car in the driveway, Brynn hesitated a bit. Sensing her uncertainty, Spencer told her it might be a good idea to include Roxy in the conversation. Brynn laughed, recalling events of the past.

"What?" Spencer asked.

"You don't know Roxy like I do," she whispered, careful not to let Blake overhear her.

"She seems level-headed to me."

"Yes, she can be. And usually is. But she's very loyal to her friends, and doesn't tolerate anyone mistreating them."

"So she's a master of revenge, huh?" he asked, causing Brynn to laugh nervously.

"You have no idea."

* * *

Ludie opened the door and invited them in. She looked at Brynn and immediately sensed something was amiss.

Looking at her nephew, she smiled. "Blake, I'm so glad you're here," she told him. "Would you mind keeping an eye on Annie while your Mom and I chat a little with the grownups?"

He was quick to oblige and asked if they could go in the backyard. Shortly, he was leading little Annie by the hand into the backyard, Sarge keeping step beside them.

"Hello, Luv, what are you up to this arvo?" Roxy puckered her lips and smooched an air kiss in their direction.

Spencer raised an eyebrow. "Arvo?"

Brynn forced a smile and explained. "It's an Australian expression for afternoon."

He nodded, the serious expression on his face making it clear he was ready to get onto the topic at hand.

Once Ludie had poured them some coffee, they sat down to talk. Ben was out for a bit, so Brynn and Spencer sat down to share the information with Ludie and Roxy.

Roxy traced the rim of her cup with her finger, never taking her eyes off Brynn as she brought them up to speed.

"I *knew* the little tart couldn't be trusted!" Roxy muttered hastily. Ludie leaned forward, her mouth open as she took in the information.

Both of them were outraged and had the same question for Brynn as Spencer had asked. *Why hadn't she told them?*

"I guess I just had so many doubts. I wasn't even sure I believed it myself. There were so many little things." Spencer squeezed her hand under the table, encouraging her.

"There were some things that happened at work, too," she added. One of the charge nurses is aware and has been watching her carefully."

"What kind of things at work?" Roxy asked.

"I'm not sure, but it seemed like she was trying to set me up," Brynn answered. "Like she wanted to get me in trouble for things I would never do." Tears swam in her eyes as she spoke.

"Well, I'm glad you know now," Ludie told her. "You can keep your eyes on her."

The four of them talked for a while, trying to formulate a plan of action. They watched Blake and Annie playing in the yard. Blake had fastened her carefully in her toddler swing and was pushing her gently. She was loving it, her little blonde curls bouncing and her mouth open, laughing delightedly. Brynn swallowed, trying to dismiss the uneasy feeling she had in the pit of her stomach.

When Brynn and Spencer arrived home later, boy and dog in tow, they noticed that there were no further signs of Piper anywhere. Apparently she hadn't been back. *Maybe,* Brynn hoped, *she wouldn't be.*

Spencer, not wanting to take any chances, went and picked up some items at the hardware store and changed the locks for both doors at Brynn's house.

* * *

On a Monday morning, less than a week later, the situation with Piper took a dramatic turn. After she'd taken Blake to school, Brynn had an unsettled feeling, wondering about Piper, where she'd gone and what she was doing.

In the afternoon, she asked Spencer to come over so they could talk. He was there in moments. He was determined to help her get through this, and he had been feeling uncomfortable any time he was away from her. He didn't want Brynn and her son alone. Not now.

Shortly after she'd gotten out the plastic sandwich bag with the linen store bill out to show Spencer, there was a knock at the door. Spencer opened it to find Roxy standing on the porch holding up a piece of paper with an address scrawled on it.

"What's this?" he asked, while Brynn came up behind him.

"Your answers," she snapped. "You can thank me later, Luv," she said with a wink, brushing past him to plant a kiss on Brynn's cheek.

Following her back inside, he closed the door firmly behind them. "Okay, I'll bite. What answers?"

"This," she said, "is the address to Piper's new apartment." Heading toward the kitchen, Roxy continued. "I could sure use a cup of coffee, it's been a busy morning."

"I can see that!" Brynn answered, smiling in admiration as she went to pour her a cup.

"Where is her apartment? How did you find it? And what else do you know?"

"Don't be looking inside horses' mouths, they don't have good teeth," Roxy said, stirring creamer into her coffee.

"That's 'don't look a gift horse in the mouth,'" Spencer corrected her.

"Yeah, whatever," she said, waving dismissively. "Just say 'thank you,' and then get over there and see what you can find out."

* * *

Just after 3:00 that afternoon, Piper ran her fingers through her hair, focusing sharply on the line of children filing off of the school bus in front of Brynn's house. She had seen Roxy leaving a little while earlier, then Brynn and Spencer pulling out of the driveway right behind her. She hoped they would be gone for a while. She knew Blake had a house key and would let himself inside to wait for his Mom. She also knew time was of crucial importance, so when the yellow school bus pulled up and let some children out, she readied herself for action.

Blake was the first one off the bus, and he started across the neighbor's yard heading for his house when, suddenly, a little girl called him back. He stopped, turning back around to listen to her. *Damn kid,* she murmured, watching closely. *Be done with it.*

Blake said something to the girl, who had gotten off the bus right after him. She walked toward him, a folder in her hands. *Hurry,* Piper whispered to herself. The kid took the folder from the little girl and stuffed it into his backpack. The little girl went next door to her own house and disappeared inside.

Piper's eyes darted back and forth between the kid and the street, watching for Brynn and Spencer to return. She shifted nervously in her seat.

Blake finally reached the front door and let himself in. Piper opened her car door and was just about to step out when Blake came bounding back outside with his dog next to him. Of course. He had to take the dog out.

After what seemed like forever, the dog finished his business and they bolted back inside.

This is it, she told herself and steeled herself for the task ahead. *It's now or never.* Removing a bottle of drops for red eyes from her purse, she squeezed a generous amount into each eye, then got out of her car. Now she had "tears" running down her cheeks. Perfect. Getting into character, she practically ran toward the front door and banged on it insistently. *Open the door, kid.*

Finally, the door eased open. Blake looked uneasy. The dog was right behind him, silently watching. The boy was clearly surprised to see her. She brought a crumpled tissue to the corner of her eye, clearly showing him she'd been crying.

"Hi, what are you doing here? Mom said you moved, and I didn't know why you didn't say goodbye." He was painfully honest. Piper noted.

"Honey, I can explain all that later, but right now you need to come with me." She'd have to play this cool. It wouldn't be easy. "Why? I'm not supposed to leave with anyone when Mom's not home, except Uncle Ben and Aunt Ludie. Your hair is a different color. Like my Mom's." His brow was knit with uncertainty, and she could tell he was unsure of how to handle this.

"Your aunt and uncle are with your Mom right now. She started getting sick, and Spencer took her to the hospital. I told them I would come and pick you up."

He nearly started crying right then. *What a pitiful little wimp*, Piper thought. *This would be much simpler than she had thought.* Apparently sensing the kid's distress, the dog emitted a low, warning growl in Piper's direction.

"Grab your backpack, we need to go."

The boy took a few steps inside to get his backpack and told Sarge he'd be back later. She peered nervously about, watching the street for Spencer's car. The damned kid was petting the dog.

"Chop, chop!" she barked, clapping her hands together twice. "We need to get going."

And trustingly, out of deep concern for his mother, he locked Sarge in the house and followed her outside to her car.

Chapter 28

Spencer had driven past the courthouse square, turning just beside the candle shop at the corner and pulled in to park behind Roxy's car. Less than a block behind the strip where the Ladybird Café and the Blackwater Creek Candle Company stood was a small apartment building. It was fairly old, judging by the siding and the quaint little porch railings. There were only two apartment units on the top and two on the bottom. Apparently, Piper had rented the one on the bottom right.

The units were furnished, all bills included, Mr. Wu had told them back when Piper was originally searching. It would've been easy for her to rent a space and get herself settled in without the worry of getting utilities connected in her name. Brynn remembered now that Mr. Wu had suggested an apartment in this building, but Piper hadn't appeared to be interested. She wanted the higher end apartment above the courthouse square.

Brynn and Spencer got out of the car and followed Roxy to the door. The three of them stood on the doorstep and knocked, waiting for an answer.

After a few moments, they realized she wasn't going to answer. Stepping behind the building, they saw a parking lot, shared with the two identical buildings behind the one with Piper's apartment. Her little blue Toyota was nowhere in sight, although she might have been parked in yet another lot behind the complex. Especially if she were trying to avoid anyone. Disappointed, they went back to their cars. They thanked Roxy, who still refused to answer how she'd found out where Piper had moved.

"Thank you," Brynn said. "I've got to find some answers, and this is a huge step."

"No worries, mate," said Roxy, who slid her sunglasses back down over her eyes and left with a smile.

Glancing at her watch, Brynn reminded Spencer that Blake would be getting home from school by now. They got into the car and headed home.

* * *

"Honey, we're back," she shouted into the house as they walked in through the back door. "Where are you?"

Sarge met them in the kitchen, clearly anxious. "What's wrong, buddy?" Spencer asked, petting him around the neck and behind his ears.

"He should be home by now," Brynn said. "The bus is never late." Her face was etched with worry. "I'm gonna ask the neighbor. Her daughter rides the same bus with Blake, maybe they're not back yet."

Cutting across the yard to the neighbor's house, Brynn couldn't help but crane her neck, looking up and down the street for any sign of her son. She knocked twice, and the door opened.

"Hi, Ashley. Have you seen Blake?"

The girl had a paper plate with chocolate chip cookies on it. A milk moustache lined her upper lip.

"Nope, not since we got home from school."

Anxiously, Brynn blurted out, "You saw him after school? When? Was he on the bus?"

"Yeah, he sat a couple of rows in front of me." The little girl was wiping chocolate from her hand onto her pants leg. "I sit back with the other 6th graders."

"Did you see him go inside? Was there anyone with him?" Brynn felt her heart hammering inside her chest. Oh, how she'd hoped for more information.

"No. He was walking in front of me, then his folder fell out of his backpack, it wasn't zipped all the way. I picked it up, and called his name. Some of the papers were loose but it wasn't my fault. I picked up what I could."

"No, it's okay, honey. What happened then?"

"I don't know, he came back when I called him. He was stuffing the papers back in, then he went home, I guess. I came inside to do my homework." She looked down. "And to eat a snack."

"Did you come back outside? Did you see him outside with Sarge?"

"No, sorry." The gravity of the situation had apparently sunk in, and Ashley seemed to be truly worried.

"Mrs. Calloway?" Her words stopped Brynn in her tracks.

"Yes?"

"I'll pray for him." She looked down at her shoes. "He'll probably come home in a little while, right?"

"Yes," she said, swallowing back a sob. "He'll come home soon."

Her breaths were coming faster and faster as she walked back home, anxiety seizing her. *He'd been home.* She had never known until now that panic had a taste, a smell. She felt it with every fiber of her being.

Spencer was waiting at the front door when she returned. He didn't say a word, but lifted a single brow in question.

"Call the police," she told him, relaying the information from Ashley.

Spencer tried to comfort her. "Maybe he went for a walk?" he told her.

"Not without Sarge," she snapped. "He would never do that." She sighed. "I'm sorry, Spencer. I'm scared." She fell into his arms and put her head on his chest. Pulling away and looking up into his eyes, she whispered. "It's Piper. She has him."

Grabbing her purse and keys again, she said, "We don't have time to call the police right now, we need to go back to Piper's. Ashley said the bus had just gotten home a few minutes ago. I'm sure she took him back there. We must have just barely missed them."

Spencer drove, while Brynn called Roxy and filled her in on the details.

"I'll meet you there," she said.

They drove up moments later. Roxy's car was already parked in front, but there was no sign of Piper. Choking back her feelings of panic, Brynn tried to reason with herself and Spencer..

"She wouldn't hurt him," she blurted out, trying to reassure herself. "I think she's just got her feelings hurt and is trying to teach me a lesson." Her face revealed her uncertainty, belying her words of confidence. Approaching the door step, they saw that the door was slightly ajar. Pushing it open, they rushed inside, calling out.

"In here!" Roxy shouted. They entered the bedroom to find her on the bed with a box open in front of her.

"How did you get in?" Brynn asked.

"I've learned a few things in my day. Don't ask. The less you know the better."

Brynn bent over and picked up a scrapbook from the box. She gave a quick glance toward Spencer, who'd followed her in. His frame filled the doorway, inadvertently standing guard in the event of Piper's return. Flipping through the pages at a fevered pace, she stopped and let her eyes settle on one page in particular. Brynn felt her blood run cold.

Spencer reached her just in time to catch her when she felt her knees give way beneath her.

* * *

Piper drove for a few minutes before Blake realized they had gone in a separate direction from the hospital.

"Where are we going?" he asked, panic growing in his voice.

"We're going on a little road trip," she told him, "just you and me."

"Where?" He gave a shallow gulp.

"Down memory lane." She tried to summon a sympathetic look, knowing he would be terrified for his mother. Not convincing enough, she knew. It's not that she didn't want to feel empathy. It's just that she didn't know how.

The boy remained silent for a few moments, his eyes big with fright. Poor kid, she almost felt sorry for him. *Almost.*

Shortly they pulled up near the small municipal airport just east of town.

"What are we doing here? We came here before. When we showed you where my Grandpa kept his plane."

"Exactly. I want to show you something."

Blake swallowed hard, trying to appear calmer and hoping she wouldn't pick up on his anxiety. He needed to be brave, for his mom.

* * *

Spencer tightened his arms around Brynn and assisted her to a sitting position.

"Take some deep breaths, Baby. We're going to get the answers we need and we're going to find him."

She sucked in a deep breath as he'd instructed and began: "She has pictures of my Dad in here. And he's with Piper's mom."

Roxy, attempting to put it all together in her mind, reverted to her thickest Australian accent.

"Didn't you tell me you were all best mates back in those days?"

"Yeah, we were. I mean, our moms were best friends, but my dad..." she trailed off. "I mean, he didn't know her too well. He wouldn't have been anywhere to have his picture taken with Aunt Sylvia." Again, she looked at the picture in her hand, studying it, searching for answers.

It was a color photo, but faded with time. The two of them stood with their backs to a railing, with a river streaming behind them. They were on a bridge somewhere.

She again tried to regulate her breathing, but it was nearly impossible with the thoughts surging through her mind. "It looks like they were on vacation, but where was my mom? They wouldn't have gone somewhere without her, that would have been weird. This doesn't make sense."

She was working her hands together, one hand in the other, twisting, clutching. She looked down at them, and caught something in the corner of her eye. A journal.

She retrieved it and opened it, the spine making a creaking sound. Spencer and Roxy waited, silently, as she flipped through the pages and absorbed what she was reading.

Brynn had opened it to an entry dated just after Sylvia had been told the cancer was back and that it wouldn't be treatable.

Mom got bad news today. Well, we both did. It seems her cancer is back and we're just out of luck. No more treatments. Just like that. She told me her financial affairs are in order, so I'll be set up just fine, I guess."

So cold, Brynn thought. So matter-of-fact. She kept turning, flipping a few pages ahead to discover more.

Get this… I just found out my mom's been lying to me all these years. My dad wasn't a truck driver at all. He was someone else entirely. And I never knew. His name was Benjamin Carston and he was Brynn's father. He flew his own private airplane and I even got to go with him. And I never knew.

Brynn's voice was reduced to sobs. "What is she saying? She's crazy!" She forced her eyes to return to the pages in front of her, struggling to focus beyond the tears.

Brynn and Ben's dad really loved my mother. He was married when he met her, and he said he had to do the right thing, whatever that was. But all along, he loved my mother more. He wanted to be with her, but he couldn't. They just had to wait, he'd always told her, until the kids were grown.

Roxy sat beside her on the edge of the bed. She felt so helpless, watching her mate suffer so. She felt no sympathy for Piper at the moment. All she could absorb was the pain it was causing Brynn.

The handwriting grew thicker, as though Piper had pressed the pen harder into the paper, desperate to get her thoughts out. Brynn didn't care. It was *her* father, and Piper didn't have any claim to him. She continued to read.

When I was a little girl and got to go flying with Brynn and Ben, did he look at me? Did he notice how much I looked like him? Because I certainly didn't. I never knew until it was too late.

Brynn threw the journal, sending it crashing into the folding closet doors across the small room.

"Why?" she sobbed. "Why did he do that? He lied to my mom, he betrayed us!" She crumbled into Spencer's arms, sobbing so hard she thought she wouldn't be able to breathe. All the feelings from his plane crash came rushing back, assaulting her again with fresh waves of grief. Her father's funeral, her mother's terrible, crippling sadness. Her own fears. Who would take care of them? she'd wondered. Who would love them now? she had asked herself at the time. Her mom had always taken care of her and Ben, but she had known instinctively that their mom was so sad she wouldn't even be able to take care of herself.

Brynn looked up to see Roxy near the closet door, picking up the pages and carefully assembling them to their original order. She handed them back to her. She opened it, desperately, flipping forward a few pages from where she'd left off.

Piper had known this. She'd known it for a while and didn't tell her. Wiping her tears with the backs of her hands she focused on the blurry words before her. Roxy patted her gently on the shoulder, offering encouragement in the only way she knew how at the moment. She sat back down on the bed, while Brynn continued to read.

So now I have a sister. And a brother. For all the good that did me. I wasn't even considered a stepchild. I was merely a bastard child with an imaginary truck-driver for a father, never acknowledged, never included. That will change. I will find them and get to know them. I admired Brynn so much. Always dreamed of having a big sister Just. Like. Her. Well now she's going to find out what it's like to lose something. To mourn for something she wants so bad and can't have. She's going to feel MY pain, and then some.

"I felt pain," Brynn whispered, so softly, in such a monotone that it scared Spencer. He'd never seen her like this.

Roxy remained silent, offering sympathetic nods, squeezing Brynn's hand gently. Her eyes met Spencer's.

"You got this?" he mouthed silently. Roxy replied with a quick nod and wrapped her arm over Brynn's shoulder. Spencer stepped out of the room into the living room to make a call. He was talking to Ben, telling him to meet them at the house. He hung up and dialed another number, pacing, then turned away from them, speaking quietly.

After his phone call, he returned, heartbroken at the sight of the woman he loved shattered, sick with worry for her son.

"We need to go back to the house," he told her gently. "Ben and Ludie will meet us there. I've already called the police."

She and Roxy stood and followed him outside.

Chapter 29

They returned home to find Ben and Ludie waiting in front of the house, holding little Annie by the hand.

"What on earth is going on?" Ben asked, visibly shaken at the sight of his sister. Ludie's face mirrored his concern.

They went inside, quietly, Spencer knowing the conversation to come would be life-changing, at best, for Ben and Ludie. Roxy went into the kitchen to give them privacy. She busied herself making coffee.

In the living room, Brynn began speaking.

"Ben, Piper's taken Blake. The little girl next door said he got off the bus and came inside, but he was gone when we got here."

"What? How do you know Piper has him?"

Brynn and Spencer exchanged a look, and then she continued.

"I need you to be calm. I don't think she'll hurt him."

"What? How can you say that? She's got a screw loose!"

"Ben, I need you to listen. Sylvia, I can't even call her Aunt Sylvia anymore, well, she knew

Dad." She swallowed, looking at him with such hurt in her eyes. "They had an affair."

"What?" Ben demanded, running his hand through his hair, looking down and then back up.

"Piper was his daughter. Our sister."

At that, Ben began pacing, at once looking furious and confused. "How can you know this? She's making this up! Where *is* she?"

"We don't know," Spencer offered. "The police are coming now to get a report. They couldn't have been gone for more than an hour."

"An *hour!*" Brynn cried. "Do you know how far they could've gotten in an hour?"

"Sweetheart, they'll find him." He wrapped his arm around her, pulling her close.

Turning to Ben, he offered more.

"We went into her apartment, and Roxy found a box with scrapbooks and a journal. There are photos."

Ben nodded. Ludie put her hands up on the back of his shoulders and gave a comforting caress. Her eyes were filled with tears. She glanced away, watching as Annie sat in front of the television playing with the blocks Aunt Brynn kept for her in a toy box. She was getting sleepy, rubbing her eyes every few minutes.

Spencer went on with his explanation.

"When Sylvia realized she was going to die, she told Piper the whole sordid story. A death-bed confession, if you will." Lowering his voice an octave, he said, "I think it's true. In the pictures, well, you can see it."

Brynn nodded. "It's true." She twisted a tear-soaked tissue in her hands. "The moment I saw, I just knew it was true. I felt it."

Ben closed the distance between them and took his sister in his arms. Hard, gasping sobs burst forth from her and she could no longer speak.

Roxy, standing by helplessly, noticed a police car pulling up out front, and went to open the door.

A tall, stocky officer came in, his expression passive from experience.

"I'm officer Baldwin," he began. "You reported a missing child? I'll need to gather some information."

"It's my son," Brynn told him. "He's twelve."

The officer scribbled something on a small, spiral-bound notebook. "Did you exchange words, perhaps? An argument that would've led to him needing to get out of the house for a while?"

"No!" she cried out. "He didn't run away! I know who took him!"

At this display of emotion, Annie started to cry. Ludie scooped her up and held her, swaying her back and forth. Comforted, Annie grew quieter, her eyebrows rising slightly as her eyelids began to close. Ludie made her way down the hall to Brynn's room to lay her down for a nap.

It was immediately obvious the officer regretted having to use those words. His gaze softened. "I'm sorry, but we have to take into consideration all possibilities. We see this from time to time and it usually turns out to be the kid went to a friend's house, mad at his parents."

Somehow she doubted that. Not in Blackwater. Maybe there were a few kids here and there that had run away, but never an abduction. Not like this.

"Her name is Piper. She was my roommate." She walked as she spoke, approaching the front window, then glancing nervously, hopefully, out the back door. Sarge paced along with her, clearly sensing the levity of the situation.

Roxy came in from the kitchen and handed the officer a piece of paper. "Here's her name, phone number and address."

The officer glanced at it, then folded it and put it in his pocket. "I'll get this info out as soon as I ask some more questions. What kind of car does she drive?"

"A Toyota," Brynn blurted out quickly. "It's not very new, it's blue."

Officer Baldwin hurriedly scratched some more notes onto his notepad.

"Excuse me for a moment." He took a few steps back into the foyer, and spoke into the radio attached to his shoulder just below his left ear. He repeated the information, and the dispatcher called it out.

When he was finished, he turned back to them. "All right. We've got people looking for them right now. We have an officer at the suspect's apartment. What more can you tell me?"

Spencer walked out onto the porch, and the officer walked out with him. Spencer was speaking in hushed tones to Baldwin and another officer who had just driven up.

Roxy came in to the living room and attempted to hand Brynn a cup of hot tea. She declined, shaking her head. "I can't drink. I can't even think," she said. "I need to *see* him!"

She suddenly turned and raced down the hallway toward Blake's room. By the time Roxy and Ludie reached her, she was on Blake's bed, clutching his pillow to her, crying softly. When she spoke again, her words were nearly imperceptible through her sobs. "I need him home!"

* * *

Shortly after, Roxy excused herself and went to her car, returning moments later with a box full of photos they'd retrieved from Piper's apartment.

"I thought you might need to see these."
Ben rushed to her, taking the box.

"I'll help you sort through them," Ludie said. There may be some clues."

They sat in the living room, sifting and sorting through photos. The box sat between them on the large, square coffee table. Each of them had a stack, including Roxy. Spencer was in Blake's room, holding Brynn. Each time she got up to pace the floors, looking out the windows, he followed her, standing closely by in case she failed to hold herself up again.

"I just thought of something!" she said suddenly. "Michael! What if he has them both?"

"Michael, the ex-boyfriend?" he asked. "I thought that was more or less something she made up for attention."

"Yeah, I did, too." She realized she'd never remembered to tell him, or anyone, about the phone call she received from Michael. She filled him in on it now, recalling the way she'd shut him down and told him never to call again.

"Do you remember when it was? Roughly? Or what kind of number it was, like where the call came from?"

"I think I know about when the call came, and it was a Houston number."

"Let's find it." He rushed into the living room and returned with her cordless home phone.

She scrolled through it quickly. "It shouldn't be hard to isolate," she said. "We hardly use the home phone for anything."

"True. Good thinking."

"Here," she said. "Here's the number."

"Should we give it to the police?"

"Let me try it first. Maybe he'll recognize my number and answer. If they don't, then we can give it to the police so they can try to track him down."

She dialed the number, and waited for it to ring. It was picked up on the third ring.

"Hello, Michael Sullivan. Can I help you?"

"Michael *Sullivan?*" Brynn was clearly puzzled. "Um, yes, my name is Brynn Callaway. You called my number a couple of weeks ago looking for Piper Hampton."

"Yes, I did. And you told me never to call again and hung up on me."

She let out a deep breath. "I'm sorry. Please let me explain."

"I'm listening."

"Piper is, *was*, my roommate. Her behavior was a bit odd, and she told me she had a stalker. His name is Michael Lopez. I thought you were him." There was a brief pause on the other end of the line.

"No, I'm not him. But I'm pretty sure Michael Lopez never stalked her."

"How can you know? How do you even know Piper?"

"Sylvia was my teaching partner. We became pretty good friends over the years, sharing our students with each other for half of the school day."

"Ohhh," Brynn sighed. "I'm so sorry for the misunderstanding. How do you know about Michael Lopez?"

"Like I said, Sylvia and I were pretty close. She was having trouble with Piper. In fact, she was at the end of her rope. Piper had these sort of, well, obsessions. Michael was the most recent of them. He worked at the school district. Maintenance. Piper took notice of him one day when she was there to bring something to her mother."

"So that's when they started dating?" she asked.

"No, that's when he shut her down. He was married, with two children. He tried to be polite about it, but she didn't take no for an answer. It wasn't her style."

"Oh my."

"Yeah, it was pretty intense. Michael ended up telling his wife about her, it nearly caused marital problems for them. Sylvia and I both went to her and explained that nothing was going on, that Michael had politely rejected her moves. That Piper had issues."

"This is really starting to add up," Brynn told him. "I can see her doing all that."

"Michael Lopez and his wife ended up getting a restraining order against her after she was caught trying to break into their back door."

"Mr. Sullivan, I apologize for my rude behavior. I never meant any harm."

"I understand. Um, do you mind if I ask? Has Piper caused you any problems?"

"I don't have time to explain right now, but yes, she has. Thank you for your help."

When she hung up, she filled in the other half of the conversation for Spencer.

He listened silently, then spoke. "Roxy brought in the photos and journal," he murmured in her ear. "I know it's hard to see them, but they might give us some answers." Together they returned to the living room and joined in looking through the photos.

Occasionally, Ben would hold a photo, squinting as though it might help him understand what was in them more clearly. There were photos of him and Brynn as children, some with Piper standing alongside them. In each of the photos, their father stood behind them. Some of them were at home, but always with their father in the picture. Suddenly, Ben had an idea. It might help his sister to see photos that would bring back good memories, ones of their mother and father *without* Piper and Sylvia.

"Brynn, do you have any scrapbooks? From when we were kids?"

"Yeah," she answered. "Mom had several." She stood and removed two of them from a bookshelf next to the fireplace. She took a seat next to her brother and they opened one to a random page. In it was a smiling Brynn, in third grade, in front of the blackboard in her classroom. It was parents' night.

Instead of comforting her, it hit her with a renewed surge of anger. Tossing it down in front of her, she asked, "How could he lie to us like that?"

"I know, Sis. I know," Ben murmured, his voice heavy with the shock of it all. Ludie stood by, watching, wringing her hands, wishing there was something she could do to comfort her husband and sister-in-law. It escaped her. All she could do was offer a silent prayer.

Another officer, this one in plain clothes with a badge pinned to his belt, arrived and began asking questions. He introduced himself as Sergeant Waldrop. At his request, Brynn furnished several recent photos of Blake. She had very few recent photos of Piper, but she offered those as well.

Over the next couple of hours, Brynn's house became a command station of sorts. Officers arrived, exchanging information with others, looking at the photos, then leaving to continue their search.

Brynn grew more restless by the minute. She was touched and comforted by the constant presence of Roxy, Ben and Ludie. Spencer was amazing. She didn't think she would even still be breathing if he weren't there, supporting her every minute.

Roxy and Ludie tried to get her to eat, but she couldn't imagine taking even a bite.

"What if my son is hungry?" she asked. "How can I eat?" Her eyes suddenly grew wide with fright as a new thought occurred to her.

"He's diabetic!" she cried out. "How could I forget that?" She slammed her hand into the wall.

"Shhh..." Spencer was at her side in a second, pulling her close. "You've had way too much information to even process today. Don't be hard on yourself." It wasn't a suggestion, it was an order and she took it, grateful for his instructions. It seemed as if she needed them, to tell her what to do minute by endless minute.

Stepping away, she returned to the front window for the umpteenth time and stared down the street. Pulling air into her lungs, she felt like she suddenly couldn't get enough oxygen.

"I'll be back," she whispered. "I just need a few minutes." She made her way down the hall and into her bedroom. Closing the door, she was heading for the sink in the master bathroom to rinse her face with cool water.

Little Annie's sleeping form caught her eye. Ludie had put her down on Brynn's bed for a nap. Brynn sat gently on the bed, watching her niece's little chest rise and fall with each breath. Her eyes filled with tears again while she studied the child, memorizing her cherubic face, her lashes splayed out across her cheeks.

Brynn brought her hand to her mouth, kissing two fingers and touching Annie's little cheek with them. She was assaulted with memories of Blake at that age, and it hurt.

Chapter 30

As the evening wore on, Brynn found herself defending her thoughts that Piper wouldn't harm her son. She tried to convince the others that Piper was just trying to teach her a lesson. Or perhaps she was trying to convince herself.

Especially now that Piper knew they were family. Surely she couldn't harm her own nephew, her own flesh and blood, right?

Sarge continued to pace, refusing to lie down anywhere and rest. His boy was gone, and he knew something was terribly, terribly wrong. The demeanors of the others in his life wasn't helping to reassure him. He sensed their anxiety. He took his job of protecting Blake seriously, and it was time for him to be home, checking his blood sugar and for Brynn to be drawing up his insulin. Sarge instinctively knew his world was turned upside down and showed it in his every move.

In the kitchen, attempting to choke down a sip of coffee, Brynn was suddenly overtaken by a stab of panic, shredding her hopes on its way through her. *His blood sugar. He can't handle this.* Blake's blood sugar was very unstable, and needed to be checked frequently. He had to eat properly, following his insulin with a protein-rich meal. She knew he hadn't had either, and it terrified her. If his glucose level went too high, he could go into a diabetic coma, if it went too low, it could mean insulin shock, and that was even more dangerous. She let out an anguished cry and crumpled to her knees. Spencer once again rushed to her side.

Ben and Ludie had already filled the detective, Sergeant Waldrop, in on the recent information they had gained and showed him pages from the journal. He was a large man, balding, face full of compassion. He was quite eager to write down any information they gave him, quickly relaying it by radio to the officers who were out searching. It seemed he instinctively knew when to spend time talking with them and when to back away and give them space.

Brynn vacillated between angrily wishing they'd search faster and gratitude that they were so diligently trying to help. She wasn't thinking clearly and she knew it.

Still trying to form a further plan of action, Spencer and Roxy kept a close eye on Brynn. Ben was out in the backyard with Sarge. Ludie stood near him, offering words of comfort. It had been a horribly stressful day and, not only was his beloved nephew missing, but he'd learned shockingly devastating news about his family.

Ben paced furiously, craning his neck over the tall, wooden privacy fence toward the front yard and street. Blake had been his little side-kick from day one. For years it had been only him and his sister Brynn raising him, and the bond he had with the boy was beyond description. He had to come home safely, Ben knew. There was no other option.

*   *   *

Brynn heard someone at the front door speaking to one of the officers that stood out in the front yard. She crossed the foyer to see Dennis coming in with bags of food from the Ladybird Café.

"Hamburgers and French fries. Birdie sent your favorites. She wouldn't let me pay for them."

Brynn was touched at the kindness of their dear friend, Birdie, and Dennis for even thinking to go pick up dinner. They were so blessed by the people God had put in their lives. She wasn't sure she could choke down a single bite, not without Blake. But for Birdie, she would try.

As the hours slowly ticked by, Brynn felt they were endless. Then at other times, she felt like she'd just seen her son off to school moments ago. *How could this be?*

Sometime after dark, Officer Baldwin came back inside to speak with Brynn.

"I've got to be going," he told her. "I have another job that needs to be covered." His tone was apologetic, and clearly demonstrated his concern.

"Your shift must have ended hours ago!" Brynn said suddenly.

"It's okay, really." He looked down and back up. "I'm off the next couple of days and I'll be out looking for him."

Gratitude overwhelmed her, and she hugged him. "That's my little boy out there," she told him. "Please bring him home to me."

Spencer shook Baldwin's hand and thanked him profusely. As the officer left, she leaned her head on Spencer's shoulder and cried. Until this, she realized, she'd never known a broken heart could literally be painful. Stabs of pain had assaulted her periodically throughout the evening, with no signs of letting up. Not until her boy was home.

* * *

Before bedtime Ludie and Ben had gone home to collect some clothes and Pull-ups for Annie and some things for themselves. They had committed to staying there with Brynn until Blake was home.

The night had slowly crept by, the phone periodically piercing the unbearable silence. Each time, Brynn jumped on it, answering on the first ring. And each time, disappointment and desperation wracked her body as she discovered it was a friend or neighbor looking for an update. Brynn wasted no time letting them know that while she appreciated the concern, they needed to keep the lines open. Word traveled quickly, and the calls soon eased up.

The police had diligently conducted searches, checking with each of Blake's friends that Brynn had told them about. The boys and their parents had been extremely cooperative and eager to help. Unfortunately, every time one of them called to offer assistance and support,

Brynn's heart sunk when she discovered it wasn't Blake or someone reporting he'd been found.

* * *

By early morning, the house had once again returned to its hectic, busy pace. Officers came in and out, asking questions, comparing notes. Sergeant Waldrop had stayed most of the night and was back early in the morning. Satisfied that this wasn't just a run-away, he'd been more than meticulous in coordinating the search. He tirelessly compared notes, studying the journals and scrapbooks.

Roxy had returned early, and got some coffee brewing. She brought donuts and pastries with her.

Dennis came by sometime in the mid-morning. He had enlisted the help of several of his friends with the fire department in the search. He'd gone to the station and made color copies of the photos of both Blake and Piper, and had even printed a photo of a car that was the same make, model and color as Piper's.

He'd distributed the photos and came by the house to check in with Roxy and to let Brynn know they were all out searching.

Brynn distracted herself for a few brief minutes with thoughts of gratitude that Dennis had come into Roxy's life and that he was so willing to help out during this nightmare.

Each time he or one of the officers or other volunteers stopped by to check in and report that Piper's vehicle hadn't been spotted, Brynn felt her heart gripped with an icy fist of fear. Panic threatened to overwhelm her, forcing her to control her thoughts. She had to be strong and to be in control to help them bring her son home.

Finally accepting a cup of coffee and a piece of toast, she took a bite of the toast. Ludie and Roxy stood looking on, tireless in their insistence that she stay nourished and hydrated. She barely tasted it, hardly noticing the texture as she forced herself to chew and swallow. She'd managed a few bites when realization once again washed over her that Blake was out there somewhere and that she wasn't sure if he'd eaten or slept.

There had been a few moments of sweetness when Annie had padded into the kitchen in her little footie pajamas and climbed up in the chair onto Brynn's lap. She had just awoken and her curls fell wildly about her face. Brynn pulled her close, smelling the sweetness that was her hair, savoring the cuddles and remembering the same moments she'd shared with Blake all those years ago when he was that age.

Spencer was relentless in his efforts. He went from officer to officer, volunteer to volunteer, handing them maps he'd printed from the computer. He'd highlighted certain areas and handed them to the volunteers, writing down the name of the searcher and the areas they'd sent them. He kept the officers abreast, and kept the phone in his hand, taking the calls and jotting down the messages. Brynn was amazed at how easily Spencer's law enforcement experience came back to him. Sergeant Waldrop commented several times how helpful he was being.

The afternoon slowly rolled around, and Brynn continued to pace. Just after 3:30, she heard someone at the door. It was Jimmy Wu and his mother.

"We brought you something to eat," he said. "Pork friend rice and spring rolls. My Mom made them."

Brynn exchanged glances with Jimmy's mom and suddenly the two of them related. One mother to another, they both knew the depth of love a young boy could inspire in a mom.

"Thank you," she told her, clasping her hands together in front of her chest. "This means so much. Blake loves having Jimmy over, and when he comes, he's always so well behaved..." her voice broke with tears.

Mrs. Wu, immediately went into action, shooing Jimmy into the kitchen. They both were carrying large containers of food. "There's more in the car," she told her. "Jimmy, come help me get the rest out of the car."

There was enough food to feed everyone there, including the officers who were in and out. Mrs. Wu had cooked from her traditional recipes from her homeland, and Brynn was deeply touched by her kindness.

After everyone had been fed, and Mrs. Wu had cleaned up the kitchen, they left. On the way out the door, Jimmy's eyes welled up in tears and he hugged Brynn tightly. "He'll be back, Mrs. Callaway. I know he will."

After they'd gone, Brynn stood and went to the couch, sinking into the cushions and bringing her bare feet up underneath her. She was sure she'd nearly worn down the tiles as she paced to the windows and back.

Annie stood at the coffee table, her chubby little hands across the clear, plastic covers on the pages in the photo album.

"Bwake," she said in her baby talk jibberesh, leading Brynn to release a new torrent of tears.

"Yes, that's Blake." She forced a smile. "And we're gonna bring him home soon."

"Home," Annie said, still looking at the pictures. "Dawg," she said, pointing to a picture of Sarge, who was never far from Blake in any of the photos. Ludie was looking on and gave a bittersweet smile at her little girl.

Brynn's thoughts had drifted away, silently offering prayers to ask God to watch over her little boy. Annie was hitting her on the knee over and over again saying something like "pain." She looked over to see the child pointing her finger at a picture on another page of Brynn and Ben and Blake at the airport. "Pwane," she was saying.

Slowly, a thought began to form in her mind. The plane, the airstrip. Her father's, *their* father's hangar, was still there. It was abandoned now, detached and separate from the other buildings on the air strip.

Brynn, hit with a sudden realization squealed out her pleasure. Annie rewarded her with a sweet, angelic smile. "Pwane," she said, nodding sweetly. Brynn nodded, saying, "Yes, plane!" Ludie was in the kitchen, but saw Annie and Brynn smiling. She didn't hear what they were talking about, but was glad her little one was providing some distraction for Brynn.

Brynn had pushed herself to her feet and crossed the room quickly to look out the window. Spencer stood in the driveway, deep in conversation with one of the police officers. She stepped outside and called out to him.

"Anything new"? she asked.

"Not yet, honey, I'm sorry." His eyes clearly showed his lack of sleep, but he managed to hold in them a look of hope. He had not resigned himself to accepting any less than good news, and she was so thankful to have him in her corner. In *their* corner.

"Can I talk to you for a few minutes?" she asked him. He crossed the yard and followed her inside.

"What's going on?"

"Alone, please." She started down the hall to her bedroom, and he was following closely behind. When they were both in her bedroom he closed the door behind them.

"Babe," she said, imploring him with her eyes. "I need you to keep this just between us, but I think I know where Blake is." She held his gaze long enough to be sure he was going to remain calm, then began getting dressed. Opening her closet, she pulled out a pair of sandals and stepped into them. Grabbing her keys and purse, she was an instant flurry of movement.

Spencer reached an arm out to still her. "Honey, where are we going?"

"We were looking at the pictures, and Annie saw the plane. I looked at them and saw an old picture of my Dad by his plane, and then another one, a newer one I had just stuck in the scrapbook recently. It was a photo I took the day we went out to the hangar to show Piper where Dad kept his plane." She held up a photo of Blake and Piper next to the hangar door, both of them were smiling.

"Wait a minute," Spencer said, attempting to gain some kind of understanding. "Why would you have taken Piper to the hangar with you and Blake? You didn't even know all this back then."

"No," she snapped, "but *she* did."

Realization hit him, and he understood. "She asked you to take her there? Weren't you curious as to why?"

"Not really, she kept telling me how sad her childhood was without a dad, and how she was always so jealous of me and Ben because we had ours." She choked back a bitter taste in her mouth.

"She actually told me some of her best memories were when she went places with me and Ben and our dad because it allowed her to pretend. I remember her going up with us and I guess it was more than a few times. She loved flying. Always made a big deal because Dad's plane was a Piper, her name."

"How did she react when she saw the hangar? Did you go inside?"

"Yes, and she got all emotional. We saw his desk, even some of his notes still on a desk calender. No one's used it since him, and aside from layers of dust, it was about the same as I'd remembered."

"Really…" he said. "Interesting.

"Yeah, and my father still had another one of his planes in the hangar, it was really not a complete plane, just the main body of one and he'd been gradually collecting other pieces and parts and adding them. He took a lot of joy in that hobby.

"So she got all sappy over it, thinking how that was *her* father, too." Spencer's face registered understanding as he put the pieces together in his mind.

"Exactly. And she seemed a little bitter, too, at times, but I chalked it up to her being jealous of not having a dad. Boy, I didn't know the half of it."

"Come on," Spencer said, "If your instincts are right, we might just be getting our little boy back." Even in the complex tragedy of their situation, it occurred to her that he had said "our little boy." It warmed her heart, breaking down the icy fear that had gripped it since yesterday.

Spencer headed down the hallway. "Let me go update Sergeant Waldrop so he can get the officers dispatched out to the hangar."

"No," she said, putting her hand over his mouth. "I don't wanna spook her. I don't trust her, she's emotional and highly strung. I wouldn't put it past her to do something crazy if she sees the police coming at her in droves."

"I don't feel good about this," he told her. "I've been in situations like this when I was in law enforcement. They know how to handle these things."

"Yeah, but I know how to handle Piper. Now that I know her backstory, anyway."

She looked up at him, imploring him with her eyes to side with her on this.

He relented immediately. "Let's go. But at the first sign of trouble, you're gonna have to let me do what I have to do, whether that means going back into cop mode or getting the whole police department out there." He locked his eyes on her. "You know I won't do anything to risk his safety."

"I know," she whispered softly. Deal."

Spencer told Ben, Ludie, and Roxy he was going to get Brynn out of the house for a few minutes. They nodded enthusiastically, said it would be good for her to get out. They assured him they would hold the fort down and would call them immediately if there was any news.

Brynn and Spencer told the officers in front they were stepping out for a bite and to have a look around. They gave him their mobile numbers in case there was news. Sarge, sensing his grown-ups were preparing for departure, went to Brynn's side, giving the clear signal that she's not going anywhere without him. He followed them to the car.

Chapter 31

On the way to the hangar, Sarge sat on the backseat, his eyes roaming to and fro, looking for his Blake. They drove around a bit, careful to give the appearance of searching the neighborhoods to anyone who might be watching them. Most of Blackwater had heard by now that Blake was missing, and so the sight of Brynn and Spencer out and about was sure to draw plenty of attention. They'd just have to make sure no one suspected anything about where they were going.

Spencer did his best to give the appearance of driving around looking for Blake in order to avoid drawing attention to their destination. When they finally arrived on the airstrip, Brynn was looking nervously about, hoping to catch sight of Piper's car. When she didn't see it, her heart sunk.

"It's not here," she murmured.

"She knows everyone is looking for her by now, she wouldn't park it in open sight."

"You're right." She nodded in agreement.

If they aren't here, she thought, *then where are they?* She knew they couldn't leave without checking it out, though. They couldn't leave a single stone unturned.

They pulled up at her father's hangar and stopped, getting out quietly. Brynn instructed Sarge to stay in the car, her voice firm. The windows were down and it was cool enough outside for him. Besides, they'd only be a moment and if it turned out to be any longer, chances are they'd need him. He sat upon command, but gave a small whimper.

Brynn raced to the side door where her father once had his small, adjoining office. The door was old, the locks and facings rusted out from lack of use. It was on a section of the air strip that was on private property that her father owned. It was near enough to the terminal and adjacent to the air strip, but separate enough that it was his own and hadn't been maintained by airport staff over the years. She supposed she and Ben should have addressed the issue after their father's death and she now vaguely wondered why the deed or the taxes hadn't been brought up when his will was probated.

Spencer turned the rusty knob, slowly peeking inside to assess the situation. The door stuck on its hinges a little, but he was able to pry it open with little difficulty. They entered, pulling the door closed behind them. Brynn had to force herself to breathe.

Cutting through his office, they peered through the window of the door that led from his office to the large, open warehouse space where he used to keep his plane, and saw Piper's car,

They quietly approached the car, hunkering down to avoid being seen. There was music from what sounded like a small, cheap radio. They still hadn't caught sight of Piper or Blake, so they continued.

Rising up slightly, just enough to peer over the car, they saw Blake. He was on the other side of the car tied to a chair. He slumped over helplessly and Brynn felt her heart in her throat. Panic engulfed her and she nearly bolted forward when Spencer stilled her with his hand.

"Shhh," he said, "wait."

She nodded her understanding, fighting the urge to burst forward and race to Blake's side. She could see him well enough to see that he was drenched in sweat. He seemed to be moaning, clearly incoherent. He hadn't seen them.

Just then, she caught sight of Piper sitting on the concrete floor between her car and the fuselage of the old plane. Piper had her back to the car, and was close enough to Blake to touch him if she reached out. She was singing along to the music in a slurred voice, applying lipstick without a mirror. Her hair was died chestnut brown with auburn lowlights, the ends turned out in small curls. Just like Brynn. *What on earth?* A closer look revealed a butcher knife resting on the ground just beside her knee. If she were to be startled, she could hurt him. She would do it, Brynn now knew. She looked at Spencer for directions. Piper was a loose cannon, and they both knew they had to proceed carefully.

Just then, Sarge bolted from behind them and brought himself up just between Blake and Piper. Blake didn't respond and, for all appearances, was too incoherent to even know they were there. Brynn gasped, covering her mouth. Spencer held her tight, waiting, watching. Piper didn't even seem to be aware of the dog's presence for a few seconds.

Sarge drew up in front of them and let out a low, deep growl. In a flurry of movement, Piper was on her feet, butcher knife in hand.

"Well," drawled Piper as she turned to face them. "I didn't know you were coming. Don't suppose your RSVP made it here." A throaty, maniacal laugh emitted from her and she looked from the dog to Blake. He still wasn't responding.

"Looks like my *nephew's* a little sick, *Sister.*" She threw her head back and laughed. "You'd think a nurse would know how to take better care of her own kid." Her speech was slurred, her pupils constricted to tiny pinpoints.

Brynn started to push her way past Spencer, but he held her firm. "Shhh…" he tried to calm her. "Wait."

"You should listen to him," Piper said. "Wouldn't want anyone to get hurt." She brandished the knife, sending a clear threat. Sarge was standing with his back to Blake, baring his teeth at Piper and barking. What happened next was a flash of movement, and was hard for Brynn to register.

Piper lunged toward Blake, and Sarge leapt up, pushing her to the ground. Her knife plunged into the dog's neck near his shoulder, but he was relentless. He held her down, and Spencer let go of Brynn and was behind Piper, gripping her wrists to keep her from grabbing the knife again.

Piper was on her back, in and out of consciousness at this point. She was clearly inebriated, grumbling incoherently.

Brynn reached her son in a flash, her hands on each of his cheeks.

"Talk to me, Blake! Honey!" She turned and looked imploringly at Spencer. "His sugar, he's in trouble!"

Piper began muttering something neither of them could decipher at first.

"Back pack!" Spencer said, still holding Piper back and away from Sarge, who was whimpering on the floor next to them. He was losing blood fast.

Somehow, Brynn had the presence of mind to tear open Piper's car door and pulled Blake's backpack from the seat of the car. Unzipping it, she turned it upside down and emptied its contents. There was a tube of glucose gel and a glucometer, along with a few other various diabetic supplies.

Prying Blake's mouth open, she squeezed a moderate amount of the sweetened gel into his mouth, talking to him sweetly, encouraging him.

"Come on, honey, wake up for me! I need you to swallow the gel."

Confident that Piper was now incapacitated, Spencer took off his shirt and tied it around Sarge's neck and shoulder, securing it tightly as a pressure dressing over the stab wound. In what seemed like one fluid motion he was behind Blake, untying him from the chair. Cradling him, he lowered him to the floor where Brynn continued working with him.

Spencer reached into his pocket and retrieved his phone, dialing it quickly, then identified himself

"I need the police, we're at the airstrip, in the old Carston hangar. My car is parked outside. We've got Blake Callaway, and he's gonna need an ambulance. Send two trucks, there's another injured person. Looks like the suspect is a possible OD."

Brynn looked helplessly from her son to Piper, then back to Sarge. The fear in her eyes tore at Spencer's heart.

"Get a vet here." He paused, listening to the voice at the other end. "Yes, a vet. We have a dog and he's losing blood quickly."

Hanging up, he rushed back to Sarge, applying pressure to the wound.

Blake was shaking his head back and forth, moaning. He was beginning to regain consciousness, and Brynn was coaxing him back every step of the way.

"That's right, Son, you've got this." She laughed out loud when he began to swallow some of the gel. "Good boy, you're doing great!"

"What?" Blake asked, looking around. "Sarge?" he called out, still obviously having difficulty focusing his eyes to find his dog.

"Spencer's right here, he's got Sarge." Brynn allowed her eyes to travel back to Piper, who lay motionless now on the concrete. A wave of guilt crushed her when she made the decision not to check for breathing or a pulse. Her son was priority one and not out of the woods yet.

Within seconds, the sound of sirens drew closer. Spencer jumped up and raced to the large, overhead door, praying it would open easily. His prayers were answered and it rose as he pushed with all his strength.

Blake's eyes were open and beginning to more clearly register what he was seeing.

"Sarge!" he cried out, pulling himself nearer and laying his head on the dog's stomach. He spoke, through his sobs. "Sarge, I love you," he cried. "You came to help me, and I need you to be okay."

It was all Brynn could take and she crumbled into sobs herself. A paramedic was hunched over Piper doing chest compressions, while a second medic bagged her with an ambu bag. Her skin was ghostly pale, and Brynn suddenly registered a wave of worry mixed with compassion. Piper was her sister, and she was sick. She needed help.

But Brynn couldn't think about that right now. She had her son to consider and he wasn't fully out of jeopardy yet. She tried in vain to control her shaking hands, fighting the tremors in an attempt to check his blood sugar with the monitor that had fallen out of his backpack. Thankfully, another medic approached, taking the meter from her hands and pricking her son's finger.

Spencer maintained his hold on Sarge, who was still bleeding profusely. Her heart was seized with fear at the sight of the pool of blood growing beneath him. She loved the dog with all her heart, knowing that he'd risked his own life to protect her son.

Just then, Dr. Dobson, the local veterinarian who had cared for Sarge in the past, rounded the corner with a medical bag in hand. Spencer assisted him in moving Sarge to his vehicle, which was waiting just on the other side of the ambulances.

Brynn was astonished when Spencer was able to speak to the police officers on scene, bringing them up to speed. She was grateful, amazed by his calmness in the midst of the ensuing chaos. She'd known all along he was cool under pressure, but this rose above anything she'd ever faced.

Blake was able to stand now with the assistance of a short, slight medic whose strength belied his appearance. He was able to speak now, and was taking sips from a bottle of water someone had handed him. He was asking about Sarge, and Spencer had returned to his side, offering reassurance.

"He's with Dr. Dobson. He said it's more of a flesh wound than it looks. Even though he lost a lot of blood, it didn't hit any vital organs."

Blake drew in a ragged breath, and Spencer instructed him to breathe easy. "He's in good hands, Son. We'll go check on him soon. He may need a little surgery, but the doctor promised he wouldn't leave his side until he's stable.

At that, Blake dissolved into tears and leaned into Spencer, who pulled him close in an embrace. Brynn's heart was gripped by overwhelming love and relief.

Finally, she allowed herself to look over at the items a police officer was placing into an evidence bag near where Piper had been lying. Pill bottles.

"What is it?" she asked.

The officer hesitated before speaking. "It's part of an ongoing investigation. We won't have any further information for a while."

"Just tell her what she wants to know," said a strong voice from behind the car. It was Sergeant Waldrop. Right behind him was Officer Baldwin, in a t-shirt and shorts, the skin on his face reddened and peeling.

He had kept his word, Brynn knew. He had been tirelessly out searching every possible location. She couldn't find the words, and he simply nodded with a smile. "I know," he told her. "It's gonna be okay."

The other officer read the labels of the empty pill bottles. They were sedatives and antidepressants and had recent dates on the labels.

She had asked for help, Brynn realized. She had seen a psychiatrist and was trying to get better. The reality of just how sick she'd been was evident. She was truly and genuinely sick, Brynn knew, the full brunt of it hitting her squarely in the chest.

Piper had wanted to be a nurse, and had yet to test for her state board exam as a nursing assistant. There would have been a background check, and Brynn knew she wouldn't have passed. She was a deeply troubled young woman with a history that would preclude it.

The most sickening realization to hit Brynn, however, was knowing that Piper had taken her son, tied him up and left him there to die before swallowing enough pills to take her own life.

Finally allowing the truth of it to wash over her, she fell, crumpled to the ground, wracked with fresh sobs. Spencer was once again at her side, helping her to her feet and pulling her to him.

She heard the ambulance doors close and the sirens beginning to wail as they pulled away. Officer Baldwin reported that the medics said Piper's pulse was weak and thready, and she was unresponsive. Brynn wasn't sure if she would survive this. She'd seen many patients after they'd ingested a large number of pills and at this point it could go either way.

She drew in some deep breaths and steeled herself as she made her way toward the other ambulance that would be taking Blake to the hospital. He had regained his coherence, speaking nervously about Sarge and his recovery.

Brynn climbed up into the ambulance and took a seat next to her son. She was grateful to the medics for allowing her to accompany him.

She couldn't help but smile as she watched Spencer walk to his car. He was a gift to her, and she silently thanked God for bringing him into her life. She knew she wouldn't have gotten through this without him. And she would need him even more after what they'd all been through at the hands of Piper.

As horrible as the situation was, she had to remember that Piper was her sister. Her actions had been horrific, but she was a very sick woman. She was in serious trouble, and Brynn wouldn't turn her back on her now. She owed it to her father to do everything she could to help Piper get better. Right now, forgiveness seemed so far out of the realm of possibility, but with time, she hoped she would reach that point.

As the ambulance began to pull away, she turned around to look at Blake again. He was sitting up talking to the medic, and seemed to be coming out of the fog he was in from the severe hypoglycemia. He barely remembered even arriving at the hangar with Piper, and everything after that was a blur. It was good that he couldn't remember the betrayal at the hands of a woman he trusted. His aunt, as it turned out. Brynn shuddered at the thought of having to explain Piper's actions.

Brynn was hit with a new wave of nausea when she thought of having to help her son understand about Piper being her sister. It was even difficult for her to understand it herself. She suppressed a chill as she remembered Sylvia on her death bed, trying to tell her something.

Had she been trying to tell her about how she had betrayed her own best friend? Brynn's mother? A flash of indignance surged through her when she considered all those years Sylvia had lied to Brynn's mother while pretending to be her best friend. Even her father had lied. That was something she was going to have to reconcile with the grief she still felt at his loss. All of this was going to be even harder for Blake, and she made the decision to get him some counseling.

* * *

When they arrived at the hospital they learned that Piper's kidneys had begun to shut down. She had a minimal brain wave and her condition was currently grave. Brynn glanced away from the doctor to see Spencer coming through the automatic entry doors of the emergency room.

No longer shirtless, he wore a black t-shirt stretched tightly across his chest. It was emblazoned with the letters "SWAT" in white.

"Nice shirt," she told him, forcing a smile.

"Officer Baldwin loaned it to me. He had it in his car."

"Well, it looks really good on you. Natural."

"Funny you should say that," he told her, taking her by the hand as they started to walk toward the room where Blake was waiting. "Baldwin and Sergeant Waldrop have already tried to talk me into going back into police work."

She turned her eyes up to his face, trying to register his expression. *Would he really become a cop again?* He was most definitely a natural, and he had seemed to know instinctively what to do next at each step of their crisis.

"Are you considering it?" she asked, drawing in a sharp breath to await his answer.

"I'm not sure. Honestly? I've thought about it. But it's something we can talk about later."

She quickly brought him up to speed about Piper's condition while they were still in the hallway. She didn't want to have to discuss it in front of Blake at this point.

When they reached his room, he was sitting up on a stretcher eating cheese and crackers. There was a small container of apple juice on the bedside table with a straw in it.

"Every bite, Son," she ordered, leaning over to plant a kiss on his forehead.

"Mom, stop," he whispered, rolling his eyes. "It's not cool."

"Well, then, excuse me while I leave you two 'cool guys' alone for a few minutes. I'm going to the cafeteria to get some coffee. I need caffeine like you needed sugar a little while ago," she said with a wink. "I'll be back in a little while."

Looking at Spencer, she added, "Call me if anything changes with him. Anything at all."

"I'm fine, Mom," Blake said. "Go." He was sitting up straighter on the side of the stretcher now, exuding an air of calm and control. *When did he get to be so mature?* she wondered.

She walked down the hallway, leaving the emergency area and turned a corner. She knew this hospital well, and wasted no time reaching the chapel.

Inside, she felt her knees start to give way beneath her and took a seat on the front row of red velvet-upholstered chairs. The room was dimly lit. A kaleidoscope of color from the small, stained-glass window reflected onto the pages of an open Bible on the altar down front.

Her mind reeled as she replayed the day's events. Blinking rapidly, she finally released the torrent of tears that had been threatening to spill over. Each time she'd fought back and gained control of the sobs. But not this time. For a few moments, she just let the tears flow.

Finally, she straightened herself in the chair, plucked a tissue from one of the boxes that had been strategically placed on every row, and wiped her eyes.

Focusing her stare intently on the blue and green lights reflected on the corner of the Bible pages, she began to pray, crying out to God in thanks for sparing her son. She had so many questions, so many uncertainties still remained. But right now, it was time to be thankful. God had given her son another chance, and her another chance as well. He'd brought a wonderful man into her life, one who loved her and would soon be her husband.

And He had given her a sister. For all practical purposes, she'd lost her before she even knew, and now the future was very uncertain.

Somehow, in spite of everything Piper had done, Brynn knew she was ultimately *her* responsibility. She was her sister. Brynn and Ben were the only family the woman had, and it was time to do the right thing. Piper, she knew, was extremely unbalanced and, if she survived, would need extensive therapy, most likely in-patient care.

After she'd finished praying, she remained in the chapel, silent and alone, for a while longer, just breathing in and out.

Finally, she came to her feet and took one more deep breath. She turned at the sound of the door opening behind her.

"I'm not surprised to find you here," Spencer said.

"I'm not surprised you came looking," she replied with a smile. "How's Blake?"

"Are you kidding? That kid of yours, *ours,* is doing just fine. He's got the nurses fussing over him. Charmer, that one. Ben and Ludie were there when I left. I caught them up to speed and they're not leaving his side. They know where you are and what you're dealing with. Roxy's still at the house with Dennis, staying busy taking care of things 'til we get home. Probably cooking up some kangaroo meat." He grinned and she couldn't help but laugh.

"Thank you," she whispered softly.

He gave a little smile. "Any more word on Piper?"

"No, I haven't been able to bring myself to go yet. They were moving her to ICU the last time I heard anything from the doctor."

"Do you want to see her?"

"Yes, but I want you with me."

"There's nowhere else I'd be."

"What was Blake talking about after I left?"

"Sarge. What else?" He chuckled softly.

"How do you think he's doing?" she asked.

"From what the vet said, it's not nearly as deep as I thought. He wants to keep him overnight, just to be sure. I'll be picking him up in the morning and he'll have instructions for us."

Together they went to the ICU and spoke to Piper's nurse. Fortunately, she knew Brynn and Spencer well and they had no problem getting in to see her.

She lay motionless, pale, and fragile in her bed. Her eyes were closed, surrounded by darkened rings. She was intubated, the tube coming from her mouth and secured with tape. IV fluids infused a bag of fluid from a pump. The monitors emitted short beeping sounds at an even rhythm overhead.

Brynn couldn't deny the protective, almost maternal feeling that overtook her at the sight of Piper lying there so helpless.

Wordless, Spencer stood by her side, looking back and forth between Brynn and the monitors. He was a man of steel and Brynn knew he would help them all through this.

Brynn gave her phone number to the nurse and instructed her to call with any changes.

The nurse asked a few questions about next of kin and Brynn drew in a quick, sharp breath. "I'm her sister."

Spencer took her by the hand, brought it to his lips and kissed the back of it. "Let's go back to ER and check on our boy."

The end.